SECRETS OF LADY LUCY

AGENTS OF THE HOME OFFICE

RACHEL ANN SMITH

PENFORD
PUBLISHING

First Edition September 2019

Edited by Victory Editing

Proofread by Gray Plume Editing

Cover design by Impluvium Studios

Copyright © 2019 by Rachel Ann Smith

Excerpt from **MYSTERIES OF LADY THEODORA** copyright © 2019 by Rachel Ann Smith

ISBN: 978-1-951112-02-8

CHAPTER ONE

"*L*ucy!"

Lady Lucille Stanford's best friend whispered harshly at the open door.

Lucy pressed herself deeper into the desk cavity. *Blast*, she had nearly been found out. She hurriedly folded and tucked the unread parchment in her hand under her garter.

"Lucy, are you in here?" Muffled steps on the plush carpet came closer.

"Lady Lucille Stanford, come out from under the desk, *now!*"

Lady Grace Oldridge's tone did nothing to alleviate Lucy's frustration at having been discovered. She smoothed out her gown and slowly rolled to her full height, all five feet two inches. "Grace, please don't be mad. I just needed a little time to myself."

Despite having successfully kept her unusual activities and investigations a secret during her first Season, Lucy was finding it increasingly difficult in her second now that her twin brother Matthew, Marquess Harrington, was intent on finding her a husband.

At two and twenty, Lucy was practically on the shelf—and far too old for this to be merely her second Season. If she had her way, she would have had none. After losing James, for years she had successfully avoided all of it—the Season, a husband. But Matthew was no longer amenable to her resistance to marriage. The only advantage of being in Town among the *ton* was her ability to access resources that facilitated what she now considered her true avocation.

Engulfed in a reassuring hug from Grace, Lucy was struck with guilt—which swiftly evaporated as she caught sight of Grace's fierce expression. "You scared us all to death when we couldn't find you in your usual hiding spots. I thought someone had... Well, never mind. We need to go back to the ballroom. I'm certain your brother is about to have an apoplexy."

"Must we go back? I've already danced with all the gentlemen Matthew coerced into asking me, and I'm no good at simpering or making idle conversation."

Lucy mentally pictured each of the suitors Matthew had deemed eligible. They totaled eight, doubled from last Season. Admittedly, all were rather dashing in their own way, but none had even come close to affecting her as James had.

Grace tried bargaining, as if she sensed Lucy was at her limit. "Perhaps we could convince Matthew to leave after the supper dance if you were to participate."

Lucy nodded and allowed Grace to pull her back into the overcrowded ballroom. She blindly followed her friend, both pushing their way through the glittering sea of ladies in silk and men in their black evening attire. With each step, Lucy mentally admonished herself for letting Grace yet again convince her to attend the Duke of Fairmont's annual ball.

The terrace doors were open on the opposite side of the room, and Lucy clasped her hands tightly, eyeing the doorway. The temptation of the night air was so alluring, yet she stood stock-still next to Grace, awaiting Matthew's arrival, confident that her brother would impart another long lecture on how Lucy was to remain in sight at all times and needed to focus on finding a suitable gentleman to marry.

Grace turned to acknowledge an acquaintance Lucy did not recognize. The movement caused Lucy's skirts to shift and the edge of the missive she'd secreted to graze against her leg. How to escape and gain a moment of peace to read the note? No matter how tempting the gardens sounded, they would not do. She needed adequate lighting. Lucy let out a slow, deep sigh and mumbled to herself, "Endure the endless balls and whatever other social events Grace wishes to attend. Eventually, my thickheaded brother will realize she is perfect for him."

Grace's piercing gaze returned to her. The look rivaled the ones Lucy's mama used to give her as a child whenever she was caught playing a trick on her brother. Lucy gave her friend a sheepish smile. Had she spoken too loudly? She really must cease the habit of talking to herself in moments of frustration.

Looking past Grace, she spied Matthew approaching. How was it that he slipped through the crowd with ease while she had to sidestep and perform pirouettes to ensure she was not trod upon? If only she had been blessed with a few extra inches.

Matthew nodded to acquaintances along the way but skillfully avoided being drawn into a conversation. Thus he was upon them in admirably quick order.

"Lady Grace, thank God you found her."

Lucy's admiration soured on being ignored and she rolled her eyes. "Grace suggested that we could all leave right after supper if I participate in the supper dance. Find me a partner, and I will happily oblige."

Matthew raised an eyebrow at her declaration. Despite his being the patriarch of the family, she was still older by six minutes. In this instance, being the older twin did not hold any weight. Lucy braced herself as her brother squared his shoulders and loomed over her. He was a full twelve inches taller, peering down on her. "I believe I've already assisted you this evening with dance partners—eight, to be exact. If you so desperately wish to leave, you will have to find your own dance partner."

"Matthew, really?" Lucy couldn't believe Matthew refused to help her. He had never denied any of her requests in the past. In fact, he was generally rather accommodating and often allowed her much freedom, which meant she was able to conduct her clandestine activities without his knowledge.

"I believe you heard me clearly, dear sister." Matthew calmly walked away to join a group of friends.

Her hands started to sweat in her gloves. Her heart rate increased at the prospect of having not only to dance again but also at the idea of trying to tempt a gentleman into approaching her. Could she even attract the attention of one?

She took a deep breath. Who would introduce her? Why was she short of breath? She was surrounded by women and men flirting with one another. If she could master the art of disguise, how hard could the task of luring a man to her side be? She needed to quickly develop the skills to take advantage of her full figure. She had seen many a barmaid employ their wiles to gain favors. She

4

peeked at her own décolletage and began to calculate her odds of success.

The only gentlemen she had been properly introduced to were in Matthew's set of friends, all with whom she had already danced. To do so a second time would provide gossip or, worse, imply an intimacy she adamantly wanted to avoid. Her shoulders, which she'd been trying to hold straight, now rolled forward as she exhaled. Rudimentary calculations led her to conclude leaving the ball early was an impossibility.

Lucy turned to Grace for support and raised her brows. *What am I to do?*

Grace lifted her chin and declared with confidence. "I'm sure we will be able to find someone suitable. Stop worrying."

Unlikely. James was gone, and the idea of meeting a gentleman who might affect Lucy as James once had caused her heart to race. She scanned the crowd; her gaze flew past a pack of young lords who were known fortune hunters and fell upon a group of gentlemen seeking new wives, all of whom at least twice her age.

Appallingly, the Marquess of Markinson filled her vision. The man was a renowned rake and notorious flirt. Lucy averted her eyes, having no wish to be entangled in a scandal that would have her superiors questioning her judgment.

Grace stiffened beside her. Lucy scanned the perimeter and followed her friend's line of sight, only to see Matthew chatting with this Season's diamond of the first water. Lady Arabelle was the younger sister of the Earl of Hereford, who happened to be on Matthew's list of eligible suitors. Glancing from the corner of her eye, Lucy caught Grace throwing daggers at Matthew with a hard stare. Meanwhile, her twin was pretending to ignore the evil glare.

Slightly amused at the interplay, Lucy predicted Matthew's next move would be to try to evoke an inappropriate response from her usually calm, reserved friend. Another sharp intake of Grace's breath drew Lucy's attention back to her brother, who leaned in closer and carried on feigned interest in the debutante. Lucy had seen that mischievous look in his eyes many a time. He winked at Grace just before she looked away.

Lucy drew Grace away from needless agony and back to the matter at hand. "Matthew has tasked me with the impossible. I hate making small talk. In fact, I don't even like to converse with Matthew's friends. I really do wish we could leave."

A fresh breeze filtered in from the garden, redoubling Lucy's desire to escape. Her gaze locked on to the terrace doors. As she formulated her plan to flee, a warm breath on the back of her neck caused her whole body to stiffen. How had she let someone sneak up on her? And who would be bold enough to stand so inappropriately close? But rather than alarm coursing through her, a strong current of energy and heat spread throughout her body.

Grace's gaze left Matthew, and her eyes twinkled as she mumbled something about a man being the answer to their prayers. Who had Grace sighted behind her? If she was acquainted with the man, why did she not greet him? Grace leaned in and whispered, "I have a plan—remain here while I find Matthew."

The stranger bent to speak close to her ear in a deep baritone voice. "It's stifling in here."

Who dared to address her so intimately? Lucy turned, only to face a starched white shirt. The man was a giant. He had to be over a foot taller than herself. To hazard a guess, she would put him at six foot three, at least.

Lucy was forced to take a step back to see his face, but

only met with his nose. She had to raise her chin so she could look into his eyes. Deep emerald green with shards of gray stared back at her. Slightly stunned by his intensity, she remained mute. Surely she had never met the man standing before her—how could she have forgotten those mesmerizing eyes?

She took another step back, placing distance between them, but his gaze kept her captive. There was a sense of familiarity about him that Lucy could not quite place. "Have we been introduced, sir?"

"It is a shame you do not remember me, Lady Lucy. I would recognize you anywhere."

Lucy had excellent recall, and she did not appreciate the insult. She turned to leave but hastily changed her mind. "Well, you have me at an advantage, Mister…"

The man had the audacity to smile down at her. Lucy so wished she could raise one eyebrow as effectively as her twin to convey a challenge. Instead, she was reduced to giving the man a hard stare. The devilish smile she received was not the response she was expecting.

"Would you care to go out onto the terrace to get some air?"

Why had this stranger made such a shocking suggestion? Lucy took inventory of her inadvertent reactions to the man looming over her. Accelerated heart rate, heat radiating from her cheeks, and an increased level of curiosity. Lucy could never walk away from a puzzle, and he was no exception.

Gone was the resounding feeling of boredom that frequently plagued her when in the company of the opposite sex. Replacing it was piqued curiosity, and now she wondered if this man had some special talent and could read minds. That he seemed to know her thoughts was confounding. He had been standing behind her as she looked at the terrace doors. He couldn't have seen the longing to be outside in her expression.

To deflect his attention, Lucy lied. "No, I'm currently looking for someone."

"Oh, who might that be? I might be of assistance." His height allowed him to see over the majority of the heads. Lucy observed him as he made a point to glance out at the crowd. A strange notion crossed her mind that had she honestly been searching for someone, he would do all that was possible to aid her.

Unaccustomed to the strange feelings this man evoked within her, Lucy pushed her shoulders back, raised her chin, and declared, "No one of your acquaintance, I'm sure."

Did he flinch at her statement? Surely not. But as her gaze fell upon his features, the man's eyes betrayed a deep hurt only to be rapidly replaced with a dullness that masked his true feelings. Calmly he replied, "You might be right. I only returned to London a fortnight ago. But perhaps you could describe the individual for me." His tone and words made Lucy question what she had seen in the depth of his eyes moments before.

She had no choice but to continue with the lie. "*He* is about so in height." She pointed above her head but just under his chin, then added, "He has brown hair, and I believe he is wearing a black jacket this evening."

A slightly rusty-sounding chuckle escaped his lips before he covered it with a cough and said, "My sweet, you have just described eighty percent of the men in attendance tonight."

Surprised by his intimate address, she gaped at him before she found her composure. "Well, I'll be off to join my friends then. Good evening, sir."

Before Lucy managed a step, he placed a hand on her

elbow and said, "Please don't run off. Allow me to escort you to your brother. Or, if you prefer, to one of his friends."

This stranger knew Matthew and his set? If he was acquainted with her twin, why was she not able to place him? Lucy pointedly stared at his hand. When her gaze returned to his, she was startled to find a twinkle of mischief in his mesmerizing green eyes.

Flustered, Lucy said, "That, sir, would be highly inappropriate, since I don't even know your name."

CHAPTER TWO

*T*he fire in Lucy's eyes made Blake want to bend down and kiss her senseless. He had recognized her right away. Her name always of mind. Though Lucy's hair had darkened since he last saw her—it was now a beautiful golden blond with honey-toned strands—her gray-blue eyes, set perfectly in her heart-shaped face, were as spectacular as he remembered. It still astounded him that while Harrington was of similar height to himself, Lucy was pixie-sized.

Perplexed by the sight of a demure young lady reentering the ballroom and submissively standing by the beauty her brother had blatantly taunted, Blake had issued himself a challenge. Could he evoke the lively sprite he had first met all those years ago at Halestone Hall?

As they conversed, he applauded his ability to make her come alive. Lucy's eyes sparkled with emotion, and he recalled the one holiday he had spent with Harrington and his family nearly a decade ago. He distinctly recollected days filled with fun—swimming, skipping stones, riding

and jumping all sorts of obstacles, and conspiring with Lucy to play numerous pranks on her brother.

Gently squeezing her elbow to gain her full attention, Blake bent to say, "I see your brother is approaching, along with your friend."

As he tracked Harrington's progress toward them, Blake tried to reconcile the carefree girl he had met years ago with the extremely cantankerous woman next to him. He admired her furiousness and clever banter, but he wondered where the compassionate girl of his memories had disappeared to. Harrington had informed him that her beloved Lord James Taylor, the Earl of Towerton's heir, had been killed in the war. Had the loss caused her to become bitter? But it wasn't bitterness he detected; it seemed she was wary of everyone and their motives. He could be accused of the same wariness, for he trusted very few. Admittedly, he was extremely guarded even with those he did trust.

Blake met Harrington's direct gaze.

"Lord Devonton," his lordship said in greeting. He immediately turned and made introductions, "Lady Grace, may I present the Earl of Devonton."

Blake snuck a glance at Lucy. Her sweet face now held a dangerous scowl, directed squarely at her brother. It was a look Blake never wanted to be a recipient of. Quite evidently, she was irate with Harrington, but why? Because he had ignored her?

Giving his head a slight shake, he returned Lady Grace's curtsy with a light kiss upon her outreached hand. "Lady Grace, it is my pleasure."

Growling, Harrington asked, "Devonton, do you miss the Continent yet?"

Returning his gaze to Lucy, Blake merely answered, "No."

Her gaze locked with his, but she remained silent.

Lady Grace interjected with, "The Continent! Lord Devonton, that must have been rather dangerous, given the war."

At the mention of war, he felt his face turn to stone. While Blake had not been on the front line, he had endured the rude reality of battle. He had been held captive on more than one occasion and interrogated by means no animal, let alone a human, should experience. Luckily, he had survived by repeatedly escaping his captors. The image that had assisted him in his darkest moments was now standing before him in flesh and blood.

He tried to repress a smile as Lucy impatiently clasped and unclasped her hands. As if no longer willing to be a bystander, she elbowed her brother hard in the ribs. Harrington rubbed his side, obviously oblivious as to why he was subject to physical prodding. Lucy mouthed, *Introduction.*

"Lucy, do you not remember Devonton? He stayed with us during the holidays my first year at Eton." Blake did not care for Harrington's scathing look nor the derisive tone he used with Lucy.

Color flooded her cheeks. She shifted her weight from one foot to the other, and her gaze fell to the floor. "Lord Devonton, I am sorry I did not recall your stay at Hale-stone Hall."

Why was Harrington behaving in such a boorish manner? Of course Lucy didn't remember him. Blake had been a lanky, bookish-looking lad of thirteen years. A mere boy compared to her intended, Lord Taylor, who was six years his senior, with the looks and body of a man.

It was extremely out of character for Harrington to treat his sister in such a manner. In a multitude of letters over the years, he had always praised Lucy's intelligence and her innate ability to assist in the management of the family estates while he was absent. So what had instigated the harsh remarks? Interestingly, Harrington's demeanor had changed when Lady Grace shifted her attention to Blake. Could the charismatic and self-assured Lord Harrington be jealous of him? Impossible.

Lucy's gaze remained downcast as Harrington tried valiantly to recover. "It has been some time since."

At the first strains of the supper waltz, Blake decided to attempt to restore a smile to Lucy's face. Bending slightly, he asked, "Lady Lucy, would you do me of the honor of this dance?" He winged out his arm and held his breath as he awaited her response.

In a voice barely louder than a whisper, she answered, "It would be my pleasure."

Desire seared through Blake as the warmth of Lucy's hand radiated up his left arm and straight to his heart. His spirits lifted as he guided them to the edge of the dance floor.

Turning to face him, she finally granted him that elusive smile he had hoped for all evening, the one he had stored in his memory for years. The one he had recalled when he most needed strength during the war. He pulled Lucy into his embrace, placing his right hand gently but firmly on her waist while his left hand engulfed hers. Since she could not quite comfortably reach to place her hand on the top of his shoulder, her hand settled near it, on the upper part of his chest.

Blake had to remind himself that while he had carried Lucy in his thoughts for years, she had only just now been reintroduced to him. Gliding about the dance floor with her felt all too natural, her soft, flowing movements in stark contrast to the stiff, mechanical steps performed by his previous partners. Was it he or his partners who had merely gone through the motions?

Blake glanced around the room at all the dancing couples, twirling, smiling, and engaging in what looked to be flirtatious tête-à-tête. Wishing he could lay his eyes upon her features rather than the top of her head, he broke the silence. "I'm a little rusty with social etiquette, but aren't you supposed to flutter your eyelashes at me or make some type of idle conversation?"

Lucy blurted, "I'm performing mathematical calculations in my head."

Not enamored with my company then. An uncomfortable knot settled in his chest as he deduced the most probable question to cause her to perform sums.

Could he impress her with his estimates?

"I would calculate it to be approximately another fifteen minutes until the dance is over. It will be another forty-five minutes before you can escape, assuming you allow me to escort you to supper with your friend and brother, and another fifteen minutes before the carriage can be out front."

Looking down at a wide-eyed Lucy, he was pleased with his own mental calculations and ability to read people. "I suggest you relax and enjoy the next seventy-five minutes, to be exact, and let me take care of you."

He was acutely aware that her body had stiffened and was now replicating those wooden movements he was accustomed to. She was apparently not at all impressed with his reckonings, nor his intuitiveness.

"While your calculations may be fairly accurate, I do not need to be *cared for*, and especially not by you." Lucy's response was filled with disdain.

Total failure. All chances of an amicable reunion were dashed. His hopes of Lucy returning his regard were crushed—pulverized. Granted, he had met her when she was only a little older than a decade, but he had allowed his adolescent infatuation to continue to grow into something more over the years. Matthew had shared with him every letter Lucy had sent during their years at Eton. Her letters had revealed a curious, brilliant, witty girl that longed to attend university. While he was away carrying out his duty to the Crown on the Continent, he had received letters from Matthew that were filled with vivid accountings of her as she matured.

Blake looked down at the woman dancing in his arms. She was not the lady he had fantasized about. But the compelling pull he had thought existed over a decade ago remained strong. *He still felt it.* Why didn't Lucy? Her facial features indicated she was oblivious. She appeared to be totally indifferent to his looks and behavior. Both her physical and verbal responses had made it perfectly clear she was neither eager nor interested in being in his company. His faith in his ability to gauge and read people was sorely tested in this instance. A heavy weight descended upon his chest. For years Lucy had represented life in England and had provided him a reason to carry on. But Blake was firmly planted in reality—the woman he had created in his mind did not exist.

Releasing a deep sigh, he loosened his hold. "Beg pardon, Lady Lucy. I'm sure you are correct—you are indeed quite capable of caring for yourself."

LUCY WASN'T sure how to handle the riot of emotions that coursed through her. Her waltz with Blake had begun like every other she had endured during the evening, in total silence. Only this time her partner seemed instinctively in tune with her movements. He was an exceptional dancer, in full control, but with a hint of recklessness that excited her. But when he had magically read her mind, Lucy had become wary of his intentions. Over the years, conducting investigations had taught her not to trust anyone.

Her body seemed to want to be closer to his—it trusted him to propel her in the right direction. His clever calculations were impressive, and her mind wanted to spar with him. It was his overbearing comment that had her bristling. But then he straightened his arm and placed an extra inch between them. Instantly, she found herself longing to be closer and feeling a little lost at no longer experiencing his radiating heat.

Blake's features were masked and entirely devoid of the intensity and interest she had seen earlier. By the end of the dance, she was fatigued and in desperate need of a few hours alone with a novel. Anything to distract her from the feelings the man had aroused in her.

He escorted her back to her brother and bowed in her direction. "Lady Lucy, I bid you a good night."

Blake ignored both Matthew and Grace and left her in their care. How extremely rude. Apparently, the man had no social graces to speak of. Yet, even though she had been the one to erect a wall of silence during their dance, she was disappointed at his leaving. Admittedly, she had behaved poorly in his company. How did he conjure in her such strong reactions?

She followed Matthew and Grace to a table where she replayed her interactions with Blake in her head. She should not refer to him by his given name, even in her thoughts, especially after sharing only one dance with him. It had started during the waltz, when he held her in his arms and she felt safe and secure. *Blake*. The man was, in fact, a conundrum.

She resolved to limit her interactions with him until she had thoroughly analyzed his effect on her.

Lucy gazed into the distance. Pretending to be preoccupied with her own thoughts, she listened as Grace conspiratorially asked Matthew, "What do you think she said to him?"

"I have no idea, but Devonton did not look pleased when he returned her to us. Let us leave right after supper."

Lucy lowered her gaze to her plate to avoid Grace's attention as her friend muttered, "I, for one, am ready to leave now."

Grace's declaration caught both Lucy's and Matthew's attention. Matthew was the one to speak first. "Are you feeling unwell?"

Intrigued to see the concern on her brother's face, Lucy waited for Grace's response.

"I'm well. I just... I'm eager to retire early this evening."

Assessing the pair, Lucy was unable to gauge the strength of the undercurrent of energy that always seemed to exist when they were in each other's presence, but there was no doubt of its existence. It appeared to Lucy that Grace was having trouble keeping her mind on the current conversation. Did Matthew have a similar effect on Grace as Blake had on her, obscuring all reasonable thinking while heightening all bodily reactions?

Matthew stood and announced that it was time for their departure. How long had Lucy been woolgathering? Glad she no longer had to convince Matthew to leave, she led the way as they returned Grace to her chaperone, who was dozing in the drawing room.

Before leaving, Lucy asked, "Grace, shall I call on you tomorrow afternoon?"

"That would be lovely. I'll have Mrs. Simmons bake some of those scones you love."

Lucy turned to face Matthew. She searched his features for any indication that his relationship with Grace was more than friendship. As if in answer, he dismissively tipped his head in Grace's direction as a form of goodbye and escorted Lucy to the foyer to await their carriage. Matthew never once glanced back, but Lucy was sure Grace's gaze remained on him as they departed.

THE WHEELS HAD BARELY COME to a stop before Lucy was jumping out of the carriage. Eager for the opportunity to finally review the missive tucked safely in her garter, she bounded up the stairs and turned to make her way to her chamber. Bursting through the door, she nearly ran right into her maid.

Carrington squeaked as she sidestepped her mistress. "My lady, I was just getting the warming pan ready for the sheets."

Carrington was Lucy's staunchest supporter of her irregular activities, and they had long ago dispensed with most of the customary formalities, with the exception that Carrington refused to address Lucy by her given name.

"Not to worry. If you could just help me out of this gown." Lucy reached down to gather up her skirts and raised them up past her garter. She retrieved the parchment and waved it in Carrington's direction. "Tonight I received a note from you-know-who. As soon as I'm done dealing with the matter, I plan to wander down to the library to retrieve a book. I might even seek out Cook and ask for a nice warm glass of milk."

Carrington moved to assist Lucy with her buttons and stays. "Will you need my assistance tonight?"

Free from her stays, Lucy stepped out of her dress. "No need, Carrington. I'm sure I'll manage—Off to bed for you."

Lucy waited for the door to click closed before lighting a candle and placing it on top a stack of books she had by her bed. Settling on the bed closest to the light, she carefully unfolded the foolscap with smooth, efficient moves, ensuring she did not smudge any of the words. Groaning, she recognized the handwriting. It belonged to none other than her superior, Graham Drummond, the Earl of Archbroke, head of the Home Office. The man may act the dandy for polite society, but he was a genius, acknowledged by all. Despite his intellect, Archbroke's arrogance and opinions regarding the female sex often prompted Lucy to provoke him into admitting she was by far the most effective decoder in the department.

Lucy went to work on decoding the contents of the note. Since it was in the code she had devised for the Home Office, within minutes she was reading:

Lady L,
Apologies for the short notice.
Meeting. Mr. Smyth. Lone Dove. Ten in the morn.
Arrangements have been made.
Anticipated return Tuesday.

She refolded the correspondence and waved it about, causing the candle to flicker. As she padded over to the fireplace, she muttered, "He asks this of me now! How does he think I'm going to disappear at the height of the Season? Men!"

Discarding the letter into the fire, she stared into the

flames and began to work on formulating a plan for her departure. With the last remnants of the missive turning to ash, she ran and jumped into her bed, extinguishing the candle. Lucy laid her aching head upon her soft pillow and closed her eyes, her book and glass of milk long forgotten.

CHAPTER THREE

$\mathcal{L}$ucy had rolled about in bed throughout the evening. Images of a faint scar just under a man's chin, the slight angle of a tooth that was set among straight ones, the freckle that was revealed under the cuff of his sleeve—all images belonging to Blake.

Unwilling to ponder the effect the man had on her, Lucy rose before the sun and went to seek out Matthew. Her brother was an early riser irrespective of the time he returned in the evenings. She wanted to take advantage of his being most accommodating in the morning, prior to frustrations of managing the estate setting in.

Predictably, she found Matthew in his study, and without preamble, she entered and said, "I received a letter from Theo. She has requested I visit her. She is in desperate need of companionship."

Matthew did not bother to look up from the estate accounts. Lucy continued, "I plan to go visit her. May I have the use of the traveling coach?"

Matthew remained focused on the ledgers in front of

him but replied, "Lucy, it is extremely early in the morn to be making demands. We agreed you would be fully engaged this Season. No more jaunts to the country and no more hiding."

Lucy retorted, "I'm not hiding, Matthew. My best friend of our childhood has just lost her papa. How can you say no?"

Was she fleeing from the one man who had managed to evoke more than brotherly affection within her? Blake had somehow invaded her thoughts throughout the night. Perhaps it would be wise to avoid his company. Her mind refused to relinquish the memory of his penetrating emerald-green eyes.

Lucy shook her head to clear her thoughts and waited patiently for Matthew to give her his undivided attention. He finally ceased writing and said, "I thought you were to pay a call on Grace this afternoon."

Perfect. He had played directly into her hand. "Matthew, I wouldn't want to disappoint Grace—perhaps you could call on her in my stead? You could tell her I've left Town to visit a friend for a few days." Lucy gave him a most sincere look, the one he could never deny.

At the mention of Grace, a twinkle materialized in Matthew's eyes, betraying his bored tone. "I'm rather busy this afternoon."

Lucy continued to make her argument. "Theo is like family. She is still in mourning and has been left on her own. Please, just a short stay this time. I'll only be away for six days. I won't even be gone for a whole week. It's not like I've attracted anyone's singular attention; no one will miss me."

As soon as Lucy spoke the words, her mind brought up an image of Blake. Was the man who haunted her dreams interested in her? Was he on the hunt for a wife?

Why was she even concerned? She had given her heart to James, and now he was dead. There would be no one who would understand her as James had.

Perhaps some debutante would capture Blake's attention while she was away. She wrapped her arms about her stomach as if it ached. She needed to cease thinking of the man.

Matthew had refocused his attention back to the ledgers before him. She knew if she offered to attend a social gathering upon her return Matthew would relent and grant his permission. But the idea of attending another ball nearly brought about hives.

But there was nothing else to barter. "I'll be home in time to accompany you to the Emsworth ball. I understand you will need assistance in gaining the right ears to listen to your new bill."

One eyebrow arched. "Very well, you may use the traveling coach, but please make sure you have at least four outriders, two footmen, and your maid."

Happy, Lucy rushed over and hugged him. "Thank you, and I promise to be back in time for the blasted ball." She released Matthew and made her way to the door.

Before she crossed the threshold, he called out, "Lucy! *I* will miss you!"

ONCE LUCY HAD Matthew's permission, her loyal contingent, which consisted of Carrington and two footmen, John and Evan, gathered in the library. She never traveled without the trio. Lord Archbroke had assigned them for her first official journey on Home Office business. After years of working together, the trio was irreplaceable.

RACHEL ANN SMITH

"My lady, the coach will be readied and available posthaste," Evan informed Lucy as he entered the room.

She shouldn't have been surprised—the trio often anticipated her orders—yet in this instance, she hadn't even mentioned a thing to Carrington as she dressed this morning, her thoughts preoccupied with Blake. Her clever maid must have figured Archbroke's note would result in them traveling. She was grateful for their efficiency, which normally allowed her to focus on the issues that required her attention, not random thoughts about a handsome stranger.

She needed to regain her unwavering concentration. "John. Evan. Matthew has ordered a minimum of four outriders, and that will be how many we will employ. You will be armed, of course, but given we are set to venture about Town, it would be a waste to hire more."

Lucy had ordered the travel coach as a ploy to divert Matthew; she sincerely hoped it would not be necessary for the entire time she was away.

She had traveled to the Lone Dove on many occasions to receive further details regarding her assignments. The tavern was a reasonably short distance located at the edge of London's city limits and at the crossroads of two main highways leading in and out of Town. She prayed her task could be completed in the comfort of one of the Lone Dove's well-kept rooms. She shuddered at the notion of being cooped up in the travel coach.

"Carrington, I expect we will be gone for six days."

"Yes, my lady. I'll ensure we are ready as soon as the coach is brought around." Carrington flew out of the library.

"My lady, it is your intention to remain inside the coach, is it not?" John bravely dared to ask.

Lucy replied, "While we remain in Town."

She began to formulate her plans. If they arrived an hour early, it would allow her enough time to change and scout the inn. She was familiar with the inn's layout and would post footmen at each entrance. That was not Lucy's concern. She was interested in who would be patronizing the inn while she conducted her meeting. Would any of her associates be present? Should Carrington accompany her to the private parlor or remain in the hired room?

Lucy decided it best to meet her correspondent alone and have Carrington arrange for supplies in the event they were indeed required to travel out of Town.

As she turned, she began, "I should…" But the room was empty.

Before lowering her voice, Lucy twirled about, ensuring she was entirely on her own, then said, "Lucy, your orders are to change and ensure the assignment is completed successfully. Stay focused. Be sure you are home in time to accompany your brother to another boring ball, for you might just run into the man who has your thoughts in a muddle."

Giggling at her own antics, she left to ready herself for the upcoming week. Indeed, her imitation of Archbroke was pitiful.

Carrington was tapping her foot, eager to get her mistress into her traveling gown as Lucy entered her room. "Carrington, really. The pale blue? It is by far the most uncomfortable dress with all the extra frills and whatnot."

"I've suggested you cease using your mama's modiste and seek out the services of Mrs. Lennox, for your entire wardrobe and not just for particular items."

"Mama would never accompany me to Mrs. Lennox's establishment. It is already a trial to convince mama to leave the house. I will employ Mrs. Lennox to outfit me when the time is right."

Lucy had always been mindful of her expenses; her modiste and milliner bills were never outrageous, and she never asked for an advance of her pin money. Rather, she used her funds for critical items that assisted her in keeping her investigations and missions a secret from Matthew, namely bribing the help. With her earnings from the Home Office and the generous allowance Matthew provided, she was never short and even managed to sneak a book purchase once in a while.

Carrington pulled her laces tight, and Lucy had to take in a breath. "Why are you determined to torture me this morn?"

"Why didn't you alert me of your plans this morn?" Carrington tartly replied.

Lucy turned and waited for Carrington to meet her gaze. "Carrington, I'm sorry."

And with that simple apology, Carrington smiled brightly and retorted, "And it won't happen again. I know, my lady."

Lucy let her maid turn her in the direction of the door and fully expected the push in the back and exaggerated her stumble, which sent Carrington into a fit of giggles.

"I'll be right behind you, my lady."

Lucy was confident that Carrington had managed to pack an outfit for every occasion imaginable and squeeze them meticulously into a traveling trunk along with all Lucy's writing supplies. One never knew what opportunities might present themselves. Since the end of the war, Archbroke rarely required her services, which had led to Lucy taking on other clients. Admittedly, assisting in the recovery of a runaway ward or lady was not as challenging as decoding for the Home Office. However, it provided Lucy with a sense of purpose, one that she would not relinquish for a marriage of convenience.

Eager to be on her way, Lucy descended the stairs where the traveling coach and her footmen were awaiting. As she climbed into the coach, her mind wandered to Blake once more. What would his activities be for the day, for the week while she was away? Were his thoughts as muddled as hers?

CHAPTER FOUR

*H*ands clasped behind his head, Blake lay on the uncomfortable and ill-sized bed he had inherited along with the long-neglected town house. He should be making lists of needed repairs or meeting with his steward, but his mind kept returning to the events of the previous evening. Cursing his inability to forget an image, he reached for his notebook. If he sketched her, maybe he could focus on other matters. But he was deceiving himself—capturing her image on paper would only reinforce his ungodly desire for the woman.

His pencil flew over the parchment as he envisioned every physical detail. Lucy had undeniably grown into a beautiful woman, but it was the spark of her invigorating energy that intrigued him. He replayed their conversation. He would have to brush up on his social etiquette, for he had clearly offended her on the dance floor. What to say when dancing with a fascinating lady?

His interactions with the fair sex over the years had been limited, for the most part having no company but his own while on the Continent. Recruited by the Foreign

Office immediately upon completing his exams at Oxford, he had spent little time these past years among the *ton*. He had built no repertoire of *bons mots* with which to flatter and flirt. All his efforts had been in service to the Crown, honing his natural skills of absolute recall and artistry.

Blake glanced at the stacks of boxes that lined the side-wall of his bedchamber. They contained numerous journals and rolls of maps he had compiled while on the Continent. Journals filled with portraits of royalty from various countries, along with dignitaries and the enemy. Some held images of key towns and their defenses. But the rolls of maps, evidence of his cartography skills, were his key possessions, for they had provided vital information for Wellington and his men. Blake understood his skills were critical to England and its allies' success; thus he had remained on the Continent until the Corsican was exiled to Elba.

Blake held the drawing up. The woman staring back at him was not the image of the lighthearted and enthusiastic girl he had carried with him all these years. Fool that he was, he had fallen in love with the girl he had met during his one and only visit to Halestone Hall. Blake had believed those feelings well buried when Harrington had informed him about Lucy's attachment to their neighbor Lord Taylor and how in love she was with him. He had been crushed to learn there was an understanding between both families that Lucy would someday marry Taylor.

Frustratingly, Blake had even liked the older boy with aristocratic good looks who was a protector of the weak when they attended Eton. Lord Taylor represented the quintessential heir to a title, honorable and well liked by all, who yet carried himself with humility and grace.

While Blake had inherited the title of earl nearly a decade ago, he was still uncomfortable among the prying eyes of the *ton*. The Continent was no different. His aristocratic features and fluency in the language had occasionally landed him assignments in the French court, but he had always been most comfortable traveling in solitude.

Returning to England meant resuming his responsibilities. And that he was no longer alone. He was constantly sought out day and night by servants, friends, and acquaintances. It was taking a toll on his nerves. An immediate solution would be to find a wife and retreat to his country estate, Shalford Castle.

After seeing and conversing with Lucy last night, he questioned if he had ever really been successful in burying his feelings for her. He had held on to her image, his perfect English lady. But did Lucy's heart still belong to her beloved Taylor?

Before his mind could engage in any further thoughts of Lucy, Blake rose to prepare for the day. Unaccustomed to being waited on, he went to his wardrobe to retrieve a clean shirt.

From the middle of his bedchamber, Gordon said, "My lord, I believe that is my duty."

Blake flinched as if he had been caught doing something he shouldn't. How long would it take to become accustomed to having others constantly nearby? Comfortable with servants at his beck and call?

"Gordon, I've dressed myself for the past decade—I'm certain I can manage without your assistance." The man's face fell, and Blake instantly wanted to retract his harsh words. "It will take me some time to adjust to being back in England. Bear with me; it will sort itself out."

"Yes, my lord."

"I need to send a message to Harrington. Could you assist me with that?"

"That would be Henderson's job, not mine."

Having been self-sufficient for his duration on the Continent and having never paid attention to these matters prior, Blake was making a hash of his reentry into English society. "Excellent. I'll speak to Henderson directly then. I aim to attend the Hereford soiree this evening. Does that give you something to attend to?"

"Yes, my lord. I appreciate you informing me with notice."

Blake glanced down at the intricately tied cravat Gordon had created without his notice. Tugging at the neck cloth, Blake said, "Gordon, I prefer simple, unassuming designs so as not to draw attention."

"Understood, my lord."

Gordon was a good and loyal servant. Blake didn't want him seeking out another household. He had better placate the man. "For today this will be a nice change." His valet must have interpreted his statement as a dismissal, for he promptly left the room.

I need someone who can assist me in assimilating back into the role of earl. Not someone, a wife. His mind had cataloged images of many beautiful women since returning to London, but only one lady remained at the forefront.

He padded over to retrieve the sketch he had left on his bed. Lucy was a confounding challenge. Could he convince her to explore the magnetic pull that was obviously evident between them?

CHAPTER FIVE

*L*ucy issued orders through the coach window. "Evan, I need you to ride ahead and ensure all will be ready for our arrival."

Evan's brow creased, but he nodded his assent. Why the displeasure? Evan was normally only too happy to do her bidding.

Sliding over to the other side of the coach, she pulled back the curtain. "John, whatever is the matter with Evan?"

"Beg pardon, my lady?"

"Why was Evan surly when I asked him to ride ahead?"

John peered into the coach, eyeing Carrington, alluding that a relationship had blossomed between her and Evan. It had never occurred to Lucy that Carrington might one day marry. She had assumed that she and Carrington would become spinsters and grow old together. Did Carrington wish for a family? How selfish of Lucy to have never asked.

Lucy considered children blessings. She often had dreams of raising a large brood, but for that to occur, it would require her to be married first. She could not fathom any gentleman of her acquaintance allowing her to continue the various activities that she believed essential. Why then did Blake's name come to mind?

The coach rolled to a stop before the Lone Dove. Lucy pulled out her pocket watch. Pleased to see she had plenty of time to spare, she smiled at the innkeeper, Mr. Barnwell, as he came out to greet her. Taking his outreached hand, she alighted from the coach.

The man's cheeks were flush as he gushed, "My lady, it is extremely good to see you. We have a chamber ready for you."

Lucy gave Mr. Barnwell a broad smile and preceded him into the inn. During daylight hours, the Lone Dove appeared more than respectable; however, as soon as the sun set, the inn began to fill with a number of interesting patrons. On occasion, Lucy had visited during the darkened hours. It was during these trips that she had been introduced to an entirely different set of society. Over the years, she had formed friendships and traded advice with pirates, naval captains, opera singers, Cyprians, hell owners, crime lords, and Bow Street Runners. Today, none of her acquaintances were present, only weary travelers.

After being shown to her room, Carrington assisted Lucy out of her traveling gown and helped her don breeches and a ruffled lawn shirt she hid under a riding habit. What would Blake think of her attire? How would he react if he found out about her association with the Home Office? She hadn't shared such information with Matthew. Theo was the only soul she had ever confided in. Lady Theodora Neale, her childhood best friend, was like a sister. Theo was always willing and able to provide her with an alibi for her disappearances. Theo's support had allowed Lucy to accomplish many a mission without raising Matthew's suspicions.

Distracted by the growling of her stomach, Lucy was overjoyed when a tavern maid scratched at the door and, upon her command, entered with a tray. Carrington eyed the contents of the tray as the maid slipped out of the room.

"Mmm. Carrington, doesn't it smell delicious?"

Carrington peered at the bowl made from bread, filled with a hearty stew. "I would have ordered a light repast."

"Evan did his best."

Carrington snorted. Strange—the two were usually inseparable and in accord. A lovers' spat. Her earlier suspicions were confirmed, for that was the only logical explanation for Carrington's volatile behavior.

Lucy sat at the table near the window and let her mind wander as she consumed the meal before her. She was back in the countryside, racing her mare and jumping over hedges. She could feel the wind biting her cheeks and the rhythmic beating of hooves.

She loved the freedom of the country, yet her work and her causes required her to often venture to London. Combined with the fact that Matthew had an obligation to attend the House of Lords, their family tended to reside in Town longer than most. He was committed to the fight for universal suffrage, as their papa had been. While Matthew gave the appearance he had taken on his role as the head of the family with ease, she sensed he was heavily burdened. This was in stark contrast to their mama's transition to widowhood eight years ago. Their mama had been pregnant at the time of their papa's death and had chosen to retreat into solitude. Even after the birth of their younger brother, Edward, Mama had remained reclusive, never attending social engagements and preferring the sanctuary of her rooms.

It was silly of Lucy to continue to associate Town life with her papa's demise. Her papa had been attacked and knifed by a ruffian trying to steal his coin. Memories of the dark days after his death began to resurface. Her whole body began to physically shake, and she stood abruptly, trying to rid herself of these unwanted feelings.

The meal no longer interested her, and she militantly walked toward the door, pausing before she crossed the threshold. "Carrington, be prepared to leave on short notice."

Continuing to the private parlor, Lucy refocused her thoughts on the meeting about to take place. By the time she reached the room, she had regained her composure and calmly stood by the window to await her correspondent.

A scratch at the door had Lucy issuing the command, "Enter."

A young man entered, similar in age to herself and with nondescript features. "Miss Jones?"

Lucy replied, "Mr. Smyth, I assume. It is a pleasure you could join me today."

The man didn't say a word but proceeded to stare. Was there a problem? Why did he not just pass on the message and leave as all the others had in the past? Mayhap it was his first assignment. She continued to be patient, but an awkward silence fell between them.

Unexpectedly, the man smirked. "Miss Jones, my apologies, but I was told to look for a lady who had many years of experience."

Lucy was smiling sweetly, but her tone was direct when she addressed him. "I appreciate your honesty.

35

However, I would prefer our business to be conducted swiftly."

When Mr. Smyth reached into an inner pocket of his jacket, Lucy tensed. He slowly pulled out a bundle of paper.

"Yes, yes. Here you are. A good day to you, Miss Jones." Despite his farewell, Mr. Smyth remained standing in front of Lucy, staring at her as if she were the most interesting woman he had ever encountered.

Reaching out, Lucy pried the packet from Mr. Smyth's fingers. Good gracious, did he not trust her in her claim to be Miss Jones? She dismissed him with a nod, and the very young Mr. Smyth made his way to the door.

Before leaving, he turned and said, "My superiors should have advised me to look for the most beautiful woman at the inn. That would have made identifying you a lot easier and would have been a most accurate statement. I hope to make your acquaintance again."

Stunned, Lucy stared at the now-empty doorway. Had Mr. Smyth really called her beautiful? She had been referred to as sweet, adorable, cute, and even pretty by some, but never beautiful. Lucy made a mental note to ask Carrington if she had done anything different with her face paint or her hair today.

Putting the curious comment aside, Lucy walked over to the fireplace. Carefully, she opened the packet Mr. Smyth had given her. The top page read:

Enclosed correspondence was intercepted from the Continent.
Arrangements for you have been made at Bloomington Inn.
They will be expecting your arrival.
Please advise upon your return to London.

Lucy threw the letter into the fire and watched as the

last of it turned to ash. She rolled the missives, lifted her skirts, and securely tucked the papers into her breeches. Smoothing out her attire, she walked calmly out of the inn and toward her contingent, who were patiently awaiting direction.

"John, we are headed for Bloomington Inn."

"My lady, that is at least another half day's ride, longer mayhap with the coach."

Lucy searched the sky. The position of the sun indicated it was a little past midday. They still had several hours of daylight to travel by.

With no time to spare, Lucy commanded, "Let's be off."

Both footmen grimaced but followed her orders nonetheless. Bloomington Inn was a fair way from London. Why hadn't Archbroke made arrangements for her to remain at the Lone Dove? She should cease questioning her superior. After all, she trusted the man with her safety. If he weren't such a pompous ass, she might actually like him.

Perched on the edge of the forward-facing seat, she reached under her skirts to retrieve the missives. She passed them to Carrington, who promptly stored them safely in Lucy's satchel. What information would they contain?

HER CONTINGENT COULDN'T HAVE BEEN on the road for more than an hour, but Lucy had already become intensely restless. She eyed Carrington, who sat reading what looked to be one of the novels Lucy had recently finished. She loved discussing the various characters and scenes with her maid, but she wasn't one to read in a coach. The jostling and effort to focus made her feel ill. "What chapter are you reading?"

"Nine."

"Oooh, that is when…"

Carrington's glare halted Lucy's speech. "Only events through Chapter Eight, *my lady*."

The emphasis on the honorific was not lost on Lucy. Not in the mood to spar with her maid, she pulled back the curtain to look out the window. Deciding they had traveled far enough for her to escape the confines of the coach, Lucy rapped three times.

Immediately, the driver yelled, "Whoa!"

"Already? You could at least warn me!" Carrington snapped the book shut and hurriedly moved to assist Lucy out of her riding habit, exposing her breeches and lawn shirt.

Carrington magically produced a fine riding jacket that had been explicitly made for warmth. The two of them were jostled about the small, confined space. Carrington fell to her knees as the coach came to a complete stop.

Lucy waited patiently for the door to open. Evan appeared, and the corner of his lips turned up as he caught a glimpse of Carrington on all fours.

Not waiting for assistance, Lucy jumped down from the coach and marched over to Evan's mount. She was about to reach for the reins when broad hands wrapped about her waist and lifted her. Once seated, she glanced down at Evan with a mischievous grin and kicked her heels, spurring the horse to take off. Lucy loved riding astride, but she reined in her mount to a trot, allowing the coach that now housed Carrington and Evan to catch up.

Now that they were beyond the city limits, the air was cleaner. Lucy breathed deeply—not a trace of ash or the acerbic smell of waste. She considered renting a room for the night at an inn. In the end, she reasoned in order to return to London on time, they would have to continue forward through the evening. John and Evan were going to be displeased with her decision. She would have to use some of her savings and pay the pair a little extra this month.

John and Lucy rode side by side, leading the coach. As customary, John had begun to share tales of his eight siblings' most recent escapades.

Lucy giggled as John continued, "...and Lotty fell face-first into the mud as she dove for the piglet."

John's family resided in the village near Halestone Hall. Lucy wondered if he would send the extra funds she planned to give him along with his monthly salary to his parents. How should she reward John? He was a selfless man. She would have to devise a way for him to person-ally derive a benefit. He certainly deserved it. She continued to ponder the dilemma, and John continued to share stories.

After luncheon, Evan and John switched places. Lucy was not as comfortable on John's steed since it was at least a hand taller, but she still preferred being out in the open. Evan did not have any family Lucy was aware of. None he told stories about, anyway. To pass the time when they rode together, they had formed the habit of creating bawdy melodies and poetry that would never be uttered in a drawing room.

Lucy was laughing so hard she nearly slid off her mount, but Evan was there to catch her and assist her to regain her seat. As he was removing his arm from around Lucy, she caught Carrington peeking from the coach window. The confusion on her maid's face caused Lucy to take a closer look at Evan. Perhaps some might call him handsome in a roguish way. He was always lighthearted but extremely diligent in his duties. She glanced back at the coach once more.

"She didn't see you falling, my lady." Evan's eyes scanned their surroundings, on the lookout for bandits or highwaymen.

His comment made no sense to Lucy—unless there was more to their relationship than both being in her employ, as she had suspected earlier.

Confirming her suspicions, Evan added, "I've been saving, but I fear she is running out of patience with me."

Lucy broke out into a genuine smile. The best reward for Evan would be to assist him in attaining a beautiful ring for Carrington. She made a mental note to send word to Mr. Rutherford, the jeweler her family had used for generations. Lucy was momentarily pleased with herself. That was before she remembered she had yet to determine what John's reward would be.

As they ventured farther north, the temperature dropped significantly. John and Evan's pleas for her to join Carrington in the coach fell on deaf ears. Lucy remained mounted through most of the night. Finally, about two hours from their destination, an exhausted Lucy accepted her fate and rode in the coach. In the quiet her thoughts were haunted once again by Blake; his image was the last she remembered before her eyes closed.

On the final leg of their journey to Bloomington Inn, Carrington woke Lucy to change into a thick traveling dress made of velvet. The soft material brushed against Lucy's goose-bumped skin. Lucy rubbed her eyes as the dawn of light peeked through the coach window. "How much longer?"

"Not long." Carrington's lips twitched right before she added, "If you catch a cold as a result of your stubbornness, I will not play nursemaid."

Lucy slumped back and propped her feet next to Carrington. "You know how hale and hearty I am. I doubt my actions will result in a sniffle."

Giving her mistress a knowing look, Carrington said, "We will just have to wait and see."

CHAPTER SIX

he coach rattled into the Bloomington Inn courtyard. Lucy had not ventured here in the past, but she had heard tales of its beginnings from fellow agents. The inn had initially belonged to a Scottish lord but had been seized and gifted to an English one. After several generations of neglect, the large manor had been abandoned and left to rot. That is, until entrepreneurial Mr. Bloomington found, purchased, and refurbished it. Upon first sight, he decided to modernize the manor to accommodate and attract the *ton*. Agents had expounded ad nauseam on how spacious the rooms were, how there were even a few with adjacent sitting areas, and had compared the inn to the king's palace.

Lucy alighted from the coach. Stepping back, she took in the sight of the inn; early morning rays of light glinted off the two rows of windows. Taking the steps up to the entrance, Lucy's mouth fell open. Large double doors were of Viking proportions. *Blake would be able to easily walk through without hunching to enter.* Why had she brought Blake to mind? Doormen swung the doors open for her. She smiled at each of them as she entered. Slowly turning in the foyer, she was astounded by the sheer size and grandeur of the reception area.

"Miss Jones?" a clerk inquired.

Closing her mouth, she nodded and approached the desk.

"We were not expecting you until much later. You and your party must have traveled throughout the night and be exhausted."

She rapidly initialed the register. The clerk motioned for a footman, who escorted her and Carrington up to her room. Over the years, her dealings with the Home Office had taught her to never underestimate her intuition. She couldn't shake the feeling something was amiss. Entering the lavish chamber, Lucy ignored the beautiful decorations, the rich textured wallpaper, the plush carpets under her feet, and the inviting bed covered in silk pillows and soft cashmere throws. She walked through the two adjoining rooms and assessed the doorways, windows, and overall layout. Why had Archbroke sent her to this luxurious location? Knowing the man, it couldn't have been out of consideration for her comfort. Or was it?

Carrington entered from the adjoining room and spun around in wonder. "My lady, this is perfect for your needs. I shall go belowstairs and bring up a tray. Coffee or tea?"

"Coffee, please. I'd like to begin working as soon as possible." Lucy stopped Carrington with one more request: "And please keep your ears open."

In a tone that indicated Carrington was offended, she stated, "As always."

Lucy had best reward Evan as soon as practical. Carrington's quick changes in disposition were leaving her flummoxed, and she did not care for the feeling one little bit.

She approached an extraordinarily elegant desk near the window. Settling into the chair, she retrieved the missives from her satchel and arranged the papers to her liking. Grateful for the sunlight streaming in, she began to study the words carefully. Without thought, Lucy reached for her writing instruments, which Carrington had already arranged. The girl was going to receive a beautiful ring indeed.

~

Lucy's HEAD rested in the crook of her arm on top of the desk that she had occupied for the past two days. Wisps of hair had long ago escaped her chignon. A stray strand moved back and forth with each breath, tickling her nose. But it was the warmth streaming through the window that brought Lucy out of a deep sleep. She rubbed her eyes. Despite having worked through the night, she still had not broken the code.

Conflicted, she was frustrated at her progress while simultaneously thrilled to be challenged. The complexity of the missives led her to believe the content must be significant, for no one went to such lengths otherwise. The frequency patterns used were elaborate and unfamiliar to her. Lucy was curious as to who could have designed the code, for the French had a terrible habit of being somewhat lax in their use of cryptography. These seemed to be using numerals not only to represent words or phrases but also something Lucy was just not able to determine.

She found herself questioning what Blake would think of this or that. The man had interrupted her peace of mind, and she needed to rid him from her thoughts.

Stretching her arms out caught Carrington's attention. "My lady, you are awake. I'll ring for a bath."

Lucy sniffed and agreed a bath would be a grand idea and would do wonders to relax her sore and tired muscles. "Carrington, a light repast and a bath would be nice."

Carrington flashed her a quick smile and then abandoned her project of organizing the discarded notes.

It wasn't long before Lucy was soaking in a warm bath. Mr. Bloomington had devised a system where hot water was now accessible on the upper floors, allowing maids to prepare baths for patrons efficiently without the assistance of footmen to bring up buckets of hot water.

Closing her eyes, she rested her head back, picturing the contents of the missives. She had already ruled out keys she had successfully used in the past. There was a familiarity in the design, yet she was unable to definitively identify the missing link. She distractedly took the sandwich Carrington placed in her hand, sloshing water as she began to eat.

Carrington broke the silence. "My lady, I have a new riddle for you. What is flat and round, has two eyes, but cannot see?"

Lucy loved solving Carrington's often wayward word puzzles. Grinning, she mulled over this latest as her maid rinsed the soap from her hair.

Carrington splashed soap and water into Lucy's eyes. "How am I to figure out the answer if you keep blinding me?"

"My lady, I've never known you to make excuses," Carrington was trying her best to stifle a giggle but failed.

Hearing Carrington's giggle, Lucy decided to tease her more. "Is it a... pie?"

"A pie? No, my lady, it's not a pie." Carrington was now drying Lucy and trying desperately not to laugh.

Stepping out of the tub, she pretended to be deep in concentration. A smirk appeared as Lucy tightened her lips to prevent the chuckle from escaping. "Alas, it has to be a... button!"

Carrington inhaled deeply and swallowed her laughter. Shaking her head, she said, "Yes! I'll have to try harder to befuddle you."

Seated, Lucy's mind began to refocus on her task while Carrington tugged and combed her hair. The riddle had given her an idea. The code contained an item she could not see.

"Carrington, I must return to work." Lucy turned to face her maid. "Thank you."

With a fresh perspective, she was close to deciphering the missive. She could feel it in her bones. Lucy walked back to the antique desk and began to review the pile of notes she had made.

Blurry-eyed, Lucy asked. "What time is it?"

"It will be time for supper soon, my lady."

Had she been working all day without interruption? Blinking, she tried to focus her weary eyes. Carrington was on her hands and knees, surrounded by papers. Had she caused that mess?

"What are you doing?"

Carrington huffed her reply. "I'm trying to put these papers in order."

Lucy should help clean up. Scrapping the chair back, she stood. But her legs buckled, and she had to lean on the desk for support.

"Carrington, you can cease organizing. I've figured it out. Certain numerals and combinations are blanks, disrupting the flow of the pattern."

"Did you not devise something similar for the Home Office, my lady?"

"Yes, and I should have recognized it days ago, but I was unaware the French had used that method in the past." Lucy was questioning the source of the missives.

"Well, what does it say?"

Lucy leaned closer to the lamp and read aloud the decoded message:

"*Imperative. Apprehend and disarm. Target: Lord D. Ensure he is not harmed. Must be in good health. Deliver on June 19. Lone Dove.*"

Odd that the rendezvous point would be the Lone Dove. It was not known as a locale where French operatives convened. She suspected the Home Office was in search of a traitor.

Further, the recipient of the missive must already know the identity of the target, for it only stated Lord D. There were multiple Lord Ds among the *ton*.

Lucy's frown deepened as she considered whether Blake, the only Lord D she was acquainted with, could be the target. Nauseated at the notion he might be at risk, she determined to find out for sure.

The missive had a target date of June 19. That gave her a month to figure out who Lord D was and formulate a plan to ensure his safety. She prayed it would not turn out to be Blake. Why she had such strong feelings for the man, she did not understand. But there was a bond that had been established when he had held her in his arms.

CHAPTER SEVEN

*W*hile Harrington pored over correspondence, Blake lounged in one of the two wingback chairs positioned near the window in the well-organized study. It had become routine for him to arrive each morn to join Harrington and his family to break their fast. At first, Blake had been disappointed to find that Lucy had decided to adjourn to the country. However, as each day passed, his intuition grew stronger that her departure was somehow related to him. Harrington had explained that his sister was visiting a friend in mourning, but he was rather vague about the details.

Blake had been waiting for days for the right opportunity to bring up the topic of Lucy. Should he disclose his longtime infatuation with his best friend's sister? His inability to forget a face was considered a boon by most. However, there were times he considered it a curse.

Lucy's image had remained at the forefront of his thoughts since the day he laid eyes on her. Every night for nearly a decade, she came to him as soon as he closed his eyes to sleep. For years he had tried to banish the vision of her, especially after Harrington had informed him of her attachment to Lord Taylor. His errant mind stubbornly held on to her features, specifically her ever-changing gray-blue eyes.

Blinking to release the image of Lucy, Blake focused his gaze on his surroundings. In stark contrast to his own cold and sparsely filled town house, this room was a mix of comfort and practicality.

Blake commented, "Your household runs extremely efficiently, Harrington."

"Now. But when I first inherited, wasn't it the same year as yourself? How old were we?"

Blake recalled the year vividly—his parents had been taken in a carriage accident. "I was sixteen, which would have made you fourteen."

Harrington's eyes darted to meet Blake's. "Well, my papa had many talents, but the management of the estates was not one of them. I tried my best, but being away at Eton made it difficult. When Lucy offered to take over, I didn't hesitate, for she has a brilliant mind. By the time we graduated Oxford, she had everything in order, which made it all the easier for me to resume my responsibilities, although I have to say it is mighty time-consuming. How have you fared while away on the Continent?"

Blake turned to gaze out the window. He didn't care to speak of his family, despite the passage of time; it was still painful to think of and refer to his parents.

On an exhale, he answered, "My papa was blessed with the talent for managing estate accounts, but he had also hired extremely talented stewards, whom I trusted to act on my behalf during my years away. I haven't visited Shalford Castle, but I've been informed that apart from having to refurbish a few rooms, all is well."

Blake didn't mention that only a few staff remained

since he had not taken up residence after he inherited. He had always managed to obtain an invitation to a friend's house for the holidays, and then he left for the Continent.

"That reminds me. Lucy should return home tomorrow."

It took every bit of Blake's self-control not to press Harrington for details of Lucy's absence. His original plan had been to visit Harrington in the hopes he would have an opportunity to apologize to Lady Lucy for not joining her for supper the other evening. But when Harrington informed him that she had left Town, he had patiently waited for her return. Tomorrow.

Lord Edward, Harrington's eight-year-old brother, bounded into the room, full of exuberance. "Lucy's to return tomorrow?"

"Yes. She promised to accompany me to the Emsworth ball tomorrow evening."

Blake made a mental note to go through his salver to see if he had received an invitation to the event.

"Devonton, would you care to join us?"

"Perhaps."

Lord Edward faced Blake solemnly. "I'd rather stay at home and read a book than have to deal with the nattering of the ladies."

Blake had never heard the word. "Nattering?"

"Yes, nattering. I heard Lucy use the term."

Harrington coughed. "Edward, you are not to eavesdrop on Lucy. In fact, no eavesdropping at all."

"Well, it isn't eavesdropping if the person is speaking loud enough for all London to hear, now is it?"

"Edward, please do not be obtuse. You know what I mean."

"Yes, Matthew. No eavesdropping."

Blake chuckled as Lord Edward crossed his fingers

behind his back while making the promise to his brother. Just as quickly as he entered, the boy exited. "Harrington, he is too clever by half. You will have to keep an eye on him and put his intelligence to good use."

Harrington groaned. "Please do not tell me you were implying I should introduce him to Archbroke."

"Of course I wasn't *implying* such a thing. More to the point, I was *stating* the fact."

Lord Edward, being the second son, would need a purpose, and if Harrington didn't believe the Home Office could use a brilliant mind, then Blake would speak to his own superiors. The Foreign Office's leaders were more broad-minded. They even employed female agents, which Blake believed was ingenious. He held in a chuckle at the idea of Archbroke employing a female to assist the Home Office. If he did, it would have to be one remarkable woman to put up with him as a superior.

Harrington's fingers tapped against the chair but stopped when he asked, "Do you miss wandering all over the Continent?"

"Not particularly."

"To have seen and experienced new cities, different languages and cultures." Harrington's voice was tinged with longing.

In an effort to keep the conversation and his tone light yet still communicate the challenges he faced during his time away from home, Blake replied, "Perhaps now that the war is over, the Continent might be a tad more alluring, but the constant traipsing from one supposed safe haven to the next was not my ideal life. Being held captive for days, weeks, on end was not the adventure I assumed I'd signed up for when I agreed to assist the Foreign Office."

"My apologies. I did not mean to remind you of those times."

"No apologies necessary, Harrington. I'm no longer a young lad seeking adventure. I am of an age now that I need to attend to my duties here in England." He had just declared he was in search of a wife. Would Harrington encourage him to consider Lucy?

"By duties, are you suggesting you want to become leg-shackled? You have only recently returned. We have time before we need to marry."

"Harrington, a wife could help me ease back into society. I'm unaccustomed to having people about, and Town life is not to my liking. I'd prefer to find a wife and retreat to Shalford Castle."

"Devonton, you are but four and twenty. We'll find you a mistress and…"

"You are not listening. I don't want a mistress, Harrington. I need a wife."

"A wife… Huh."

"Yes, one that has a mind."

Harrington chimed in. "A bluestocking?"

"A woman that can easily converse on varied topics, fashion, politics…"

"Not a bluestocking then."

"A lady who is beautiful inside and out."

Had Harrington not realized Blake was describing Lucy? Did he not deem Blake worthy of his sister's hand? Blake considered Harrington like a brother. Could it be that Harrington viewed Blake more like a brother to Lucy than a potential suitor? If that was the case, did she see him in the same light? He would seek her out later this eve and try to uncover how she perceived him.

Eager to return to his town house to look through his salver, Blake bid Harrington goodbye.

CHAPTER EIGHT

*L*ucy hadn't taken but a few steps into the foyer before Matthew accosted her. "You're home! How was Theo?" He bussed Lucy on the cheek, then stepped back and took a harder look at her. His concern was written on his face. "Lucy, is everything all right? Did you have an issue on your trip? Was there an incident?"

Lucy had dark circles under her eyes. The journey home had exhausted all her remaining energy, and now she was totally drained of any patience she might have had left.

"If you would just let me speak, I'll be able to answer your questions." She sighed and walked into the drawing room. As she passed Kirkland, the butler, she glanced up and smiled. Hopefully the man would return with coffee, but she knew it was more likely Kirkland would bring tea, as a proper lady would drink.

With Matthew following on her heels, she turned and said, "I'm well, just a little tired from the travel. Theo has decided she should enter half mourning and will not come to London for the Season even after her mourning period is over. I was dreadfully disappointed and spent days trying to convince her otherwise. After all, misery does love company."

In fact, she had corresponded with Theo over a series of days. Not only had Theo confirmed she would happily provide Lucy with an alibi, as she often had in the past, but she also faithfully wrote reassurances of her belief in Lucy's abilities. Theo was a stout supporter of Lucy's involvement with the Home Office, and she was ever grateful for her childhood best friend.

She sank onto the settee and curled her legs under her skirts as she used to as a child. She closed her weary eyes. Her mind was awash with memories of when she and Matthew used to play in the drawing room instead of up in the nursery. Matthew would pretend to be her guard. He would keep watch and listen for footsteps, but as soon as he sensed or heard someone approaching, he would wake Lucy up and help her to the chessboard, making it appear that they had been playing for hours.

The fond memories had Lucy smiling until Matthew muttered, "I had hoped you would return rested. You know we have a number of commitments to attend, and I need your support as I'm launching a new bill."

When had he turned into such a stick-in-the-mud? "Matthew, what you need is a wife! She can then attend to all your initiatives, and you know the lords do not take bachelors seriously."

This was an old but frequent argument the two of them had had for the past two Seasons. At the onset of Lucy's first Season, Matthew had declared he was not going to consider marriage until he ensured she was married and suitably settled. Which was absolutely ludicrous since she was quite capable of taking care of herself.

As the words rolled about in her mind, she thought of

Blake and their conversation. Perhaps she should share her plan to set up her own household with Matthew, and then he might cease his insistence on her marrying.

She was about to outline her plan when he stubbornly announced, "Lucy, I've not the time today to discuss the issue. We both know my position on marriage, and it will not change. You are my sister, and you will be betrothed by the end of the Season. Please rest, and I'll be back this evening to escort you to the Emsworth ball."

Lucy remained with her eyes closed for if she opened them, they would be rolling backward, which would only infuriate Matthew more.

Assuming he was leaving at the sound of his boots hitting the floor, she opened her eyes. However, he was leaning over her with concern marring his features. "If you are really too tired, I will understand."

Never one to not fulfill a promise, Lucy said, "I will be ready. Will all your friends be in attendance also?" She hadn't wanted to call particular attention to Blake, but she was interested in finding out more about the man and in turn rule him out as the intended target.

With a narrowed gaze, Matthew replied, "Yes, I believe most of my set will be there in support. One never knows about Devonton. He tends to be somewhat of a recluse."

At the mention of Blake, Lucy had fluttered her eyelids closed and faked a yawn, to mask her interest in Matthew's response. The click of the door confirmed Matthew's departure. Eyes already at rest, it was only moments before she was sound asleep.

SEARCHING THE CROWDED BALLROOM, Lucy spotted Grace and Grace's aunt, Lady Emily Allensworth, by the terrace doors. As Matthew and Lucy's arrival was announced, Grace turned toward them. Did her gaze linger a tad longer on Matthew than normal? Matthew's penetrating stare brought Blake to mind. Blake had mysteriously provided Lucy with a whole new perspective.

As they made their way through the crowd, Matthew bent and whispered, "I'm headed for the card room. I expect you know who you are supposed to acquaint yourself with."

He did not even bother to wait for her confirmation before he hied off in the opposite direction.

When she was within speaking distance, Grace asked, "How was your visit? You look exhausted."

Lucy had chosen to wear an evening gown in lavender. A bold choice for an unmarried woman in her second Season, but she continued to wear the color out of loyalty to James. While James rarely entered her thoughts these days, she had yet to meet a man that made her feel as he had, secure and confident in her abilities. Since she was set on not marrying, Lucy had decided to wear colors that pleased her and not what was at the height of fashion.

She hid a yawn behind her gloved hand. "It was pleasant." Trying to stifle another yawn, she admitted, "I hope to decline the first gentleman who asks me to dance so I can beg off for the rest of the evening."

"Lucy! You know how important tonight is for your brother!"

Why was Grace so defensive of Matthew? Her feelings for him must be much stronger than Lucy initially believed. Testing her theory, she said, "I don't know why he is being stubborn. He should just marry. That way I wouldn't have to attend all these society events with him. All he has to do is find some politically minded bluestocking and make her the happiest of ladies. He hounds me to find a husband, but he doesn't even pay the least attention each year to the lovely fresh debutantes. There are a number who would suit him rather well this year, yet he hardly ever dances with anyone."

Grace's features had transformed from calm and serene to tortured and heated. Why hadn't Grace confessed her attraction to Matthew? Lucy considered Grace one of her best friends—they should be able to confide in one another. Was Grace keeping other secrets from her? Admittedly, she had never shared with Grace her involvement with the Home Office, and Grace never pried or questioned Lucy's impromptu trips.

The color in Grace's cheeks was beginning to dissipate as she said, "You two are both extremely stubborn. Matthew will marry when he is ready. It is not common for a man of his age to be ready to… how do the men refer to marriage? Leg-shackle themselves."

Curious to find out the true depths of Grace's feeling for her brother, Lucy said, "No one will take him seriously in the House of Lords if he doesn't settle down and breed an heir. He has sound positions, and I want him to succeed. You should hear some of his speeches. He is brilliant."

Admiration and pride flashed across Grace's features. Had she heard of Matthew's positions? The smirk upon her face indicated she was familiar with Matthew's addresses. How could that be possible? Matthew only practiced in his private study.

But instead of a confession, Grace changed the topic entirely. "Lucy, Lord Hereford and Lord Archbroke are both young, handsome, wealthy, and very honorable. Why do you continue to treat them more like brothers than suitors?"

"They *are* like brothers! I know them better than they know themselves, and they…"

"What? Out with it, Lucy."

"They… They don't make my heart race." Lucy paused, searching for the right words. "I want to look into a man's eyes and see desire flare when he looks at me. I want…"

"You have been reading too many Minerva novels. Are you seeking lust or love?"

Lucy frowned as she replied, "Are they not linked? Don't tell me you believe they are both independent. If you loved someone, do you not think you would also crave his physical attention?"

The lines in her forehead deepened. Now that she had spoken the words, did she believe them? She had loved James, hadn't she? She had given her promise to marry him—how could she not have given him her heart as well? She tried to recall the brief moments James had held her. What had she felt? Nothing as memorable as the tingling sensations she had experienced while dancing with Blake. Perhaps Grace was right. Maybe it was one or the other. But to think love and lust were mutually exclusive did not bode well with Lucy.

She continued to debate out loud. "Although, men might argue that one should lust after his mistress and love his wife. Hmm… Perhaps love and lust might be considered independent emotions, now that I have given it more thought. I should also take into consideration that the probability of a marriage based on love is, well… near nonexistent."

Lucy glanced at Grace, curious about her reaction to her monologue. Her features were as serene as ever, not even the slightest hint of a blush given the topic of discussion.

One of these days I'm going to break through her masquerade of total control. It was always this way. The more controlled Grace became, the more Lucy's own actions spiraled out of control. The hairs on the back of Lucy's neck started to rise.

She glanced up to find Lord Devonton staring directly at her. He was standing alone, slightly hidden from sight by a potted plant. Why was he hiding? He had taken one of her favorite hiding spots, which raised her ire. Had he taken up the position on purpose? While he took on the appearance of being relaxed and unassuming, Lucy suspected he had ulterior motives. Was he spying on her? Now that he'd spotted her, why was he not coming to ask her to dance?

Their gazes locked. Lucy wondered why it was she could not draw her eyes away from him. Was he casting some sort of spell on her? Was Blake a mind reader? His actions at the Duke of Fairmont's ball and the familiarity with which he addressed her had driven her to distraction during her assignment. Not to mention her imagination running wild with visions of him paying court, flirting, and dancing with another caused her heart and stomach to ache in a way she had never experienced before.

All her reactions to Blake made no sense. She hardly knew the man, but every time he was in her proximity, she was drawn to him. But was he as attracted to her?

CHAPTER NINE

$\mathcal{D}$espite having entered through the side door, Blake found himself cornered by his hosts.

Lord Emsworth said, "Devonton, it is a pleasure to finally see you back in Town."

"My lord, we are glad you are here this evening." Lady Emsworth's eyes raked him over and then shone with pride. The couple had always been generous toward him. They were among a small group that were close friends of his parents, who had provided support when he needed it most.

"Lord Emsworth, it is a pleasure. Lady Emsworth, you have outdone yourself tonight. The ball is a crush, and I can see there are many lovely ladies in attendance."

Her ladyship gave him a curious look but politely replied, "Please allow me to make any introductions you might seek."

Perhaps in his haste to please the woman, he had overstepped. For there was only one woman he was interested in seeking out.

"My thanks, Lady Emsworth. Excuse me. I must find

Lord Harrington." Blake briskly made a retreat and set out to find a private location from which he could observe the crowd.

Having found the perfect spot, he took full advantage of his height and scanned the ballroom. As soon as Lucy was in his sight, he mumbled, "Goodness, she is beautiful."

She was wearing a silk gown that shimmered as she moved. What could she be possibly discussing with Lady Grace? Lucy's hands fluttered about in the air, her animation transforming him from bored to curious. Blake's full attention was caught when she ran her gloved hand up along her arm, followed with a fluttering motion near her heart. He wished he could read lips, but from her expression and the slight blush on her cheeks, he imagined it was not a discussion on the latest fashion.

After what felt like an eternity, Blake finally caught Lucy's gaze, and once he had it, he was not going to be the first to break contact. He could look into those ever-changing gray-blue eyes all night if need be. Blake had missed her. Had she really left Town to visit a friend in the country? An unsettling feeling in his gut caused him to believe the excuse for her disappearance right after their meeting to be a ruse.

What am I doing standing here? I should just walk over and ask her for a dance. He was about to give up the prime spot from which he could see everything and everyone when Archbroke sidled up to him. In the end, it was Blake who broke his gaze from Lucy, which promptly made her smile.

Blake was cursing under his breath. "Of all the people to cause me to lose to Lucy…"

Archbroke greeted him with a knowing smile. "Devonton, glad you are out and about tonight. We haven't seen you about Town in the past week or so."

Apparently, it had been noticed that he had not

attended a single event while Lucy was away. "I'm still getting used to Town hours and becoming reacquainted with everyone."

Blake glanced at the Home Secretary's ensemble. His waistcoat was of a color similar to Lincoln green, the cravat so intricate he likened it to a puzzle, and shirt points that were plain ridiculous. When had Archbroke become a dandy?

Frowning, he asked, "Do you still fence? I need to find someone to practice with. Harrington is no longer a challenge."

"Fencing?" Archbroke's high-pitched voice caught Blake by surprise.

He blinked, clearing his vision. Stunned, he tried to reconcile the dandy standing before him and the master-mind who ran the Home Office. Few knew of Archbroke's involvement. Was acting the fool really the best disguise?

Archbroke continued in the annoying tone. "Harrington is by far one of the best in our set. If he is not up to snuff, you will be hard pressed to find another as skilled as him. However, I recently joined Gentleman Jackson's. I find I quite enjoy watching the fights. Are you a member yet?"

Blake replied, "I'm surprised you are a fan of pugilism. Seems rather barbaric, does it not?"

"Perhaps you are right. I should take up fencing again rather than risking this lovely face of mine in the ring." Archbroke turned his head to show Blake his profile and gave him a lopsided grin. "Speaking of lovely faces, spying on our Lady Lucy over there, were you?"

Guilty. Blake responded a little too quickly, "Who?"

"Don't play games, Devonton. You were gaping at Harrington's sister. It is common knowledge you never forget a face, so what's what?"

Blake tried to compose a calm, aloof response. "I have no idea to what you are referring. Lady Lucy and I have only recently become reacquainted, and as you pointed out, she is Harrington's sister, after all. I imagine he wouldn't appreciate me taking an interest in her."

As if letting him into a secret, Archbroke resumed what Blake knew to be his natural tone. "Harrington can't wait to get Lady Lucy married off. He told us all at the beginning of this Season that if any of us could convince her to marry, he would be glad to have us as a brother. Mind you, that was not his tune the year she came out. That Season, he clearly instructed us to protect her since she was still grieving. But apparently he has had a change of heart and all but dared one of us to succeed in wooing her."

"Then why have none of you asked her to dance tonight?"

"Lady Lucy has just returned from one of her trips to the country. She is never in a good mood upon her return. We all know to give her a day or two before even daring to go near her, or she will give us the cut direct."

Had Archbroke issued him a dare? Devonton never backed down from a challenge. Lady Grace and Lucy were still standing by the terrace doors. As he made his way over to her, he hastily devised a plan to woo Lucy.

BLAKE HALTED JUST to the right and bowed. "Good evening Lady Grace, Lady Lucy. It is a pleasure to see you again."

To Lucy's irritation, Grace performed a perfect curtsy, which only made her own appear hasty and poorly executed. Making matters worse, Grace used her most alluring tone. "Lord Devonton, it is always a treat to be in your company. Lady Lucy has just returned from a quick jaunt to the countryside to visit a friend. She was regaling me with some of the events of her trip."

With a single brow slowly raised, he asked, "Lady Lucy, where did you venture to?"

"Nowhere of interest to you."

Grace poked Lucy hard in the arm and admonished, "Don't be rude."

Lucy relented a little and plastered a smile on her face. "Lord Devonton, please excuse me; I'm feeling a bit parched." She turned her back to him. "Grace, I'm going to the refreshments table."

As she turned to leave, a heavy hand stopped her. Lucy cried out, "My lord, unhand me!"

Blake bent down to speak into her ear. In a low, sultry voice he said, "You are making a scene. I'm sure if you continue, your brother will inquire as to whether or not he needs to meet me at dawn. If you allow me to escort you to the refreshments table, all will go easier."

With a deep sigh, she knew he was correct. Defeated, she placed her hand on his winged arm, practically running to keep up with his long strides. She turned to seek help, but Grace wasn't right behind them as expected. Instead, she was now in the company of Matthew, who was standing a little closer than what propriety would allow. The two were oblivious to their surroundings. How had Matthew materialized out of thin air? He did have a habit of appearing next to Grace quite often.

Lucy turned her attention back to the man who was basically dragging her to the refreshments table. Why was he behaving this way? Where was the attentive Blake she remembered from the Duke of Fairmont's ball? Or had her memory played tricks on her? She looked up through her lashes, only to see him gazing right down on her bosom. The nerve of the man. He should be behaving like a gentleman. Yet at the same time it made her feel wanton, and it was exciting.

Daring to be bold, Lucy inquired, "Do you see something of interest?"

Blake's eyes flared and his lips formed into a wicked smile that was designed to tempt its recipient. "Yes, I do find you of interest. I enjoy viewing you from all angles, but particularly from this one."

Raising a hand to the side of her neck, a vein beat against her fingertips erratically. The slight buzzing in her ear was accompanied by dizziness. If Blake could inflict this type of physical response with the simple insinuation that he liked observing her, it would be dangerous to continue to verbally spar with him. None of Matthew's other friends were able to challenge her except for Archbroke, but he was her superior. She could feel the pink in her cheeks and the tops of her breasts, like his gaze had scorched them. Reaching for a glass of punch, he brushed the back of his hand across her stomach. The contact caused a jolt of electricity that ran throughout her entire body.

Instinctively she took a half step away and peered up at him. Seeing the smug look on his face, she snipped, "Lord Devonton, do you not have to locate someone else? Surely you have a dance partner eagerly awaiting you."

"In fact, my sweet, I have not promised any of the lovely ladies a dance and seek your guidance on those I should honor tonight."

Lucy raised up onto the balls of her feet. Her eyes instantaneously fell upon a set of ladies standing by the wall. "Well... there is Lady Olivia over there, the brunette. It is her third Season, and she is a lovely girl with a dowry of ten thousand. Lady Marjorie, the blonde—while she is shy, she can converse in five languages and has a dowry of twenty thousand... and then there is..."

Blake interrupted, "Who is the lovely lady with the mahogany hair standing all alone over there?" He discreetly pointed out the lady in question and added, "She looks to have a fine figure and..."

She glanced over to the spot he indicated. Lady Mary. A wave of jealousy hit her. She liked Lady Mary. She was kind, intelligent, and beautiful. Most men found her intelligence a deterrent, but she sensed Blake would find it attractive. Why did it bother her that he showed an interest in someone other than her? Hadn't she just encouraged him to dance with another? She really needed to sort through these conflicting thoughts and emotions.

Lucy assumed a disinterested tone. "That is Lady Mary. She is the daughter of the Duke of Seaburn. She is musically inclined and plays the pianoforte well. Unfortunately, she only has a moderate dowry. She is in her fourth Season and has been referred to as a bluestocking, which just means she has more intelligence than the men she's conversed with."

As she rattled off the details, Blake's gaze never once left Lady Mary. While she searched his features, her jealousy turned to pain, which was exacerbated when he asked, "Would you be so kind as to introduce me?"

Her sight blurred, but her voice remained calm. "It would be my pleasure, if..."

"What is your hesitation?"

"I would want to make sure your intentions are honorable. I consider Lady Mary a friend, and I wouldn't want to be responsible for any heartbreak."

Blake's teasing tone had returned. "It is only an introduction. I don't intend to seduce her right on the dance floor. What type of cad do you take me for?"

Lucy's mind went blank. She had never imagined anyone talking to her in such a manner, and to even think about seducing someone on the dance floor would imply he was a rake.

"Lady Lucy, do you really think Lady Mary would fall in love with a plain gentleman such as myself?"

Eyes wide, she stood and stared at Blake. Her mind was a jumble of questions. Did Blake just refer to himself as plain? Was he just being modest? Or was that indeed how he viewed himself? Plain would be the last word Lucy would use to describe Blake. He was at least a few inches over six feet, with disheveled, short-cropped ash-brown hair that just begged to have her hands run through it. Combined with arresting green eyes and an aristocratic nose that he seemed to always be looking down at her with, Blake was nothing less than striking.

"I do believe women are more likely to swoon for a handsome rake. I was under the impression ladies believe reformed rakes to be the best husbands. Was I mistaken?"

Taking her time, she continued to contemplate his looks. Perhaps his overall appearance could be described by the masses as plain, yet the more Lucy observed him, the more appealing he became. As she was taking in his full measure, an idea occurred to her: was his intention for her to take a closer look at him? What a devilish plan, yet if that was his intent, he was far more intelligent than she had given him credit for.

In the end, Lucy found her voice, and rather than answering his question, she merely stated, "Lady Mary is a self-proclaimed wallflower. I'm sure she would appreciate a gentleman, even one as plain as you, to pay attention to her this eve. Shall I make the introduction now?"

~

HIS HEART RIPPED APART when her eyes began to mist. The flash of sadness came and went in such a flash that if he didn't possess the ability for exact recall, he would have questioned what he had seen. He had set out to charm her, not upset her. Few women were able to rein in their features as well as Lucy had.

What was he doing, admiring a woman who had just called him plain? She had remained quiet while he attempted to tease and flirt with her. She was willing to introduce him to a friend. Had he not returned to society to seek out a bride who would be happy with a marriage of convenience? But the challenge of winning Lucy over was too hard to resist.

He arranged his features into a mask of innocence before asking, "And what if my motives are not honorable? What if…"

He could almost feel the wave of heat and anger roll off her as his words sank in. No, the woman standing before him would never be amicable to a marriage of convenience.

"Lord Devonton, you have been away on the Continent for an extended period, but I would hazard Matthew would never associate with a man who would not share his gentlemanly honor."

Did he hear her correctly? He found her bold declaration heartwarming. Here was a lady whom he had just become reacquainted with, but she was willing to defend his character. The volatility of his thoughts and emotions only caused his interest and determination to increase.

Lucy grabbed his hand. Delighted at the physical contact, he paid no attention to where she was leading him, nor did he care. He would follow her wherever she desired.

They had only managed to move a few steps forward

when they were approached by Lord Waterford. "Devonton, you are monopolizing Lady Lucy. What are the two of you discussing? Maps, geological formations, site elevations?"

Blake responded, "Who sounds like the cartographer now? Since when did you take any interest, Waterford?"

Waterford's eyes blazed, and in them Blake recognized pure loathing. What had he done to deserve such hatred? Blake hadn't seen the man since their days at Oxford. While they had not been best of chums, they were at least friendly back then. Blake and Waterford had never crossed paths despite both of them having been on the Continent for the duration of the war.

Ignoring Blake entirely, Waterford turned to address Lucy. "Well, my lady, are you enjoying Devonton's company or is he being a total bore?"

She shifted slightly closer to Blake, and he placed his hand on her lower back as reassurance. Was Waterford drunk? His eyes were clear, and there was no evidence he was inebriated. Blake did not care for the way he was making Lucy uncomfortable.

Bless the woman's heart, she tried to lighten the mood. "Lord Devonton was actually making inquiries into the characters of this Season's wallflowers. He claims his appearance would be more attractive to those who stand along the wall."

"Well, I'm not sure any would find his appearance attractive, but I'm sure they would appreciate his bluestocking conversation far more than the diamonds of the Season. I too may be interested in hearing more about these paragons. While I may not be of the same intellect as Devonton here, I believe I could hold my own with any of them."

What was the man implying? Blake had always

achieved excellent grades—it would be difficult not to, with his recollection—but Waterford had achieved high marks right alongside him. He couldn't figure the man out.

Lucy carried the conversation once more. "We were discussing the esteemed Lady Mary over there."

Waterford's spine stiffened. "Ahhh, Lady Mary. It is her third or fourth Season out, am I correct?"

Apparently, the implication that Lady Mary was long in the tooth did not sit well with Lucy. She sharply reminded Waterford, "It is her fourth, and there is nothing to be ashamed of in having experienced more than one Season."

The trio stared in Lady Mary's direction. The poor woman looked around her. When she found she was alone and the sole recipient of their obvious attention, she nodded in their direction, acknowledging their rather rude behavior, and walked directly out of the ballroom.

Lucy moved away, but before she could escape, Blake placed a hand on her elbow.

"Lord Devonton, you will need to excuse me. I need to… well, I need to find Lady Mary."

He bowed and whispered quietly, "Please extend my apologies if I somehow made Lady Mary uncomfortable. That was not my intent."

Blake released her. Lucy's eyes locked with his just before she turned and headed toward the hall Lady Mary had disappeared into. The sadness in her eyes made his heart ache.

AFTER ENTERING THE LADIES' retiring room, Lucy searched for Lady Mary. She found her standing in front of a mirror.

Lucy approached the woman with her gaze lowered. "Lady Mary, please, if I may…"

Lady Mary's hand rose and halted her speech. "Lady Lucy, how nice to see you again. What were you and your contingent of admirers whispering about me?"

Well, Lady Mary didn't hold back punches.

Opting for the truth, Lucy replied, "My companions noticed you and were interested in seeking an introduction." Before Lady Mary could make a comment, Lucy rushed on to say, "However, I advised them I would only introduce you if you agreed and only if they had honorable intentions."

Lucy held in a breath as she shifted from one foot to the other, awaiting a response. When none was forthcoming she asked, "So, would you care to be introduced to Blake Gower, the Earl of Devonton, and Gilbert Talbot, the Earl of Waterford? They are by and large honorable, but I wanted to seek your approval first."

She bit her cheek to remain quiet, in agony as she waited for Lady Mary's reply.

Finally, Lady Mary put her out of her misery. "I'm already acquainted with Waterford. He was formally introduced to me in my first Season. Perhaps I am forgettable."

Quickly, Lucy replied, "It was Devonton who requested the introduction. Waterford just happened to join us. I'm sure he remembers you and would like to become reacquainted."

Lady Mary stared directly at Lucy, who was a few inches shorter. "Lady Lucy, I do not care to be the butt of any jokes, and while I appreciate your friendship, I do not wish to offend. An introduction to any of your brother's cronies holds little interest."

Lucy was taken aback by the direct response. "My apologies, Lady Mary. I did not intend to disrupt your evening. I will take my leave, and I hope you will forgive me. I hope you enjoy the rest of the Season. I shall not bother you again."

Darting out of the retiring room, a sinking feeling settled in her stomach. Had she lost a friend? She didn't have many to start with. As her eyes began to water, Lady Mary called out from behind her, "Lady Lucy... wait." But the tears were already flowing.

Widening her stride, she ran to seek out one of her hiding spots.

CHAPTER TEN

*B*lake spied Harrington guiding Lady Grace from the dance floor. Why was he continually scanning the room? Was there a threat?

Blake remained standing by the refreshments table as the couple approached.

Harrington reached for a glass of lemonade and handed it to Lady Grace. "Damnation, why does she always sneak off? I'm tired of hunting her down at every social event. We will have to split up. You check the usual places, and I'll start on the terrace."

Lady Grace accepted the watered-down refreshment and gave an impermissible nod. The woman was not at all phased by Harrington's blustering.

As the marquess released Lady Grace, he gave her hand a small squeeze, which did not go unnoticed by Blake. Before his friend could begin his search, Blake spoke up. "Harrington, how are you this evening?"

"I'm in search of my twin yet again. Have you seen Lucy?"

"She went to find Lady Mary, not ten minutes ago."

"Oh, well, at least she is not off reading a book and hiding somewhere. She is supposed to be assisting me with my newest bill. By the by, I'm happy to have you reside with us next week. Shame about the roof leak at your town house."

"What? Take up residence with you? Whatever for?"

Harrington dropped his voice to a whisper. "I received orders I must ensure"—his eyes scanned their surroundings to see who was about—"your safety."

"I do not need a nanny. I am quite capable of ensuring my own safety." Blake had received word from the Foreign Office that the Home Office had intercepted correspondence that indicated he might be the target of a planned abduction. They had cautioned him not to take undue risks and advised him not to leave Town.

"Well, I have my orders. I'm sure you will receive yours shortly."

Momentarily stunned by the turn of events, Blake remained rooted to the spot as Matthew took his leave through the terrace doors.

PACING WHILE WAITING in the foyer for his carriage to be brought around, Blake was still unsettled by the fact that the Home Office felt it necessary for him to reside with Harrington. He didn't even work for the Home Office, but since he was now on English soil, he presumed it had jurisdiction over the Foreign Office.

He had survived years on the Continent with little to no support. He had mapped and worked with Wellington to devise safe routes. He had been a witness to many villages brought to rubble. During his entire military career, he had traveled with no batman and no valet, just alone with his travel bag. He was not used to being around the same set of people day in and day out. He was also not a complainer. But to have others run interference in his life now was rather inconvenient.

He inhaled another deep breath to gain patience. A flash of lavender caught his attention, and the click of a door closing sharply piqued his interest. That lavender gown Lucy was wearing was delectable. What was she doing abovestairs? Was she meeting someone?

Curiosity got the better of him as he took the stairs two at a time, soundlessly approaching the door he guessed she had entered. He could clearly hear someone sobbing. Why was Lucy crying?

He crept into the dark room, closing the door behind him. Leaning against solid wood, he waited for his eyes to adjust before whispering, "Lucy, my sweet?"

He reached out for her in the darkness. His hands met with air and then fell to his sides. The scent of lavender tickled his nose. She was near. His muscles simultaneously tensed and tingled. He needed to touch her, make sure she was well.

She drew in a breath and replied, "Lord Devonton, I do not believe I have given you leave to call me by my given name, nor is it appropriate to call an acquaintance by such an intimate endearment."

"Lady Lucy, are you crying?"

"I never cry. I have no idea what gave you the notion. Why are you here?"

"Perhaps I should ask the same of you."

"I needed to repair my dress, and I could not find the ladies' retiring room."

Jealousy spurred Blake to ask, "So you are not meeting someone?"

"With whom would I be having an assignation?"

"There are a number of lords here this evening who would love the opportunity. I'm sure if you were to show even a little interest, many wouldn't mind being caught in a compromising situation with you." He took a step closer. "Can I be of assistance with your dress?"

"I do not believe you have the necessary skills to assist me. However, if you would kindly leave before we are found together with the door closed, I would greatly appreciate it since I do not wish to endure a scandal of any sort."

"Why would there be a scandal? Unless we were found in an exceedingly compromising position, there would be nothing to gossip about." In fact, that would not be the case, and Harrington would surely call him out.

Eyes fully adjusted now, he took another step closer, which brought him within inches of Lucy. She could have retreated, but she chose not to.

"Lord Devonton, I ask that you leave immediately."

He reached out, turned her by the shoulders and tried to view her dress. He could see nothing wrong with her dress in the dark. He put an arm around her waist and gently pulled her back. Lowering his head to her ear, Blake teased, "I'm unable to find fault with your dress. Perhaps there is a problem with another article of your clothing." His breath was hot and his voice silky.

Did the chit just shiver in his arms? The tension in her body began to dissipate, and she leaned back into him. It felt right.

Turning to face him, she uttered, "What do you know of women's clothing?"

He grinned and skimmed his hand down her spine,

inching one button at a time until his palm rested on her lower back, which he began to rub in a circular motion. "I confess I know little of women's fashion, but I can assure you I'm an expert in divesting women of all their clothing in a very efficient manner."

He could feel her muscles relaxing. But then, as if realizing the illicit nature of their meeting in a room alone, she stepped away. "If you will not leave, I must return to the ballroom and find Matthew so we can depart posthaste."

Did he want to force the issue with Lucy? No, his preference would be for her to come to him of her own free will. When she moved to open the door, he didn't stop her.

"Do not follow me too closely. Wait a while before leaving."

Lucy peeked out into the hallway, and then, before he could blink, she was gone.

He had to give himself, and certain body parts, a minute to recompose. Lucy's light lavender scent remained, making it difficult. Having had her in his arms, he was determined to have her in them again, and soon. Perhaps residing with Harrington might not be such an inconvenience after all.

As she descended the stairs, Lucy spied her brother below. The groan she exhaled had Matthew gazing up at her. She placed her foot on the last step and steeled herself for the barrage of questions from her twin.

"Where on earth have you been hiding? Were you abovestairs with someone? It better not have been Arch-broke or one of the others—I'll call them out!"

"Matthew, you have this annoying habit of asking

questions without pause. Please let me explain, and all will be well."

Annoyingly, he raised one eyebrow, the skill Lucy had always been unable to achieve.

"Well, you see, I lost my way, and I was looking for Lady Mary to apologize, and I…"

"Lucy, you have the best sense of direction I know. There is more lead in your nose than most. I'm not an idiot. Please tell me the truth."

Clearing the lump in her throat, Lucy replied, "The truth is there are very few ladies who I would like to be friends with, and tonight I think I have offended Lady Mary… I'm just exhausted and out of sorts. Can we please leave?"

It was frustrating that ladies were not afforded the same opportunity to form as close friendships as gentlemen, for girls were not sent to study at schools as excellent as Eton or Oxford. She had been fortunate her papa had not objected when she started to attend lessons with Matthew. Glad to have company in the schoolroom, Matthew always encouraged her. Oddly enough, she excelled in the subjects he struggled with and vice versa. Matthew was never one to boast, was always extraordinarily patient, and assisted her in mastering topics that left her feeling like a dullard. It was also during this time they realized that they shared the ability to sense each other's strengths, weaknesses, and if they wanted, to anticipate each other's thoughts.

With Matthew's nod, Lucy released the breath she was holding, and relief flowed through her, knowing he fully understood her dismay.

She followed her brother back to the ballroom. Assuming they were to say their farewells to their host and Grace, her focus remained on Matthew's tailcoat, ignoring inquiring stares. She walked directly into his back when he came to an abrupt stop.

"Devonton! I would ask a favor of you. It is such a crush tonight, and it will take some time for our carriage to be brought around. Lucy is exhausted and would like to return home summarily. Would you please escort her there? I still have a matter to settle in the card room."

Lucy turned abruptly and glared at him as she spoke. "Matthew, it is not proper for Lord Devonton and me to be alone in the carriage. There will be gossip."

"Lucy, I trust Devonton. He is like a brother to me."

Blake addressed Matthew directly over Lucy's head as he winged his arm toward her and she placed her hand on his bicep. "I'd be honored to escort Lucy home. She will be safe with me."

When Matthew turned to leave, Blake gave Lucy a devilish wink. It sent shock waves throughout her body. Deciding that there was no other choice but to go with Blake unless she wanted to make a scene, she shuffled her feet, willing them to move through the throng of guests who waited for their carriages. Avoiding eye contact, she wondered what pressing issue Matthew could possibly have that he would leave her in Blake's care. But if Matthew trusted and regarded Blake with such respect, perhaps she should too.

"Ready?" Blake asked as his carriage, marked with a distinctive crest, moved to the forefront. As he handed her in, she couldn't help but note the strength that resonated from this man. His eyes were hypnotic, and when she gazed directly into them, her pulse quickened. It reminded her of how he incited emotions and thoughts that were a puzzle to her. He was a mystery to her, one she would have to figure out.

Lucy settled on the forward-facing seat and expected

Blake to take the one opposite. Instead, he made room for himself next to her, forcing her to move over a tad. She could feel his large, muscled thigh through her gown; his broad shoulders were the perfect height for her to rest her head on, like a pillow. She was trying to deduce why she had this overwhelming need to seek comfort in his arms. The warmth emanating from his body was too much to resist. Lucy leaned into him, and he reached out to cover her hands clasped in her lap.

Lucy did not pull away. She enjoyed the simplicity of his large hand engulfing both of hers. Lost in recollections of their past encounters, she began counting how many times she and Blake had conversed. Five. How could it be so few? She felt a kinship with him, and after each happenstance, she was eager to know more about the man that made her body tingle.

Blake broke her train of thought. "Lady Lucy, I'm pleased to have the opportunity to become better acquainted with you and your family in the coming weeks."

"Pray tell what do you mean?"

"Did your brother not inform you that I will be residing with your family while the roof of my town house is being repaired? Having been away for so long, some of the maintenance on the house has been overlooked."

Surely Matthew would have advised her of such arrangements despite Lucy having just returned. Skeptical at the sudden turn of events, her mind turned over the implications of having another man in the house. "Are… are…" She took a calming breath before she tried again. "How long do you expect the repairs to take?"

As if finding her flustered entertained him, he grinned. "Until all the damage can be assessed, I'm uncertain as to the length of time. However, the workmen will be ready to start next week."

"Next week!" Not only was Lucy's mind whirling around like a tornado, but so were her emotions. What would it be like to be always near him? With familiarity, would these tingling sensations subside? Would he continue to make her insides knot and her bones turn into pudding? He shifted his weight, and again with his touch a wave of heat rioted through her body.

The carriage rolled to a stop. He squeezed her hands that were now hot and sweaty. As the footman opened the door, Blake exited and turned to assist her. Once her feet were planted on the ground, she twisted to bid him good night but found she was expertly being guided up the stoop to the front door.

A step above him, she turned and they were face-to-face. Blake leaned in and whispered, "Pleasant dreams, my sweet," and then left.

Staring at Blake's retreating back, she stood fuming. My sweet! The audacity of the man. Admittedly, for a brief moment, she had thought he would kiss her, and now she was left to contend with this peculiar feeling of disappointment.

NOT READY TO RETURN TO his lodgings, Blake headed to Brooks's to enjoy a late-night drink to wind down and relax. Why was it Lucy could tie him and his muscles into knots? Even with a simple look, she had his body wanting to reach out and touch her in ways only a husband should.

He was getting way ahead of himself—first, on his return, Lucy hadn't even recognized him, and second, she had made it obvious she had no interest in him whatsoever.

But there was no denying her physical reaction to him. Her eyes had dilated, the pulse in her neck quickened, and the color flooded her cheeks.

As Blake downed the last of his brandy, Harrington entered the club and made his way over to a chair next to Blake that afforded both men a view of the entrance.

At the sight of Harrington's scowl, Blake asked, "What has you at sixes and sevens?"

"Nothing, really. Tomorrow I will need to search out Roxbury."

"Remind me. Who is Roxbury?"

Harrington sighed and answered, "He is Lady Mary's older brother."

"Ah, you are going to run interference then?"

Harrington rubbed his temples. "I dislike it when Lucy is upset."

Blake felt some responsibility for his part in causing a rift between the two lovely ladies. "Would you like assistance in tracking the man down?"

"If you would like to accompany me to Tattersalls tomorrow, I'd appreciate the company."

Harrington's mention of his company prompted Blake to say, "I was wondering if we could discuss my living arrangements for next week. I'm not certain your place would provide the best solution."

"What are you implying, Devonton? My town house is not good enough for you? I'll have you know—"

"It's not the town house!" Blake exploded uncharacter-istically. "It is that I do not want to endanger your family. Edward is still a mite, and your mama and sister are also in residence. I'd hate for any harm to befall them as a result of my staying with you."

Harrington reeled back and stared at Blake for a moment. "I'm aware you are unaccustomed to sharing quarters, but all will be well. If everything goes to plan, it will only be for a few weeks."

Neither of them would disobey a direct order. Restless, Blake stood and began to pace.

"Devonton, you are making me dizzy. Will you cease with the pacing?"

"I think better when I'm on the move."

"I don't fully comprehend why now and why you."

Those were the exact same questions Blake had asked himself over and over throughout the night. Why would anyone have a need to kidnap him?

He confided in his friend. "My theory is they need someone with intimate knowledge of a particular area. Since I've toured and can navigate the terrain surrounding various holdings on the Continent, I believe it is that knowledge that they seek."

"I was told all your travels had been well documented. Why not just obtain the necessary maps? Why do they need you?"

Could the man limit himself to one question at a time? Blake mulled over Harrington's queries. "Not all the maps are available. Some are under protection at the Guard House. And who is to say they only have one plan in motion?"

Blake could see the cogs of Harrington's brain churning and his gaze darting around the room. When there was no one close enough to hear their conversion, the marquess said, "I've heard reports of increased activity in several of the known smugglers' dens. In particular, near Sandgate. Perhaps we should…"

"We should what?" Was Harrington implying they directly disobey orders? It was unlike him to suggest such a thing. Orders which stated the men were to remain in London. Blake brought to mind a picture of Sandgate and the surrounding area. "Harrington, did you receive an invitation to attend Lord and Lady Redburn's house party?"

"Redburn. Hmm… Redburn. Yes, I believe we did. However, I typically avoid house parties, and I would never leave Lucy here unescorted."

Not wanting to pass up an opportunity to do some investigating himself, Blake suggested, "Perhaps Lucy would like to attend the house party."

"Are you serious? I can't even get her to agree to attend a ball without having Grace spend days needling her into acceptance. Lucy would be quite content to stay at home with a good book and play games with Edward. If it were not for Grace, she would have sequestered herself to the country and not come to London for the Season. Why do you have an interest in the Redburns' party, anyway?"

Harrington's gaze put Blake on edge. Had he somehow detected Blake's interest in Lucy? To lust after your best friend's sister was not done. Masking his thoughts and emotions, he merely answered, "Redburn's property is in the vicinity of Sandgate."

BLAKE HADN'T BEEN to Tattersalls in years. He would have to consult with his steward as to the status of his stables. A pair of matching grays caught his attention, and he was immediately drawn to them. Their coloring reminding him of Lucy's eyes. Before he could make his way over to the pair, Harrington drew him in the opposite direction, toward a gentleman not much older than themselves.

"Roxbury, good to see you," Harrington greeted.

Roxbury's appearance resembled nothing like his sister, Lady Mary. The lady had warm mahogany tresses with honey-brown eyes, while Roxbury had golden-blond hair with clear blue eyes.

"Harrington." Roxbury turned to face Matthew with a slight frown marring his forehead. "My sister shared a rather interesting story about your sister and some of your friends at a ball she attended recently." He slid an accusing gaze toward Blake.

"Roxbury, please allow me to introduce you to Blake Gower, the Earl of Devonton." Harrington carried on, saying, "I'm not certain of the details; however, Lucy was distressed that she had somehow offended Lady Mary. I'm certain my sister would appreciate the opportunity to make amends, but convincing Lucy to attend any social event is a feat in itself."

Empathy was written all over Roxbury's features. "Well, my mama and sister will be attending the Redburn house party. I swear my mama is at her wits' end to marry Mary off, and if she can contrive a plan to compromise my sister, I'm sure she would at this point."

It was evident both men cared deeply about their sisters' welfare and future. How nice it must be to have a sibling.

With a conspiratorial smile, Harrington quipped, "I might have to join forces with your mama, as I'm having the same issues with my own sister."

Roxbury confessed, "Sisters with above-average intelligence can be a challenge, but since I married a woman of similar disposition, I'm of the mindset that Mary just needs to find a gentleman who can see beyond her mantle. None of my set can even keep up with her." Roxbury's gaze fell upon Blake once more.

Harrington leaned against a stall. "In that case, I sincerely hope I can convince Lucy to go to the Redburn house party."

"Good luck, Harrington." Roxbury left with a broad smile on his face.

"Interesting fellow," Blake commented. Roxbury's regard for women with intelligence was rare. Why had he received pointed looks from the man at the mention of his sister? Roxbury knew nothing of him.

"Devonton, interesting doesn't even begin to describe that man."

CHAPTER ELEVEN

*L*ucy had been busy directing a guest room to be cleaned and aired out for Blake when the sounds of a horse and carriage caught her attention. She peeked out the window to see a valet alight carrying two valises. Interesting. The man traveled light. Perhaps his conservative style did not warrant multiple trunks. Or did he act with an ulterior motive?

Lucy still found Blake to be confounding. The man he presented to the *ton* could easily be referred to as nondescript. His clothing was conventional, nothing garish or out of style. She peered over at the wardrobe she had ordered to be cleared for him and determined it would definitely be adequate.

Her gaze wandered to the bed. Would Blake fit? Did he sleep in a nightshirt? She had overheard one of the upstairs maids share tales with another that her own brother opted to sleep in only his smalls. Images of Blake's large form brought heat to her cheeks. She really shouldn't be picturing Blake in his smalls, but it was an entertaining distraction.

She jumped as the door swung open.

"Beg pardon, my lady." It was the valet she'd seen from the window. He bowed and began to withdraw.

"No—do come in. Are you Lord Devonton's man?"

"Yes, my lady."

At his hesitation, she attempted one of Matthew's eyebrow lifts, hoping for more information. "And?"

"Mr. Kirkland was detained belowstairs, my lady. I'm Riley, if your ladyship pleases, at your service."

"We are pleased to have your master with us." Lucy smoothed out her skirts. "I should go check on Kirkland."

"I believe Lord Edward has him occupied."

"Oh, well then, he should be up shortly. If you need anything, please advise Kirkland. I'm sure he will come to show you the servants' quarters."

"Yes, my lady."

As Lucy left the room, she heard Riley mutter, "Finally to be among those who value English tradition."

What a peculiar statement from a valet! What exotic habits had Blake picked up during his travels? An electric shiver ran down her spine. The *ton* often shuddered and ridiculed foreign practices.

She really should refrain from woolgathering about Blake, but her mind refused to relinquish him as a topic. It was his eyes that mesmerized her. Or was it his innate confidence? Unlike the other gentlemen of Matthew's set, Blake was more interested in her and her thoughts than his own.

Absently, Lucy wandered down the hall to her room. What she should focus her attention on was gathering a complete list of all the possible Lord Ds and not on one particular Lord D.

~

Nose buried in her copy of *Debrett's*, Lucy lost focus when there was a commotion out in the hall. Resisting the temptation to peek out, she pressed her ear to her door.

Kirkland's stoic voice reverberated. "Lord Devonton, it is a pleasure to be of service to you. Lord Harrington has bid you see him in his study. I'll be happy to show you the way."

When the sound of footsteps descending the stairs became faint, she popped her head out of her door, only to see Edward, was doing the same.

He rushed to her. "Was that Lord Devonton?"

"Yes, it was. He is to reside with us while repairs to his town house are made."

Her younger brother's excitement was palpable. It would be good to have another male role model for Edward. Matthew was always preoccupied with estate affairs, and he rarely saw Edward. Lucy tried her best to carve out time for him since their mama was all but absent. Lucy had taught Edward how to dance and play chess and the pianoforte, but she sensed he would prefer to be riding or fencing with Matthew.

Edward pushed his way into her room and said, "He has the most interesting tales of the Continent."

"And how would you know?" Lucy maneuvered him back out into the hall.

Walking to his room, Edward replied over his shoulder, "He came to visit every day while you were in the country." He wagged his eyebrows at her before he closed his door.

Lucy found this bit of information of interest. What had prompted Blake's visits? What were her brother and Devonton up to? Had Matthew been encouraging Blake to pursue her? Was he that desperate to have her off his hands?

~

OCCUPIED with compiling a complete list of Lord Ds, Lucy had managed to avoid Blake for days. Wrinkles appeared on her forehead as she read over the list once more:

The Marquess of Dunhill
The Earl of Devonton
Viscount Dumont
Baron Draven...

The list continued with names of eldest sons of dukes, marquesses, and earls, all who held titles.

With her copy of *Debrett's* and the social columns she hardly ever read, she had eliminated half the names on her list, those who could not be of age, were too old, or were unlikely to have any connection to the Continent. There remained a few who could not easily be eliminated, Blake being one of them. She was frustrated with her lack of progress and cursed not having paid better attention at social gatherings, since it was an excellent source of information on gentlemen and their activities.

Lucy felt the pressure of time running out. She needed to notify the lord of the threat, for she was aware Archbroke often took the stance that individuals were on a need-to-know basis and would feel justified in dealing with the matter without alerting all parties involved. Blake remained on her list of potential targets. Why was she hoping that there would be another more likely? If she approached Blake, would he believe her? Would he take the threat seriously or dismiss her claims as ludicrous?

She needed a break. Pulling out one of her Minerva novels, she tucked her notes away and curled up on her bed to read. She was so deeply engrossed in the book that she didn't hear Matthew scratching at her door until he asked, "Lucy, may I come in?"

He was always a stickler for privacy, and Lucy could count on him to give her ample time to hide whatever she was working on or make sure she was appropriately attired. Taking a moment to hide the lurid novel, Lucy hopped off the bed and then stood in the middle of the room.

"Please come in."

The door opened, and Matthew drew in a deep breath as he crossed the threshold and then began, "Lucy, I've received an invitation to the Redburn house party. We will leave on Monday and stay for the week. Lord Devonton will be accompanying us."

Lucy threw her hands in the air. "A house party! Nothing virtuous occurs at house parties. You are not trying to marry me off, are you?"

"You have been hiding in your room for the past four days! It was Devonton's inquiry into your health this morning that made me realize you have not joined the family for any meals."

Had it been four days? Was Matthew insinuating she was behaving like their mama? Hiding and absconding from family responsibilities? Lucy had taken all her meals alone in her chambers in an attempt to elude Blake. Despite her efforts to avoid the man, he was a constant distraction. His footsteps had a distinct pattern, slowing each time he passed her door. Questions of where he was in the house or where had he ventured to when he left plagued her. The man was inevitably driving her mad.

Lucy replied, "You know I am in perfect health. I prefer privacy."

While she had remained behind closed doors, Carrington had kept her fully informed of Blake's coming and goings. He was an early riser. Lucy had spied him meeting with Edward every morning from her window. The two of them would gallop off, with Edward always eagerly setting the pace. But they never failed to return in time for her brother to start his studies.

Edward was another source who willingly provided updates. Every evening before retiring to bed, he would stop by Lucy's chambers and regale her with the day's events. It warmed her heart to see Edward happy. Unexpectedly, images of Blake with children of his own floated before her.

Lucy's gaze snapped up to meet Matthew's as he tapped his glove against his thigh. Had Matthew asked her a question while she was woolgathering? Deciding it best to speak first, Lucy continued to explain, "I've just been preoccupied with a new novel I purchased. Actually, a couple, to be honest."

"Only two?" Abruptly Matthew's eyes flared, and he asked, "You haven't been hiding from Devonton, have you? He's like a brother."

Lucy wasn't about to share that her feelings for Blake were anything but brotherly. Ignoring Matthew's question, she said, "I'd rather not attend the Redburn house party. I could stay here in Town with Mama and Edward. I promise not to attend any social events without a chaperone while you are away."

His brows drew together, and Lucy sensed Matthew's patience was coming to an end. "Lucy, I've told you that I will not force you to marry, but if you do not leave your room, how are you ever to find someone to love? Please, attend the house party with me and try to socialize. I believe Lady Mary is attending, and perhaps you can renew your friendship."

Matthew's last remark had Lucy eyeing him carefully.

"Are you certain Lady Mary will be in attendance? Will Grace be attending also?"

"I know for a fact Lady Mary has accepted; however, Grace has declined."

Of course, Grace was not attending—she had firm opinions about the activities that occurred at house parties and vowed she would never be a guest at one.

Matthew's eyes followed Lucy as she paced and weighed the arguments for and against attending the house party. It would be an opportunity for her to mend her relationship with Lady Mary. The Redburns were well connected and might provide information to assist her in narrowing the list. The less formal setting would allow her to discreetly spend more time with Blake—but was that an advantage or disadvantage?

Turning to face Matthew directly, Lucy declared, "I will attend the Redburn house party."

CHAPTER TWELVE

*B*lake and Harrington maintained memberships at both White's and Brooks's. While Matthew favored White's, Blake felt more comfortable at Brooks's and had spent most of his days there to avoid both Stanfords. Blake's mind refused to release the memory of Lucy's body in his arms. He constantly pictured the lush curve of her lips and often caught himself fantasizing about kissing her, and then his imagination had her fully undressed and lying on his bed. Her sleeping only a few doors away from him each night did not help.

Blake occupied his usual high-back chair near a fireplace which afforded him lines of sight to both entrance and exit.

"Devonton."

Who had addressed him?

His gaze shifted towards the door. It was none other than the head of the Home Office. "Archbroke."

Settling into the chair next to his, Archbroke nodded to the paper in Blake's hands. "Busy?"

"Always."

"Haven't seen you come by Gentlemen Jackson's or attend many social engagements lately."

Harrington had convinced Blake to accompany him to a few dinner parties, a soiree or two, but all were private affairs hosted by close friends from Oxford. At every event, Harrington had introduced him to a variety of eligible young ladies, but none could hold his attention. Quite rudely, his thoughts often strayed to Lucy and what she was doing holed up in her rooms.

"Is that all your set does?" he asked Archbroke. "Attend races? Play Cards? Thrash each other in the ring?"

While Archbroke had not attended Oxford, he was deeply ingrained with those who had.

The Home Secretary glanced at the other members nearby. "What else could you possibly be interested in doing?"

One eyebrow raised, Blake rattled the paper in his hand. "Get involved in the building of factories? New industries? Better conditions for those who work our lands?"

Archbroke scoffed, "Preposterous! That sounds like work."

Blake chuckled. "Yes, work."

Accustomed to working, he missed having a particularly defined purpose or mission. Now he must define his own assignments and tasks. First, he must marry and beget an heir. Immediately he envisioned Lucy.

Archbroke leaned over the arm of the chair and asked. "Shouldn't you be out courting a lady?"

Had Blake somehow revealed his thoughts? No, he was a master of blank expressions. However, Archbroke was considered a genius. Or had the man acted upon a hunch?

"I have the entire Season to make my choice." It was a lie. Blake didn't have time to waste—he needed to return to his country estate with enough time to effectively implement some of the farming techniques he had learned over on the Continent. Crop yields for the past two years had dwindled, and his tenants would greatly benefit from the new methods.

With a smirk, Archbroke taunted him. "If I remember correctly, I don't believe you succeeded in convincing Lady Lucy to dance with you at the Emsworth ball."

Apparently, Blake wasn't the only one with an excellent memory. Why was Archbroke intent on goading him? Of what benefit would it be to him if Blake was to take an interest in Lucy?

"You are correct, but Harrington did grant me the honor of escorting her home."

Seeing the shock in Archbroke's eyes, Blake regretted disclosing that last piece of information. He didn't want to jeopardize Lucy's reputation in any way. Despite being drawn to the woman like a magnet, she was Harrington's sister. But could he deny his attraction to her? She was a complete enigma. She showed no apparent interest in him, yet there was an undeniable pull that existed between them.

Archbroke rose and, in an authoritative tone, said, "Devonton, it appears you have spent too many years away."

Why did the man have the uncanny ability to access a situation and sum it up succinctly? Blake had come to the same conclusion just the other day. He would have to decide soon what do to about Lucy. If by the end of the house party she showed no further interest in him, he would have to consider some other lady. Mayhap Lady Mary, whom Lucy had recommended to him.

CHAPTER THIRTEEN

*A*fter her conversation with Matthew the day before, Lucy refused to be considered as someone cowering or hiding. She awoke and informed Carrington she was going to break her fast with the family.

"Do you have a preference for either the lemon or the mint day dress?"

"Why is it that you must reference food in some fashion when discussing my attire?"

"It's the only way I know to make them more appealing."

"Carrington!"

Her maid's eyebrows rose in innocence.

"Very well, mint it is."

Lucy made her way down to the breakfast room and was taken aback by the sight of her mama seated at the table. Since when had she removed herself from her rooms? "Mama?"

"Lucy, dear! Lord Devonton has provided Edward with a delightful challenge. Edward must find some obscure town that Devonton has visited on a map. If Edward can locate it, Devonton will share with us a story from his adventures in that very location."

Edward was kneeling in his chair and hunched over a large map of the Continent spread out on the table. "Lucy, come help me find Evora. What country should I even start searching?"

Without blinking, Lucy replied, "Portugal." She settled into her chair, and a footman placed a pot of hot tea in front of her.

"Are you familiar with the location, Lady Lucy?" Blake rose and sauntered over to the sideboard. He piled eggs, sausage, and toast on a plate, skipping over the kippers. As he set the plate before Lucy, he grinned and in a light tone imparted, "I hope all is to your liking."

He turned to return to the sideboard, and his hand casually brushed the back of her neck. An intense shock went through her all the way to her toes. Had he touched her intentionally?

"Well, Lucy, how did you know Evora was in Portugal?" Edward questioned.

Matthew ambled into the room as if he hadn't been up already for hours and casually stated, "Lucy has always excelled in geography."

Matthew joined Blake by the sideboard. After both men had piled enough food to feed an army on their plates, they returned to take their seats. Each eyed the other before eating. How were they communicating without words? She often could anticipate Matthew's thoughts, but they were twins. Blake wasn't even related by blood.

Lucy placed her hand on the spot on her neck where his hand had brushed up against her only moments ago. She was curious to see if he was as unaffected by their brief touch as he appeared. Only the slight bob of his Adam's apple as he glanced at her belied his remarkably calm demeanor. But what had he felt? An electric jolt? Tingling sensations?

Her mama's smile caught her attention. What was she smiling about? Had Lucy missed some part of the conversation? No. The men were shoveling food, and Edward remained focused on finding Evora. Her mama's knowing look unsettled Lucy. Her parents had had a love union, and it was her mama's and Matthew's wish for her to find a similar union. But the reality was love matches were as rare as four-leaf clovers.

"Lucy, are you sure it is in Portugal? I can't find it," Edward whined.

Giving Matthew a look she was sure would rankle, she asked, "Matthew, would you like to show Edward where he could find Evora on the map? Or should I?"

"By all means, sister, please do the honors."

Lucy rose and placed her napkin next to her plate. There was no room to stand between Edward and Blake, forcing her to round the table. Edward and the map were on the opposite side, causing her to lean over the table to point to Evora. Blake's gaze was not on the map, nor her face, but fully trained on the neckline of her bodice. Making sure no one else noticed, she bent a little farther, allowing her dress to gape a tad more. When he finally raised his gaze to meet hers, his eyes had notably darkened. What had prompted her to act so coltishly? Why did she seek a reaction out of him?

"By Jove, Lucy, you found it!" Edward exclaimed, and Lucy stood up quickly.

She did not think the feelings Blake evoked in her were love but, more accurately, pure physical lust. If she acted upon these feelings, she would be ruined. She couldn't marry and lose her independence. But what of a secret affair?

After she walked back to her seat, her eyes landed on Matthew, who appeared happy. Happier than she had seen him in a long time. Matthew, the dutiful son. If he could take on the title and remain dutiful, she could also do her duty to the family and avoid ruin and scandal at all costs. She would have to ignore Blake.

Seated, she averted her gaze and resumed drinking her tea.

With a broad smile, Matthew said, "I have news of the house party we are to attend. You will be happy to hear that in addition to the normal variety of parlor games and activities, there will be outdoor competitions, an outing to the beach, and tours of the local village. Lord Redburn has even orchestrated a display of fireworks for one of the evening's entertainments."

For the first time in a long while, Lucy didn't have to feign excitement when she responded, "Fireworks? That is truly exciting. Had you mentioned that at first, I wouldn't have hesitated to agree to go. Lord Devonton, have you ever seen fireworks?" Why had she immediately included him in the discussion? Moments ago, hadn't she decided to ignore Blake? What was wrong with her resolution these days?

In a gravelly voice, he replied, "I have had the pleasure of experiencing firework displays at Vauxhall Gardens as well as in Rome and Brussels."

Lucy sat in awe as she gazed at Blake. Her inquisitive nature made her want him to share all the details with her, but she couldn't trust the effect he had on her judgment. Forcing her gaze back to the table, she focused on the remaining slice of toast on her plate.

Edward's eyes were wide with excitement. "I want to see the fireworks, Matthew! May I come too? Please…"

Matthew's smile fell from his face as he delivered the answer; he would surely disappoint his young brother. "Sorry, not this time." He pulled out his pocket watch. "Look at the time. Head up to the schoolroom—Mr. Trenton will be waiting for you. Off you go."

A dejected Edward walked slowly to the door. Before he crossed the threshold, he asked, "Lord Devonton, will you tell me your tale of Evora this afternoon?"

"I'd be glad to. I'll meet you in the library, and not only will I tell you of my travels to Evora, but I will also show you my drawings of the fireworks displays."

The boy's eyes nearly popped out of his head at Blake's response. Hopeful, Edward asked, "Lucy, will you be joining us also? I'm guessing Matthew has estate business to attend to, and Mama will want to return to her rooms, but it would be nice if you could be there."

Edward's enthusiasm was infectious, and Lucy found herself saying, "Of course, Edward. I'll look forward to seeing you both later this afternoon."

She politely excused herself, pausing when her mama gave her an odd look. But Mama remained silent as always and nodded her consent as Lucy rose to leave.

THROUGHOUT THE DAY, Lucy kept checking the timepiece in the library. Was it broken? Why was time moving slowly today? As each hour passed, she was increasingly anxious to see Blake again. Why did she miss him? Seated by the window, she ran her hands across her thighs and adjusted her skirts for the hundredth time. Lucy intentionally directed her gaze out the window, but she found herself turning to see if the needle had moved. *Not even a minute!*

Edward burst into the library and flopped onto the settee. With all the dramatic flair of an eight-year-old, he complained, "Latin has to be the worst language spoken. Why must I learn it when it is no longer used? I'm sure Matthew makes Mr. Trenton teach it to me as some sort of punishment." He was pausing for breath when Blake entered the room.

"All the great classics are written in Latin," Blake said as he sat next to Edward. Lucy spied a travel bag full of journals.

Edward sat up in a flash and gave Blake his full attention. Blake's gaze went to Lucy, and without saying a word, he beckoned her to come join them. She rose and proceeded to sit in a chair opposite Blake. Lucy crossed and recrossed her ankles before making a show of adjusting her skirts.

Blake turned to Edward and asked, *"Esne paratus incipiat?"* Are you ready to begin?

Edward nodded.

Blake began in Latin, *"Instar castelli moenibus munita mandamus,"* then translated to English, "Like a castle, Evora is protected by walls."

He continued in Latin. *"Ebora speciali duplicem murum circumdatum."* And then again in English, "Evora is special, surrounded by two walls."

Edward was captivated and said, "Lord Devonton, please continue."

"Antiquissimis temporibus fuisse romanam positae. The oldest is said to have been erected during Roman times. *Romani callidus est.* The Romans were a clever lot. *Turris disposito sunt in varietate figurarum, quadratum, circularis et polygonalibus.*

Towers were designed in a variety of shapes, square, circular and even polygonal."

At first, Lucy assumed Blake was translating for Edward's benefit, but midway he turned and spoke to her directly.

"Lord Devonton, there is no need for you to translate. I'm fluent in Latin."

Edward spoke up. "But Lucy, I'm not. What is polygonal anyway?"

Blake answered before she could, "It is having a shape with straight sides, as few as three, but most of the time five or more." He pulled out a sketchbook and illustrated a few shapes for Edward.

Edward remarked, "Ah, those Romans were clever fellows."

Lucy leaned forward to peer at the drawings. Blake had not only sketched a variety of shapes two-dimensionally, he had also provided a three-dimensional version that he had described might be set along the wall that protected Evora.

Blake continued his tale. "The walls protect the most astonishing cathedral. The colored glass in its windows contains all the *colores arcus caelestis*, that is, colors within the rainbow." He sketched as he spoke, bringing it to life on paper.

Pleasantly surprised Edward did not complain as Blake wove Latin into his story, Lucy relaxed and found herself engaged entirely by the man and his tale. It was a side of him she had never seen at social gatherings, where he seemed somewhat aloof with very little to say. Did he prefer to listen to others' natterings? They weren't half as entertaining as his story.

From the travel bag, Blake pulled out a journal that held his drawings of Evora. As he shared the pictures of the town, Lucy's jaw slacked open. The illustrations were extremely lifelike and detailed.

Edward peered over a drawing, a finger tracing over a peculiar-looking form within a column. "Lord Devonton, what is that?"

"A skull."

Brows knit together, Edward replied, "Why is there a skull in the... well, it looks like a pole in front of a church."

"The chapel dates back to the sixteenth century, and it is believed to be constructed from the bones of over five thousand monks."

Lucy shuddered. "Your drawings are rather thorough."

Matthew had commented on Blake's ability to make a picture come to life numerous times, but this was the first time she had been privy to Blake's work. Engrossed in his illustrations, she decided to spend the rest of the afternoon with him and Edward with the hope she would learn something of the man that would allow her to eliminate him from her list of targets.

As Blake flipped the pages, Lucy spied the unique annotations in the corners. What did they signify? It occurred to her there was so much more to the man sitting opposite her than a lord who would sit in parliament and tend to his estate.

Blake continued to turn the pages, but Edward stopped him and asked, "Is that a coat of arms?"

"Indeed, it is, Edward. You do have a natural knack for identifying some of the more gruesome aspects of Evora's history."

Edward turned to Lucy. "Lucy, do you see it?"

Peering over the replica, she tried not to squirm at the sight of two severed human heads. Lucy asked, "See what?"

"Lucy, there are figures with no bodies. Their bodies,

gone!" Edward with eyes wide open made a slicing motion across his neck. Turning to address Blake, he asked, "Have you ever seen a dead body?"

"I've seen cave drawings depicting dead bodies. Would you like to see those?" Blake's body had stiffened, but only ever slightly. He had been on the Continent during a war —he must have seen some of the devastation. She was grateful he had not answered Edward directly, but she wondered at the horrific sights he had been subject to.

"Ooh, yes, please." Edward eagerly waited for Blake to reveal the picture, then his features fell as he inspected the stick figures. "This is it?"

The depictions were in stark contrast to the images Blake had drawn, which were full of detail and somehow came alive. How did he manage to make lines on paper appear real?

Edward's whole demeanor changed as Blake explained, "These are remarkable prehistoric images from a time when there was no parchment. Stories were recorded on the walls of caves."

Blake switched journals and asked, "Would you like to see my illustrations of the firework displays?"

He hadn't managed to turn but a few pages before Edward stuck a finger between sheets and inquired, "What city is depicted here?" Half the buildings on the page were crumpled piles of rocks. There was a heavy darkness to the picture.

"Just one I traveled through to see the fireworks." Blake quickly brought up an image he had drawn using pastels. It was bright and colorful, a stark contrast to the one Edward had just inquired about.

Blake shared, "Brussels is an extraordinary city."

"Did you see Wellington and his army in Brussels?" Edward innocently asked.

Lucy eyed Blake closely. Brussels was extremely close to Waterloo, the final battle site where Wellington succeeded in leading coalition forces defeating Napoleon. Had Blake been involved?

"Wellington strikes an impressive figure upon a horse."

What a clever response Blake had formulated, neither confirming nor denying having seen Wellington. Why would he not meet her gaze?

Lucy asked, "Lord Devonton, is it true that it only took the duke but a few hours to prevail?"

She read Blake's lips as he mumbled, "I wouldn't consider eight a few." Turning, he finally faced her and replied, "I too heard it was reported a quick victory."

Another shrewd answer. The dullness in his eyes confirmed her suspicions he had been present, but it did not explain why he continued to provide only vague answers. What had he truly seen and experienced while abroad that caused the haunted look in his eyes?

A longing to comfort him had Lucy moving to sit next to Blake. Her leg grazed his as she shifted to gain a better view of the journal. Looking up through her lashes, she was delighted to see a spark reappear in his eyes once more. What did that spark signify?

She would have to devise a strategy to extract the information she needed to be confirmed. Based on the evasive answers he had provided this afternoon, she would not be able to strike Blake's name from her list of possible targets. With a heavy heart, she would have to move his name to the top as most probable.

The notion of Blake in danger had Lucy scooting even closer to him, which in turn caused Blake to arch an eyebrow in her direction. She smiled and returned her attention to the volume on his lap as she happily listened to Blake answer Edward's endless questions.

CHAPTER FOURTEEN

*E*arly Monday morning, Blake, Harrington, and Lucy set out for the Redburns' house party. Blake turned to wave farewell to the young Lord Edward as they made their way down the drive.

"I'm glad Mama ventured from her rooms to escort Edward back into the house," Harrington muttered.

"What was that, Harrington?" Blake asked.

"I don't know what has brought about the change in my mama, but I'm glad she's been making more of an effort to interact with the family."

Blake too was glad to see the Dowager Lady Harrington come out of hiding. He felt compassion for the woman. She was widowed when pregnant with Edward. During his visit to Halestone Hall, he had observed the tender looks, the frequent loving embraces, and most memorable was the spark in the eyes of Matthew's parents when they were in each other's company. Blake's own parents had shared a similar bond. Was it an intangible bond that compelled him to continuously seek out Lucy?

Outriders led their contingent, followed by the coach

carrying Lucy and her maid. Mounted, Harrington and Blake trailed close behind. Interestingly, John and Evan flanked the coach, close enough to the window for them to converse with Lucy or her maid.

Blake slowed the Arabian he was riding, and Harrington immediately adjusted his pace to match, giving them space away from Lucy's footmen and the rest of the entourage. Blake wanted to discuss in private their plans for the week. For the first half hour, he listened as Harrington outlined the location of various smugglers' dens and descriptions of the leaders. But his attention was drawn to Lucy's two footmen. The pair rode with an uncommon familiarity. They behaved more like outriders, scanning the woods and the roads with a keen sense looking out for danger. It was as if they were protecting Lucy from threats that went beyond highwaymen.

How often did Lucy travel without Matthew? Were her visits limited to the countryside? Their behavior left him with an unsettled feeling he did not care for.

Harrington asked, "Are you even listening to me?"

"Yes. I agree with your plan. We shall ride out early tomorrow morn to do some preliminary scouting. How regularly does Lucy journey on her own?"

With an incredulous look, Matthew replied, "What?"

"How frequently does your sister travel on her own?"

"I don't keep a record of her comings and goings. Why do you ask?"

Blake didn't answer but continued his inquisition. "How long have those footmen been in your employ?"

"John and Evan? I believe Lucy hired them. Again, why are you asking?"

"I need to bolster my staff and was curious as to how you came about such skilled footmen. I shall have to discuss the matter with Lucy."

Matthew eyed him disbelievingly. "She would prefer to be riding; they are just keeping her entertained."

That's how it appeared, but Blake was skeptical. He rode closer to see if he could listen to their conversation, but their chatter ceased as soon as he was close. Very odd indeed. They continued on with Blake sneaking glances at Lucy through the window whenever possible.

As their party approached the drive of Redburn Manor, Blake shook his head at the long line of coaches waiting for guests to alight and greet their hosts. He and Harrington rode around to the stables and then walked to the front to join Lucy.

"I was under the impression house parties were more private affairs," Blake said.

"Alas, how many house parties have you attended?"

"This is my first since my return."

"Then I shall be the bearer of bad news. Guests at these events can range from a few couples to half the *ton*, depending on the size of the venue and the host. Never fear, Devonton, I have it on good authority Lady Redburn used utmost discretion, as we are one of a half dozen parties in attendance this week."

One of six? Good gracious. Blake had hoped to find peace and quiet in the country. He secretly hoped it would also allow him to sequester Lucy away from prying eyes and discover if they would rub along well or if he needed to abolish all thoughts of the woman.

Lady Redburn greeted their party as they moved to the front of the line. "Lord Devonton, Lord Harrington, Lady Lucy. I'm delighted you have all arrived safely."

Lord Redburn gave his wife a hard stare and expounded, "We have heard of other parties having troubles with highwaymen on their way here. I will have to contact the magistrate."

Harrington, the more social of the lot, spoke up first. "We too are glad for an uneventful journey."

"Mr. Hartley, please escort the gentlemen to their rooms. Lady Lucy, come with me." Lady Redburn linked her arm with Lucy, but before leaving she gave one last order: "Henry, dear, please greet the rest of our guests and try to make them feel welcome."

She leaned up and bussed her husband's cheek. It was not the norm for a wife to publicly show affection. It was widely known by all that the Redburns were a love match, and they didn't care what the *ton* thought of them or how they behaved. Blake could only hope for a union such as theirs.

MR. HARTLEY ESCORTED Matthew and Blake in the direction of the guest wing. Lady Redburn gave Lucy a slight tug, propelling her to walk with the lady. "How have you been, dear?"

"Well, Lady Redburn—"

"There is no one about. You can call me Eleanor, as always."

Archbroke often arranged for Lucy to stay with the Redburns either on her journey out or back into Town. She didn't know to what extent or how exactly they were associated with Archbroke, but over the years, they had become surrogate parents to Lucy.

As they made their way to Lucy's usual assigned suite near the family rooms, Eleanor asked, "Does Archbroke know you are here? We did not receive word from him."

"Archbroke always tends to be aware of my whereabouts." *Most of the time I inform the infuriating man.* Lucy had chosen not to send word to Archbroke of her jaunt to the country since she was attending for personal reasons, to amend her friendship with Lady Mary. Plastering a smile on her face, Lucy continued, "Thank you for the kind invitation, Eleanor. I needed to escape the social route."

"We have invited your family for years, and this is the first time Lord Harrington has ever accepted. Is all well?"

"At first I too questioned my brother's motives, especially with all the stories and activities you hear occurring at these events. Oh, Eleanor, I meant no offense."

"Lucy, I cannot enforce moral behavior from my guests, but if I or any of my staff get wind of such activity, both Henry and I immediately ask them to depart."

"My thanks for allowing me to stay close to your rooms."

"My dear, you are like a daughter to me. I wouldn't allow anything to happen to you while you are under my care."

"Eleanor, I am working on a project currently."

"One that Archbroke is unaware of?"

"Technically, I have already alerted him. However, I was not specifically instructed to pursue my investigations. I have a... a feeling it is important for me to continue. Will you make the necessary excuses for me if I fail to attend an event or meal where I'm expected?"

"Of course, my dear. If you need anything else, let me know directly."

Lucy gave Eleanor a hug and entered her room. Closing the door behind her, she leaned back and rested her head. She had run scenario after scenario as to how to best apologize to Lady Mary while stuck in the coach. But every time she peeked out the window, her gaze fell upon Blake. She couldn't help but admire how well he rode. Or how strong and muscular his thighs were, as if he was guiding his mount with the barest movement of his knees.

The entire trip he appeared relaxed, but she was certain he was acutely aware of his surroundings.

Trying to dislodge images of Blake, she shook her head. Carrington was tapping her foot impatiently as Lucy disrobed. How long had Lucy been woolgathering? With Carrington's assistance, she was bathed and dressed with time to spare before dinner.

Lucy walked into the drawing room, where the other guests were gathering. Searching for Lady Mary, she positioned herself in a corner with the hope it would give her an advantage of spotting the woman when she entered. To Lucy's surprise, Lady Mary had somehow managed to sneak up next to her and was standing only inches away.

Lucy decided it was now or never. "Lady Mary, I wanted to…," she began, determined to try to mend their friendship.

However, Lady Mary interrupted her apology with, "Lady Lucy, where is your usual gaggle of admirers?"

Lady Mary was not one to hold back a thought or comment, but if she thought she would use that sharp tongue of hers to scare Lucy away, she was in for a surprise.

Glibly, Lucy replied, "I've left them in London. And to be honest they are not my admirers; they are all in one way or other acquaintances of my brother. It would actually be flattering if a gentleman actually saw me for me and not just as Lord Harrington's twin sister."

Lady Mary stared into her eyes and asked, "Why are you so honest with me?"

"What have I to lose? I've already insulted you beyond forgiveness. You are the only one here who has any common sense and more intelligence than a potted plant. It was knowledge of your attendance that swayed me to agree and attend, myself."

Lucy's skin on the back of her neck prickled. Her gaze instantly searched the perimeter. Blake was at the threshold, about to enter the room. She quickly turned to directly face Lady Mary.

Lady Mary stared and asked, "Are you avoiding someone, Lady Lucy?"

She looked past Lucy with a frown. Lucy raised a hand to rub the back of her neck. Why had she not been more discreet? What caused her to react rashly when Blake was in the vicinity? Her whole body came alive as soon as he was near. Lucy detested irrational thoughts and emotions. She preferred her life to be well planned and logical. Her marriage to James would have been based upon friendship and a mutual desire to create an alliance between neighbors. Rational. Her attraction to Blake was illogical. But the man challenged and thrilled her, nonetheless.

Lady Mary's eyes widened and then swiftly narrowed. "Perhaps... Lord Devonton?"

Lucy's mouth fell agape. The woman was extremely astute.

Lady Mary asked, "Why would *you* want to avoid *him?*"

Lucy attempted to don a mask of indifference as Lady Mary's eyes raked over her features. *Don't look too hard, for even I don't know the answers.*

Lady Mary's gaze shifted and remained on a spot to the left of Lucy's shoulder. "Gossip is he has a rather ordinary disposition. Some of the ladies have even described him as a total bore. They claim he never talks, hardly even makes eye contact, and when he dances, his hold is nearly imperceptible. His aloof demeanor has deemed him unworthy, despite being one of the few younger eligible earls on the hunt for a wife. But he looks perfectly harmless to me."

Lucy muttered, "Harmless as a honey badger."

Lady Mary continued as if she hadn't heard Lucy's comment. "You always seem rather comfortable in the presence of men, yet you are definitely trying not to draw Lord Devonton's attention."

It took every ounce of Lucy's control not to reveal her thoughts. Searching her memory, she recalled an earlier conversation she had with Blake when he had referred to himself as plain. Did others see him that way too? It would appear so, based on Lady Mary's comments. Yet, as she turned to look at him, all Lucy saw was an impressive Corinthian. Lady Mary was still frowning at her as Lord Devonton approached.

Blake bowed. "Good evening, Lady Lucy."

Lucy curtsied and gave Blake a weary smile as his gaze slid to Lady Mary.

Why was he staring at Lady Mary? Realizing he was waiting for her to make the proper introductions, Lucy blurted, "Oh, yes! Lady Mary, if you please, may I introduce Blake Gower, the Earl of Devonton." She was sure she had mucked up the introduction but was at a loss how to correct her error.

Lady Mary stared directly into Blake's eyes as if issuing a challenge of some sort and then said with a wicked smile, "Lord Devonton, it is my pleasure to finally meet you."

Lucy's gaze shifted back and forth between the two. Was Lady Mary flirting with Blake? Why did he not remove his gaze from her? Did he find her attractive? Were they having a staring competition? Surely not.

Lady Mary's lips curled into a devilish grin as Blake turned to ask, "Lady Lucy, have you seen your brother? I haven't seen him since we arrived."

Lady Mary recaptured Blake's attention by answering first. "I believe Lord Harrington is in the card room."

Lucy's hands balled into fists at her side. Why was she

reacting this way? What did she care if Blake took an interest in Lady Mary? The question caused her chest to tighten, and she blinked as a sharp, stabbing pain shot through to her heart. She was jealous.

Blake shifted his weight to the balls of his feet and rocked back on his heels as he said, "Perfect. Well, if you will excuse me, ladies, perhaps you will both save me a dance later this evening."

Before either of them could agree or decline, Blake turned and made his way out of the room.

Lucy gave Lady Mary a piercing look. "To my point, Lady Mary, no gentleman seeks me out for myself but rather as only a connection to my brother."

Contradicting her statement, Lucy's cheeks turned bright red as Blake looked over his shoulder and winked directly her.

With a chuckle, Lady Mary said, "Well, Lady Lucy, I believe I might have been misinformed about Lord Devonton's disposition. Now that I have met him myself, I'm of the opinion he might have a devilish streak in him. However, I'd say it was only evident around you."

What did Lady Mary mean, only around her? Did she feel the sparks Lucy experienced when Blake was close by? Reeling from the statement, Lucy felt herself blush all the way to her scalp and suggested they take a stroll in the gardens before dinner.

As they were turning a corner, she could see in the distance her brother and Blake were riding out of the stables. Where on earth were they headed like the devil was on their tails?

CHAPTER FIFTEEN

*L*ater that evening in her room, Lucy looked down at her notes, a mass of papers with crisscross markings, her sole intent to eliminate one Lord D at a time. She was meticulous, not wanting to make an error. There was too much at stake.

Her eyes were starting to blur. She needed rest. Lucy lay in bed, tossing and turning until the sheets were a tangled mess. She gave up on the idea of sleep and decided to go down to the library to find a book. As she made her way through the halls, she was relieved that Lord Redburn had ordered the candles to remain lit. As she neared the library, light seeped from under the door. Had a footman forgotten to bank the library fire?

Swiftly calculating the risk of a house fire and that of being found in only her nightgown and robe, Lucy leaned in close and placed her ear to the door. *No sounds from within.* Slowly opening the door, Lucy checked to see if it was occupied. A log fell and crackled in the fireplace. Lucy jumped and crossed the threshold. Once her heartbeat returned to its normal rhythm, she closed the door behind her and locked it. Safe from being found.

She trailed a finger along the edge of a shelf that housed books that she longed to read. Lord Redburn was an avid book collector, and his library was filled with rows and rows of books.

A flicker of light caught her attention.Firelight glinted off a shiny hessian boot. Someone was in the room with her. Tiptoeing closer, she recognized the gentleman. It was Blake. He had fallen asleep in the chair, but what caught Lucy's full attention was the sketchbook in his lap.

It shouldn't have surprised Lucy he would sketch while attending a house party. She had seen the volumes of notebooks filled with his drawings stacked in his rooms back in London. Always curious, she had snuck in and flipped through them and had found Blake sketched all sorts of items ranging from the mundane—leaves, horse-drawn carts—to intricate structures adorned with exotic carvings. There were also a number of portraits.

Inquisitive in nature, Lucy bent down to take a closer look at the sketchbook, only to see a picture of her and Lady Mary, tucked behind a potted palm. Lucy grinned as she remembered the two of them earlier that evening, giving a running commentary on the evening's dancing from their sequestered spot. Lady Mary's quick wit and scathing tongue, never uttered with malice but in bold truth, made for the most enjoyable evening Lucy had had in years.

Why would he choose to draw a picture of Lady Mary? An image of Lady Mary in Blake's arms had all the air leaving her lungs and made her stomach ache.

Why did it cause her pain, the idea of Blake with another? She did not want to marry. She couldn't risk losing her independence and the ability to work for the Home Office.

Lies—she did want to marry and have a family. She hadn't believed it possible until now.

With her emotions in a jumbled web, she turned to leave. Blake's hand snaked out and grabbed her wrist. *Blast.* When had he awakened? Tumbling into his lap, she expected to land on the picture she had just seen, but his quick reflexes had her between his thighs and the sketchbook neatly on the floor beside the chair.

BLAKE WAITED for her to stop wiggling and then admonished, "What are you doing, roaming around in the middle of the night?"

Lucy answered breathlessly, "I couldn't sleep. I came down to find a novel."

What had he been thinking of, pulling her into his lap? Just moments before, he had been dreaming of her, and now she was here, warm and inviting and severely testing his control.

"Are you sure it was a book you were seeking?" His voice was still gravelly from sleep, or was it due to her lush body being in his arms?

Before she could answer, he had the back of her head cradled in his hand and was massaging her neck. Her muscles felt tight. What caused her to be so tense?

She leaned back and rolled her neck. An "ooh" slipped out. Blake couldn't resist any longer. He gently placed a kiss upon her lips. But when she moaned, he kissed her hard, leaning into her, with her back pressed against the arm of the chair. She instinctively responded and parted her lips. As soon as he had entrance, his tongue dipped, and he tasted her. He would have expected her to taste like honey, yet surprisingly she tasted more spicy than sweet. How shocking but at the same time entirely appropriate. It was what he suspected: she might appear innocent, but under that façade she was a bundle of surprises of fire and spice. It was he who released a guttural sound of desire first.

His free hand shook as it moved from her waist to lightly rest on her breast. He had been with women before. Why was he nervous? Steady. Her soft full bosom filled his palm, and he gently squeezed. She stiffened and tried to sit up, pushing on his broad chest for leverage. *Damn*. He had brought up her defenses again. Relaxing his hold on her, he tried to suppress his increasing inner anger at his lack of self-control.

Lucy squirmed in his lap until she was upright so he no longer loomed over her. Instead of pushing him away as he expected, she was clutching at his lapels, bringing them closer. A burst of relief at her invitation banished all thoughts. Acting on instinct, he massaged the back of her neck and angled her head to allow him to kiss her deeply.

It was like sinking into a warm bath. His muscles began to relax but immediately tensed as Lucy pressed her body up against his. Chest to Chest. She snaked her arms up over his shoulders. She drove her hands through his hair and raked her fingertips over his scalp, setting every cell on his head alive. Her innocent movements were driving him crazy. Lucy's sigh only increased his urgency for his hands to explore her body. He trailed his fingers down to her hip and back up to her chest, lightly at first and then with more intensity. Her nipples grew taut, and she pressed herself into the curve of his hand.

He didn't want to stop. Excitement flowed through his veins. Blake pressed light kisses on her closed eyelids and then kissed and nibbled behind her ear. He found a pressure point on her neck that had Lucy gasping. Music to his ears. He wanted to hear her gasp again and began to nibble and suck on her neck, knowing he would leave a mark, but he couldn't stop himself. He wanted to satisfy her silent pleas, but she was an innocent and likely not aware of what her body was desperately seeking. Lucy began to wiggle, her bottom and her legs becoming restless. Blake's desire to push up her skirts and touch her intimately nearly overruled his resolve to put an end to their activities.

He broke the contact and pushed her slightly away. "Lucy, we have to stop."

"Stop?"

"Yes. If we continue, I will want to kiss and touch you in ways I shouldn't."

As soon as his meaning sank in, she jumped up, scurrying to the door.

Blake rose and gently grabbed her by the shoulders. "Lucy, look at me." He tipped her chin up so he could gaze into her eyes. "Please don't regret anything we did tonight. I won't. It was all very natural and wonderful. I have been fighting against my attraction to you, as I was unsure of your feelings for me. But tonight I realized I want you, and from your response, you want to get to know me more also. Don't look so sad, Lucy."

"I'm not sad. I'm just a little confused. I've never behaved... I never felt like this before. You make all my senses jumbled, and at the same time, I feel more..."

Blake finished her sentence for her. "More alive. Like we complement each other in a unique sort of way."

He could read the confusion in her eyes and then the recognition that they both shared the same feelings, thoughts, and fears. When Blake bent down to give her a reassuring kiss, she rose on her tiptoes and pressed her lips to his chin. Then she reached up and placed her hand behind his head and guided him to her. Without hesitation, she kissed him as thoroughly as he had kissed her.

When Lucy broke the kiss, her cheeks were rosy, and her lips were swollen. Breathlessly, she said, "Good night," and then she fled the library.

CHAPTER SIXTEEN

$\mathcal{T}$he next morning, Lucy was greeted by a rather subdued Lady Mary. "Good morn, Lady Lucy. It appears your family are all early risers."

Confused by Lady Mary's comment, Lucy replied, "A very good morning to you, Lady Mary. Have you seen my brother already?"

"No, I rose early to go for a ride to clear my mind. I overheard the stable master grumbling at the fact that Lord Harrington and Lord Devonton had taken up the habit of riding out before dawn. He was none too pleased since on occasion they had tried to attend to the horses themselves."

Lucy's frown disappeared. Matthew never stood on ceremony and could do without the assistance in the stables; he was an accomplished horseman. But he wasn't one to rise early unless required to. Why were he and Blake out riding before anyone was about? Where did they venture to?

Lady Mary stiffened.

"What was plaguing you that caused you to go out

riding before dawn?" Lucy noticed Lord Waterford had entered and he was making his way to join them.

"Nothing of importance. I just needed some time alone and fresh air to rid myself of..." Lady Mary stopped midsentence as Lord Waterford appeared but then quickly asked, "Lady Lucy, would you care to join me for a stroll in the gardens?"

Without waiting for Lucy's reply, Lady Mary rose and left. Ignoring Waterford's scowl, Lucy rushed to follow her friend out the terrace doors. Why had Lady Mary given Waterford the cut direct?

As she fell into step next to Lady Mary, she caught a glimpse of her friend's features. She could clearly see Lady Mary was not in the mood to converse. Lucy let her thoughts wander as they walked through the garden. Why had Matthew and Blake ridden out early this morn? What were the pair up to?

When she and Lady Mary had returned from the gardens, Lucy kept an eye on the stables from the drawing room, where all the ladies were taking tea. As soon as she spied Matthew, she made her way to the stables. "Matthew, where did you and Lord Devonton ride to this morn?"

"We were out taking advantage of Redburn's excellent stables before being subjected to the blitherings of marriage-minded mamas." Matthew's answer did not appease her.

She let him go but kept an eye on him as he made his way back to the house. He could never get anything past her if she persisted. Lucy decided to take a different approach to the matter. She turned and approached the stables. She peeked into one of the stalls, where Blake was rubbing down his horse. He had his coat off and his shirt-sleeves rolled up to expose his forearms. His shirt was tight across his broad chest, and her eyes continued to take in the ripple of his muscles. She couldn't tear her gaze away from him.

Blake caught her staring, turned, and devilishly gave her a wink. "Lucy, how are you today? Your brother and I just returned before the weather came in." To her disappointment, he rolled his sleeves down and shrugged back into his coat.

Ignoring the question, she asked, "Where did the two of you go?"

Blake offered his arm and answered, "Oh, we just went out for some exercise with no particular destination in mind."

Lucy's brow furrowed. It was telling how similar his response was to her brother's... as if it were a coordinated lie.

She placed her hand on Blake's forearm, and he led her out of the stables. She didn't want to return to the house and the other guests. What she wanted was to spend more time with Blake.

As if reading her mind, he said, "I was just heading to the lake. Would you care to join me?"

"Yes, I'd much prefer to stay out of doors if you think the weather will hold."

Following him to the lake would provide her an opportunity to question him further. What was his motive for drawing her away from the house party? Had his thoughts strayed to their interlude in the library as hers had?

While they walked toward the lake in silence, Lucy attempted to refocus her thoughts back to the question of what activities her brother and Blake could have been engaged in this morn. But she was distracted by the warmth of his hand as he placed it over hers. It was an intimate gesture, one which she found both comforting and electrifying at the same time. As they approached the water, Blake took off his coat and laid it out for them to sit on under a tree. They were far enough away from the house that they had complete privacy.

～

BLAKE'S THOUGHTS were focused on what had occurred the night before in the library. Lucy had seen his sketch of her. Did she wonder what had prompted him to sketch Lady Mary and herself? It was a question he was trying to decipher himself. His attraction to Lucy was undeniable. She had responded to his kisses but gave no indication she would be open to the proposal of marriage. He needed a wife. While Lady Mary did not evoke the same responses within him as Lucy did, she was a smart, eligible lady of the *ton*.

He lowered himself to the ground and leaned against the tree, waiting for Lucy to sit. Looking up at her, he patted space next to him. "Are you going to join me?"

She hesitated another moment before lowering herself to the ground. As she tucked her legs under her skirts, Blake caught a glimpse of her pale pink stockings. Pink, not white? His hand itched to feel the silk against his palms. He put his hands around her waist and pulled her back to lean against him. It was highly inappropriate, but it felt right.

Lucy relaxed into his embrace. Neither said anything but gazed out on the lake for a while, their breathing slowly becoming in sync. Eventually, Lucy closed her eyes and breathed.

Blake reached over, picked a white daisy, and gave it to her. She proceeded to pluck the petals one by one. He remembered her skipping through Halestone Hall when she was a girl, chanting, *He loves me, he loves me not*.

Ultimately, Lucy pulled off the last petal. "He loves me."

When she glanced up at him, there was a teasing sparkle in her eyes. He bent his head down to give her a kiss. It was a slow, seductive kiss, so dissimilar from the one the night before—light touches and the barest of pressure.

Lucy broke the kiss and turned her gaze to the lake. He wasn't finished tasting her, so he continued to nibble at her ear and down her neck.

"Lord Devonton…"

"Lucy, after last night, please call me Blake—or at the very least, Devonton."

Her brow furrowed, then arched and finally came to rest naturally as she said, "If you wish. Blake… do you have any family?"

He smiled and gave her the serious answer she was looking for. "None living. My parents married unconventionally young, especially my papa at the age of one and twenty, and my mama was five years his junior. I was not blessed with any siblings, and my mama and papa passed in a carriage accident when I was sixteen." He kept his voice totally devoid of emotion. "I've been on my own for many years now. I was sure my title and lands would either go to a distant relative since I wasn't entirely sure I'd return from the Continent."

It was a good thing she was facing the lake and not him. Otherwise, he was certain he would have seen pity in her gaze. He waited for the typical response, "I'm sorry for your loss," but it never came.

"Having Matthew as a twin, I've always felt like half a person when he was not around. I know it is selfish, but I was glad he did not venture off like you. I find it odd that you were on the Continent during the war unless you were there to help with the fight. With no family, why did you decide to go?"

Her reply totally took Blake by surprise. To lighten the conversation, he said. "I wouldn't call traipsing across the Continent and mapping cities and routes as fighting."

"I would. Superior information would give the British the upper hand to defeat Bonaparte." She turned to look into his eyes. "But you didn't answer my question." She continued to search his features as if trying to see into his soul, and soon he leaned down to kiss her. But she pulled away and shook her head.

"I too have an excellent memory, and I will not let my question go unanswered. Before the house party is over, you will tell me." She flashed a wicked smile as she was learning how to wield the power she now held over him.

Since it was apparent there was to be no kissing, he said, "Hmm… if you and Harrington are a whole, you are by far the better half for company." He nibbled and sucked on her earlobe, trying to elicit a moan from her.

"Blake, you are like a puzzle to me. Matthew has mentioned you over the years, but I feel like I only have some of the pieces… the corner pieces, but with some of the border missing. I'd love for you to give me the rest to make the picture whole, but I'm not sure you are willing to share. Are you?"

"Lady Lucy, I'm not some mysterious rake or scandalous rogue. I'm an open book. Just ask, and I'll tell you."

"Really?" Seeing the twinkle in her eyes, he suspected her questions were going to be rather tricky. "Are you enjoying the house party?"

Best he only reply either in the affirmative or negative. "Yes."

"Do you currently have a mistress?"

Blake didn't flinch before stating quite adamantly, "No."

"Have you ever had a mistress?"

He pondered why Lucy was asking such bold, intimate questions but promptly answered, "No."

"Why?"

He couldn't stick to the one-word answers for this question. Honesty would serve him best. "I've never been in one place long enough to maintain a mistress."

"Are you a virgin?"

He tried not to laugh. "No."

As if on to his scheme, Lady Lucy changed her line of questions. "What is your favorite color?"

"I don't have one."

"What hobbies do you enjoy?"

Should he give her the gentlemanly answer or the one that would make her blush? He remembered she was Harrington's sister and modified his answer. "Well, I do enjoy sketching…"

"Why did you do a sketch of Lady Mary?"

"It was a sketch of the two of you, not just Lady Mary. And whatever the two of you were discussing made for interesting conversation, for everyone else in the room could see there was a true connection of like minds. I was trying to capture the moment. If I am to be completely honest, I don't think I've ever experienced that type of camaraderie with anyone."

The smile Lucy gave him told him he had revealed a lot more than he intended. It was getting late; they needed to return to the house and change for dinner.

"Will you be joining in the festivities this evening?" Lucy asked.

Had she noticed he often disappeared after dinner? He had thought she would assume he and her brother had retired to the card room or to play billiards. Perhaps they had not been as clever at hiding their activities as they believed.

"My skills at charades are awful. I prefer to avoid the game and hide in the billiards room. Let's meet out here again tomorrow, and you can finish your inquisition."

Lucy gave a slight nod of agreement. Would she look forward to spending time alone together as much as he did?

CHAPTER SEVENTEEN

*L*ucy smiled as she turned to Lady Mary, who was staring up at the night sky. "I've enjoyed our time here. House parties are not as torturous as I had imagined."

"That is because you have landed yourself the best partner for these silly activities, while I've been subject to Lord Waterford's grumpy disposition."

Blake was a fantastic partner. He often provided witty commentary and on occasion invented challenges for them both. Lucy's favorite was reciting cities that began with each letter of a peer's name. She had named Lady Roxbury and was in complete awe as Blake rattled off, "Rome in Italy, Oberhausen in Germany, Xifias in Greece, Bilbao in Spain, Utrecht in the Netherlands, Rheims in France, and Yekaterinburg, Russia."

Lucy had to admit Blake's company guaranteed an evening full of interesting lessons. Unwilling to admit that Lady Mary was correct, she said, "Waterford isn't all bad."

"Gilbert is the most arrogant, high-handed, opinion-ated man I've ever known."

Had Lady Mary just referred to Waterford using his Christian name? Accustomed to addressing and calling him Waterford, it took Lucy a moment to recognize the name Gilbert. What could have occurred between Lady Mary and Waterford for her to make such a statement?

Lady Mary turned and pointedly stared down at her. "Devonton is *always* extremely attentive."

"You can make me blush, but no one will witness it in the dark."

Lady Mary's laughter, was no genteel giggle, it had her bending at the waist. Tears streamed from her eyes. Why did she find Lucy's statement hilarious?

Taking a deep calming breath, Lady Mary regained some of her composure. "Who would have guessed that the ever-rational, level-headed Lady Lucy would fall victim to my teasing? I am curious to know. What interesting facts have you learned about our dear Devonton during your stolen moments alone?"

"What are you talking about?"

"Lady Lucy, you are not five, and you do not need daily naps."

"Naps?"

"Yes. It is the excuse Lady Redburn has used for the past three days for your absence in the afternoons." Lady Mary was relentless. "What does Devonton enjoy? Kisses, perhaps?"

Lucy was sure she was blushing as she answered, "Devonton enjoys the outdoors. He is a marvelous story-teller, and when he speaks of his travels, it feels as if you are right there. He is well educated…"

"In kissing?" Lady Mary teased.

"Yes, he is an excellent kisser, and when…"

"Lady Lucy, may I have a moment of your time?" Blake croaked.

How did he appear without detection? She had perfect hearing and usually could sense someone approaching well before they came face-to-face.

"Lady Mary, please excuse us for a moment. Perhaps we can partner for the Jonesy contest."

Lady Mary eyed them both with interest. "I'd be delighted to partner with you if you are still available."

Ignoring Lady Mary's comment, Lucy turned and let Blake pull her farther into the gardens. He gently placed his hands on her shoulders and bumbled, "Lucy, I'm not sure how to ask this of you."

"Ask me what?" Lucy craned her neck so she could see into his eyes. He appeared nervous. She told herself to be patient with the man.

"I'd like to court you if you would be amenable to the notion."

"Blake, I thought you already were. Why have we been sneaking to the lake every day if not to learn more about each other to see if we would suit? It wasn't just because you wanted to kiss me, was it?" Lucy wasn't sure, but had she managed to make Blake blush?

The rustling of branches had Lucy peering into the dark. Who had joined them? Matthew materialized from behind a topiary that resembled a snake balancing a ball on its head.

"Why are you two sneaking about in the gardens?"

Blake's hands dropped to his sides. His abrupt release left her wobbling. Lucy easily regained her balance, but she caught the conflicted emotions that flew across Blake's features. What was he worried about? It wasn't as if Matthew would call his best friend out for having his hands upon her. Matthew's narrowed gaze fell upon Blake, and he raised an eyebrow.

Blake regained his voice first. "Well, Harrington, I…"

"Oh goodness, Matthew. Blake and I have been doing whatever one does at house parties," Lucy announced, not really knowing what she was implying.

"*What?*" Matthew shouted loud enough that those on the terrace turned to look. He poked Blake in the chest and asked directly, "Did you take advantage of Lucy? Have you…"

Before Matthew could go on, Blake was shaking his head adamantly, "Harrington, no. I would never dishonor Lucy, and I would never risk our friendship like that."

Lucy stepped between them and pushed Matthew back. "Matthew, how could you accuse Blake of such behavior? You of all people should know he would do the honorable thing should something like… like that occurred between us." She was blushing and honestly a little lost as to how to explain what was happening between herself and Blake.

Blake calmly wrapped an arm around her waist and gently pulled her back to put some distance between her and Matthew.

Oddly, instead of seeming further enraged, Matthew eyed Blake's protective motions and ordered them, "I expect you both to behave while we remain at Redburn Manor."

His directive was in stark contrast with the bounce in his step as he returned to the drawing room through the terrace doors.

Lucy felt Blake's chest rattle and turned to see him chuckling. She slapped him on the chest and said, "I think that went well."

Blake interweaved their fingers and led her to the lake.

~

CHEEKS ROSY AND LIPS SWOLLEN, Lucy returned to the house to participate in the Jonesy contest.

"Lucy. Lady Lucy." Lady Mary poked her elbow into Lucy's ribs. "If you could stop daydreaming, we might have a chance at winning."

Lucy apologized. "Sorry, I'll focus."

"What rhymes with *enough*?"

"Love?"

"Lucy, if you don't stop thinking of Devonton, I will…"

"Devonton? What has Devonton and love got to do with enough?"

Lady Mary blinked as if Lucy were talking in riddles. "Lucy, you are in love with the man!"

Shocked, Lucy replied, "In love? I can't be. We've only recently begun to get to know each other."

"Devonton can appear to be rather standoffish and boring, but if you watch him and listen closely, he always has a purpose."

Lucy narrowed her eyes at Lady Mary. Had Lady Mary taken a particular interest in Blake? He *was* a master of hiding out in the open.

Lady Mary echoed her thoughts, saying, "He is an expert at blending in and influencing discussions without bringing attention to himself. Exceptionally sneaky is what I call him, and when you look beyond his mask, he is rather handsome."

Handsome? Striking was a better description of Blake. But it wasn't his features that impressed Lucy the most. It was his keen mind and ability to blend into any environment, like a chameleon. Having to master the skill herself, Lucy was fully aware of the vast control and patience required to perform such a task. Lucy had benefited on more than one occasion from remaining hidden in plain sight. The insight into which investments were likely to bear modest returns had allowed her to accumulate a small fortune, enough for her to set up her own household. *Independence. Freedom from marriage.* After meeting Blake, were those still her wishes?

Lady Mary continued, "Lady Lucy, the man has eyes only for you. Women have been casting their lures at Devonton the entire house party, but he pretends to misunderstand their invitations or politely declines the more overt offers."

"He has?"

"Why do you think all the others titter behind their fans when you enter a room? They are jealous. You have captured the interest of a young earl who has recently returned from his tour. If rumors are to be believed, gentlemen who have traveled to foreign lands are much better lovers than those who have never left our shores. He is a mystery, and they want what you have: his attention."

Did she? When Blake was near, she was aware her own focus became rather singular. The man she had spent afternoons with was warm and funny, anything but boring. Now that she considered the matter, Blake did take an extraordinary interest in her opinions and feelings. During their time alone by the lake, he had proven that he was unlike other gentlemen—he paid attention and truly listened. He had gained her trust. Lucy had even confessed her secret wish for a family, but after James's death, she hadn't thought it possible.

She did have Blake's attention, and Lucy wasn't about to lose it.

"Lady Mary, Lady Lucy, do you have your riddle ready?" Lady Redburn inquired.

Lost in the myriad of questions Lady Mary had brought to mind, she had not focused on the Jonesy contest. Thankfully, her mind was filled with riddles. "Yes, Lady Redburn."

Lucy searched the room, and when her gaze landed on Blake, she began. "A king was to grant one knight the honor of marrying his only daughter. She stood in the middle of the room upon a large rug that was wider than a man's body length. The princess had selected the four knights the night prior, and each stood in one corner of the room. The king declared the knight who kissed the princess's hand would receive his blessing. However, they must not use anything, nor were they allowed to touch the rug upon which she stood. After long moments, one knight placed his lips upon the princess's hand. How did he accomplish it?"

Lady Mary whispered, "Do you think he will figure it out?"

"I certainly hope so. If not tonight, soon."

Waterford, who was seated next to Devonton, called out, "The knight ordered the princess to come to him and present her hand for a kiss."

Giggling at Lady Mary's shocked expression, Lucy replied, "Well done, Lord Waterford. You are correct!"

Waterford performed a cursory bow, but there was a hard, unfamiliar glimmer in his eyes as his gaze fell upon Lady Mary. The tension between the two was palpable. Was it hatred she sensed?

The pair ceased scowling at each other as Lady Mary turned to Lucy. "That man has a terrible habit of ensuring I never win."

"Lady Mary, you must admit it was rather clever of Waterford to figure it out."

"Lord Archbroke would have solved it faster."

Lucy conceded Lady Mary was right. Lord Archbroke, pompous genius that he was, would have had the answer before she even finished relating the riddle. No longer a contender in the Jonesy competition, Lucy relaxed and listened as each team shared their entries. It was amusing to see Lady Mary, Waterford, and the others battle to answer first.

When it was Blake and Waterford's turn, Lucy shifted to the edge of her seat. Would Blake be the one to perform? The pair communicated between themselves without words. Ultimately, it was Waterford who cleared his throat before beginning:

"I was traveling down a path when it split into two.

One path lead to war and death. One path lead to rest and peace.

Two soldiers sat by the paths. One was known to never tell the truth, the other never spoke a lie.

What one question would I ask of them to lead me down the correct path?"

What a peculiar riddle to share. Did Waterford mean it to be a hidden message for someone? No one among the group offered an answer.

Lady Redburn said, "My lords, I believe you have stumped us all. Pray tell, what would the question be?"

Blake replied, "Lady Redburn, I should ask, what would he say was the path to my salvation and peace? And I would travel down the opposite path to which he pointed."

The confused features of the group were plain for all to see.

Lady Redburn clapped her hands as if to break the spell that had been cast by Blake and Waterford. "I declare Lord Waterford and Lord Devonton the winners of the Jonesy contest. Well done, my lords."

Once the applause from the group subsided, Blake

approached, and Lucy stood to greet him. His eyes were ablaze as he asked, "Would you care for a refreshment?"

Lucy turned to ask Lady Mary to join them only to realize that they were completely alone. When had everyone left?

Placing a hand on his chest, Lucy said, "Congratulations on the win."

"My thanks. Would you consider granting the winner a kiss?"

"Kiss Waterford? Never!" Lucy loved Blake's surprised look at her reply. She slid both hands up his chest and stood on her tiptoes to pull him down for a kiss. She had intended to kiss him senseless, but it was she who was left with no rational thoughts.

As they parted, Blake growled, "You are a minx. I shall escort you to your room."

Nodding in a daze, she allowed him to guide her. Lady Redburn was pacing in the foyer. As soon as they were close enough, her hostess scolded, "What were you two about in there? No, don't answer me. Lucy, come along with me. We shall retire for the evening." But before leading Lucy away, Lady Redburn pointed down the opposite hallway and said to Blake, "Off with you."

The reference to Blake's riddle had Lucy grinning. Had Lady Redburn instructed him to go down the right path? *Heaven? Or hell?*

CHAPTER EIGHTEEN

Staring at her list of Lord Ds, Lucy dipped her quit into the ink pot. She had received missives late in the evening resulting in her eliminating two more potential targets. She drew a bold line through Lord Draven's name. Theo had sent word that Lord Draven was of a similar age to Edward and had only recently inherited the title. Lord Dunhill's name was also scratched through as her informant from the north had confirmed he remained ensconced in Scotland with no indication he had traveled to the Continent or attended the House of Lords in years.

Blake's name was one of two remaining. Lucy weighed the facts: the number of years and the timing of his stay on the Continent. Her suspicions of the true nature of his purpose had not waned and had, with each passing day, increased. It was plausible that Blake had made enemies as he sketched his way through each country.

Shoulders sagging, head bowed, she fought back tears as she concluded that it was more than likely Blake was indeed the intended target. She desperately wanted to confront him today. Fear of the answer had her wishing to postpone the confrontation. She was about to head to the dining room to break her fast when a footman in the hall approached her with a silver platter.

"Lady Lucy." She peeked up at the footman and recognized him to be the messenger from the Home Office, Mr. Smyth. Why was Mr. Smyth disguised as a footman?

She took the missive from the platter and placed it in her pocket. As if Mr. Smyth had appeared out of thin air, he vanished in the same fashion.

Lucy retreated to her room and opened the missive. Instead of it being a message hidden within a passage, it was written in numerals and symbols. This meant it must be of an urgent nature. She sat at the bay window of her room and began to puzzle out the code.

Absorbed in the task before her, she started and felt her heart jump out of her chest when Blake's raspy voice called through the door, "Lady Lucy."

She hurriedly tucked the missive under some pillows before replying, "Come in."

Blake opened the door but remained at the threshold. "Lucy, I waited by the lake. When you did not arrive, I was concerned."

She rushed to reassure him. "Oh, Blake! I'm sorry. I lost track of time. I apologize for worrying you, but I'm well, just a little distracted."

Blake quietly slipped into the room. He closed and locked the door behind him. There was a glimmer in his eyes; it was a look that was becoming more apparent as they spent more time in each other's company. She sensed it to be more than longing and lust, but she wasn't entirely sure.

Lucy rose and walked toward him. She didn't stop until she was mere inches away and reached up to put her arms around his neck. She leaned into him so he would feel every inch of her body as she raised up on her tiptoes and pulled his head down for a kiss.

Blake did not return her embrace. Was he angry at her? Had he worried she no longer wanted to meet? Had her riddle not given him a clue as to her feelings for him? He had shared with her his fear of letting people come close. He had lost everyone he had loved. She suspected he had erected solid walls around his heart, and it was those walls that enabled him to live in solitude for so many years.

Relief washed through her as Blake's arms began to wrap around her. But when he stopped and gently pulled back, it filled her with worry.

Blake caught her attention by looking directly into her eyes. He asked, "Distracted?"

Could he see the depths of her desire?

He gave her a wicked grin and said, "Perhaps I could provide a better distraction." Blake bent his head and placed soft kisses, starting at the middle of her forehead, down her nose, and finally he fulfilled her wish to have his lips on hers.

Lucy had enjoyed the kisses they had shared the past few days, but she longed to feel the hot sensations he had brought about while they were in the library. As if he read her mind, he ran his hands down the row of buttons at her back, then rested them on her plump bottom. He squeezed her cheeks and brought her closer to him. His physical response to her was immediately evident. She wanted to remove all the barriers between them and began to feel a warm wetness between her legs. She moved to get even closer to Blake, and in doing so, he slipped a leg between hers and slightly lifted her. Her tiptoes barely touched the floor.

The pressure between her legs felt delightful, and Lucy

let out a moan. In her daze, she could only focus on Blake's touches—speech was impossible—his hands seemed to be everywhere on her body. He let out a growl in her ear when she began riding his thigh. The groan encouraged her to continue taking bolder moves, and she pushed his face down to bury it in her décolletage.

Blake expertly kissed the tops of her breasts. His finger circled her hardened nipple. Lucy cursed the material that prevented him from touching her. She arched her back, pressing farther into his caress. When he pinched her pebbled nipple, she couldn't prevent a moan from escaping. The sensations she experienced overwhelmed her, as he continued to stroke her, soft sighs and primal sounds she had never uttered escaped her lips.

Lucy was endowed with large breasts and plump hips and thighs, and as Blake's hands roamed every inch of her body, his touch set off flutters of delight that mixed with twinges of anxiety about her figure. Would he consider her desirable? But as the moments passed his caresses became more urgent until she couldn't think of anything but the exhilarating sensations he was provoking within her.

He grabbed her skirts and pulled them roughly up to her waist, telling her gruffly, "Hold these here."

She removed one of her arms from around his neck and did as she was told, holding the material up out of his way.

His hands caressed her inner thighs and moved upward as if seeking out her core. Ashamed of the wetness he would find, Lucy buried her head in his neck, and she began to kiss her way up, eager for his lips again.

He picked her up by the waist, and she instinctively wrapped her legs around him. Blake walked backward to the bed, kissing her the entire time. The sound of his calves hitting the frame only registered when he fell back with her on top of him. Rather than try to get off him, she positioned herself so that her soft, rounded bottom sat upon his stomach as she straddled him. She pinned him with a gaze that brooked no arguments and clearly indicated he was to stay where he was.

Lucy reached for his cravat first and removed the material from around his neck, only to dangle it in front of him. While she had no idea what to do with a man beneath her, she followed her natural instincts. Blake loved it when she teased him during their talks, so she decided to do the same now. He reached for his cravat and grabbed it from her to put it under the small of his back.

He then tried to grab her hands to still them as she was working the buttons on his shirt and pulling it out from his breeches. "Lucy, do you have any idea what you are doing to me?"

She rocked a little and replied, "I have a fair idea."

Her dress and corset fell to her waist. She hadn't even realized Blake's nimble fingers had undone her buttons and laces. In one swift move, he rolled and had her pinned under him.

"Lucy, I want to make you mine, but…"

She moved under him and changed their positions, which placed him right between her legs. In this position, she could see his face clearly. Desire burned in his eyes, but then he shook his head. She tensed. Did he think she was trying to trap him? No, it was like he was deciding what to do next. He had told her he wasn't a virgin. He must know what to do.

He took her head between his hands and stared directly into her eyes, asking, "Do you trust me?"

She tried to nod, but Blake wouldn't let her. "I need to hear you say the words. Do you trust me?"

"Yes, Blake, I trust you," she breathlessly answered.

"Good, now do as I say."

Why was he ordering her about? Was this how he had interpreted her riddle?

Her body ached for his touch. With a frown, she answered, "Very well, I'll do as you say."

Blake found his cravat and gently raised Lucy's arms above her head and bound her wrists. "Now, leave your hands above your head, no matter what."

She was sure her confusion was written all over her face. Blake's features were contorted, as if he was at war with himself. Did he need control or her trust?

At his hesitation, Lucy said, "I trust you. I want you to kiss me again."

All remaining doubts fled from his features as soon as she uttered the words.

Lucy did as she was told and left her hands above her head. Blake bent to give her a teasing kiss, a kiss that left her wanting more. She needed to feel his tongue in her mouth, and when he began kissing her again, she didn't hold back. She sought out his tongue and then sucked hard on it; it seemed to break all of Blake's restraint.

He kissed her with such intensity her core temperature soared to feverish heights. With his teeth he nipped at her skin, traveling down her neck, then following the line of her collarbone, and when he reached her breast, he rolled her nipple between his lips and caressed it with his tongue. Lucy arched her back and let out sigh after sigh. Blake's hands skimmed the skin along her arms, on the inside of her elbows, and with a featherlight touch down her side all the way to the middle of her thigh. His mouth moved down her body, licking, kissing, and biting his way to her pelvic bone.

He slowly removed her drawers. Gently he spread her

legs to accommodate his wide shoulders comfortably between her thighs.

Goosebumps danced along her skin as his tongue grazed along lips that had never been touched by another. She instinctively tried to clamp her legs shut, but his hands gently guided her knees to relax and for her to open up to him. He placed his palms and fingers under her bottom, while his thumbs were massaging her core. Blake continued to lick and tease her until her body bowed with tension. Every movement magnified the sensitivity of her core. She nearly came apart as he slid a finger inside her and began to slowly pump it in and out, going deeper with each stroke all the while his tongue flicked her sensitive bud. When he added another finger, her muscles tightened around them, and her eyes closed so tightly stars appeared as an explosion of sensations shuddered throughout her body.

She floated back to reality, as Blake caressed and kissed the inside of her wrists as he unbound her. His touch made her skin come alive and sent pleasing sparks all over her body. She couldn't speak; her mind was blank, and all she wanted was for Blake to hold her.

He moved to lie beside her. She loved the fact he was in tune with her wants and needs. Together, they lay facing the window, not speaking, just catching their breath. She enjoyed being in Blake's arms. Content, it didn't worry her that she was totally naked in bed with a man she wasn't married to.

After a while, Lucy broke the silence. "Blake, that was... was exceptional. Having grown up in the country, I believe there is more to the experience."

"Your virtue is intact; however, your innocence is... well... I'd say you are more enlightened."

She turned to face him. "I have..." She wanted to tell

him a multitude of things, but her mind was preoccupied with her concern for his safety, and she was starting to fall in love with him, but those thoughts were weighty and she dared not bring them up.

Blake placed a finger on her lips to prevent her from talking. "Shhh. Let's rest before I have to leave. I'm sure your maid will be here to assist you in getting ready for supper."

Lucy snuggled into his embrace and placed the curve of her bottom into his groin.

Blake let out a groan. "Lucy. Stay. Still."

Lucy instantly quit moving, and before long she'd fallen fast asleep.

BLAKE WAITED until Lucy's breathing had evened before untangling himself from her lush form. He pulled the sheets higher, ensuring she was fully covered. "Sleep well, my sweet." He tiptoed out into the hall.

He left her room intending to seek out his own chambers to sort out the turmoil of thoughts and emotions rolling about in his mind. He needed to decide what he was going to do about Lucy. He wanted to trust his instincts and go and seek her hand, but fear her heart remained with James prevented him from acting. She physically desired his touch and wanted to know him in the biblical sense, but was that enough for a lifetime of marriage?

Blake's parents had married for love. The affection and companionship they shared was something he craved. Could one assess if another was compatible based on a few weeks of acquaintance? The intangible lure and a feeling of rightness remained every time he was with Lucy. When she wasn't near, a sense of emptiness and a longing to see or be with her overwhelmed him. Blake was so lost in his thoughts, he nearly walked past Harrington.

Harrington's features were drawn taut, and the relaxed, amicable gentleman was nowhere to be seen. "Devonton, why are you near the family wing? Were you in Lucy's chambers? Alone?"

Blake was conscious of the fact his cravat was untied, and he must look like he had debauched his best friend's sister.

Harrington glared and growled, "We don't have time to discuss this right now. I have the horses being readied. We need to ride out—there has been activity near the cave."

Without hesitation, Devonton turned, and they ran to the stables.

Confused, Lucy rubbed her eyes and scanned the room. She was alone. The spot beside her indented but cool. Blake must have left some time ago.

In short order Lucy had put her clothes back on as best she could by herself and then summoned Carrington. She didn't feel like dining with the other guests this evening, so she requested her supper be brought to her rooms.

Remembering the missive, Lucy retrieved it from the window seat and began to decipher the message. An hour later she read the transcribed passage:

We have intercepted five more missives.
Need your immediate assistance, deadline approaching, please make arrangements posthaste.
Mr. Smyth is at your disposal.

"Five! Good God, how am I to manage? And so soon after the last trip."

Carrington entered her room, balancing a tray with her supper.

"Carrington, we need to return to London. Please make the necessary arrangements for us to leave in the morning."

"My lady, we cannot leave without notifying Lord Harrington. What are you going to tell him? Perhaps now would be a good time to tell him the truth."

"Tell Matthew?" Lucy looked at Carrington as if she'd completely lost all her senses. "He would banish me to a nunnery in a heartbeat if he knew of my involvement with the Home Office."

Carrington persisted, "I'm not so sure I agree with you, my lady. He would never want to be that far from you. Please consider it. We need to leave the house party, and we cannot leave without your brother's consent."

"I'll tell him I've heard from Grace and need to go back to London."

"Lady Lucy, his lordship has strong feelings for Lady Grace. It would put him in a panic, and he would insist on returning and seeing her himself."

How did Carrington know of Matthew's feelings for Grace? Admittedly, servants did tend to be well informed about such matters. Pacing back and forth, Lucy said, "Oh, Carrington, what am I to do? I must think of something…"

Carrington arranged Lucy's supper on the desk.

"I know what you're thinking." Lucy glared at her maid.

Carrington had been hounding her to confess to Matthew for the past year. What would his reaction be? Was she being overdramatic or would he really banish her?

No, deep in her heart she knew Matthew would never do that to her. Thinking on it, perhaps her brother could assist her. What if she told Matthew, and he shared with Blake her involvement with the Home Office? Certainly, Blake wouldn't want a wife who worked. Even if he was to over-look her activities, he wouldn't understand how important it was to her to remain an agent.

Lucy was lost in her own musings as Carrington ushered her to the table where she began to absently eat her meal. With a deep sigh, she relented. "Very well. I'll find Matthew and tell him tonight. Be ready to leave at first light."

It was dark outside when Lucy made her way to the stables. She had not been able to locate either Blake or her brother anywhere in the house, conservatories, or the surrounding gardens. It had been hours since Blake left her rooms, and Lucy was beginning to worry for the safety of them both.

She was in the process of saddling a mare when the stable master came in. "My lady, may I be of some assistance?"

Lucy was glad to see him. "Yes. Did Lord Harrington and Lord Devonton ride out earlier today?"

"Your brother had two steeds readied, but I did not see them leave." He looked down the row of stalls. "Appears the govs have not returned, my lady. They are both excel-lent horsemen; I'm sure they will return soon."

"I will need the escort of either an outrider or footman, whoever can be ready to accompany me in the next fifteen minutes."

A shadow appeared and Mr. Smyth presented himself.

"I will accompany you, my lady." He disappeared into the stables and reappeared mounted with an efficiency that surprised Lucy.

She grinned and led her horse to the mounting block. "Let's be off."

Maneuvering his horse next to Lucy's, he inquired, "Which way, my lady?"

Lucy frowned as she scanned her surroundings. She had no idea which way Matthew might have gone, but as the minutes passed, a feeling he was in danger had crept into her bones. The last time she'd had this feeling Matthew had fallen and twisted his ankle in the woods; it had taken her hours to convince their papa to help her search for him.

Lucy gazed up to see only stars and a quarter moon. It would be difficult to track them at night. Facing Mr. Smyth, she said, "I'm not very familiar with this area. However, I know Lord Devonton and my brother have been going out riding and most times have been gone for at least three hours, so they must have targeted sites that are approximately forty-five minutes to an hour's ride out. Are you familiar with the area, Mr. Smyth?"

"I've only been this way once or twice. I do know there are smugglers' caves about a hard hour's ride out, but in the opposite direction, there is an old abandoned castle that I've had to venture to once before."

"We can split up—one of us should head to the caves and the other to the castle."

"No, my lady. I will not leave you. If I had to make a choice, I'd venture to the caves. It is only a quarter moon…"

Before he could say more, Lucy spied two steeds meandered down the lane toward them. "Mr. Smyth, those horses are returning to the stables, but they are without riders."

Dread and a cold shiver ran down her spine.

"We need to decide which direction quickly. Lady Lucy, where to?"

She leaned over her mare and nudged it to a gallop. "The caves."

CHAPTER NINETEEN

*B*lake pried open his eyes, but as light filtered through, he flinched. A sharp, stabbing pain pierced through his brain. Sealing them shut again, he utilized his other senses to ascertain where he might be. The ringing in his ears made it hard for him to listen to his surroundings.

His head ached. Lifting his hand to his ear, a warm, thick, sticky substance covered his fingers. He raised them to his nose and confirmed it was blood. He tried to recall what had happened, but the strain intensified the throbbing pain in his head.

Salt. Seawater.

Running his hand over the ground beneath him, his fingers and palm grazed over hard, packed sand and rock. It was moist. He must be in a cave. How close was he to the entrance?

He tried to call out, but all he could manage was a hoarse whisper, "Harrington?"

Silence.

Disoriented, he tried to move, but his stomach revolted,

and his head pounded, and within seconds he slipped back into the darkness.

~

THE ROAD WAS NARROW, and Mr. Smyth was in the lead. *Where are they?* Lucy's heart beat in time to her mount's hooves. She was trying to remain calm, but the possibility of the two men she cared for most being harmed had her wits in a tangled mess.

"Over there!" Mr. Smyth yelled and pointed slightly off the path and to the right.

Lucy squinted at the spot he'd indicated. She couldn't see the man's features, but she knew it was her twin. Matthew!

She dug in her heels and took over the lead.

Matthew sat up and removed what appeared to be a twig poking him in the most uncomfortable of places. He shook his head and surveyed his surroundings. He seemed to have enough of his wits about him that he was aware of the approaching pounding of hooves. Lucy slowed her mount. Matthew scrambled to his knees. Mr. Smyth's was right behind her and dust and dirt kicked up into Matthew's face.

"Matthew!" Lucy cried out as her brother shielded his head with his arms.

The horse snorted as Mr. Smyth pulled up on the reins to make a quick turn in an attempt to avoid trampling Matthew or colliding with Lucy. The horse bucked and sent Mr. Smyth to the ground. Mr. Smyth jumped back up to his feet and brushed the dust from his clothes. With only a slight limp, he made his way to Matthew.

Lucy jumped down from her mount. Kneeling at

Matthew's side, she began patting him down, trying to assess his health.

"Matthew, what happened?" She really wanted to ask about Blake, but first she needed to understand what had occurred.

In typical Matthew fashion, he questioned without pause, "Devonton? Is he hurt? Where is he? We must find him."

"We've only just found you. It doesn't appear Blake is close by. Matthew, you need to tell us what happened and stop asking questions."

"We…" Matthew hesitated.

She wanted to yell and scream *now is not the time to keep secrets!* But theatrics would not get her the information she was desperate for.

Lucy's patience was worn thin. It was time to come clean and tell him all. "Matthew, I need to know the truth. Mr. Smyth here was sent by the Home Office to assist me. Now please, tell me what happened."

"Home Office? Why would the Home Office send *you*, Mr. Smyth?" With a slight turn of his head, his eyes widened with recognition. "*Mr. Jones?*"

Anger was not what Lucy was expecting from Matthew. Who was Mr. Jones? How many pseudonyms could one have?

"Yes, I'm Mr. Jones and Mr. Smyth. I have many aliases. But Lord Harrington, this is not the time for questions. We need to understand the situation so we can help Lord Devonton, who I believe is in grave danger."

Shaking his head, Matthew drew a deep breath and began, "Devonton and I have been monitoring and watching for activity in the cove and the caves. We were hoping to intercept plans. My orders from the Home

Office were to protect Devonton as there was a suspicion he was the target of an abduction…"

"*You* received an order from Lord Archbroke? You *knew* it was Blake, and still you risked…" Lucy couldn't continue. The shocking revelation that the pair had been so irresponsible had her wanting to strangle her brother. Why would they put Blake's life at risk? Seeking out the smugglers was like handing him over on a silver platter.

"Yes, we were informed he was at risk, but he didn't just want to wait in London like a caged pigeon. We agreed it would be better for us to assess the situation personally rather than wait in ignorance."

Lucy just shook her head. Why did men feel like they always had to "do" something or "fix" the situation when it might be best left to others? "Matthew, I was the one to decode the message revealing the planned abduction. They are…"

"*You!* Since when have you been involved with the Home Office?"

"Matthew, please calm down."

"Calm down! I want answers, sister!"

"And so do we. I'm guessing you will not be helpful until we have this discussion. To start, I've been working with the Home Office for many years, assisting them throughout the war in decoding messages and devising the code used for correspondence. I'll explain in more detail later. I would also like to understand *your* involvement and role at the Home Office, since you are already acquainted with Mr. Smyth. However, right now we need to help Blake. How long ago were you attacked?"

"I just awoke to the sounds of your horses' hooves." Matthew rubbed the back of his head. "Blimey, my head hurts." Eyes closed, he continued, "I remember Devonton hearing voices in the woods. We dismounted and tethered the horses to a tree and continued on foot. We came upon three men around a campfire and spread out so we could approach from both sides. Devonton was to move in first, but as he did, a man attacked him from behind, swinging a large branch and knocking him out. I was getting up when I heard a noise from behind me. They must have knocked me out too."

Matthew began patting himself down.

Lucy asked, "What are you searching for?"

"My pistol. My coin."

"Obviously, they are gone along with Blake," Lucy said as she walked away to address Mr. Smyth. His features were blank as Lucy ordered, "Please search the area."

Based on Matthew's recounting, there were at least five men in the group. Lucy scanned the ground—there were both hoof and footprints. She joined Mr. Smyth, who was crouched and peering at a hoof print. The deep impression was a telltale sign that one of the horses carried something of significant weight.

Lucy's heart sank.

Blake had been kidnapped. They were too late. She had to find him.

"Mr. Smyth, were you able to find any indication of which direction they headed?"

"The tracks are fairly fresh, so they cannot be too far ahead, but they are well covered, and some appear to have been made in a circular fashion to mask their true direction. We are not dealing with amateurs."

Matthew joined them surveying the tracks. "There are two caves which have had recent activity. Devonton and I were headed to the first. Let's continue—"

Mr. Smyth interjected, "Lord Harrington, if in fact there are five men, we are outnumbered, and you are injured."

"I'm well. We need to find Devonton before he is moved."

Mr. Smyth was correct in his assessment of the situation. With Matthew hurt, the odds were not in their favor. Lucy was torn. Her heart begged her to pursue Blake. But she rationalized the best chance of recovering him was to return to London and hope the correspondence she had been summoned to decipher would identify Blake's kidnappers.

She had to convince her brother to see reason. "Matthew, Mr. Smyth is right. You need to recover. We only have two mounts, and if we proceed, we could be headed in the wrong direction if in fact there are two possible locations. We cannot waste time; we need to return to London without delay. I received a summons earlier requiring me to assist with another five missives. Perhaps from those, along with the earlier note that indicated Blake was to be taken to the Lone Dove, we can formulate a plan to recover him and apprehend the French operatives."

Matthew paced, mumbling under his breath. Why was he taking so long? They didn't have time to waste and wait around for him to come to his senses and admit she was right. Lucy noticed that he was limping slightly as he paced back and forth and decided to give him a little longer.

Ignoring her brother for a moment, Lucy instructed, "Mr. Smyth, when we return to Redburn House, please have the carriage readied right away. I will have Matthew write a message for Lord Redburn explaining we had to depart due to a family situation in London and have him instruct both his and Lord Devonton's valets to pack and return with my maid."

She was deciding what other items needed to be seen to when Matthew announced, "I'm not returning to

Redburn House with the two of you. It will look suspicious if…"

Lucy interrupted her brother's speech. "Matthew, the two mounts you and Blake rode out on have already returned to the stables. If you do not come back to assist me in explaining that we are to depart immediately, there will be more queries as to where the two of you went and questions regarding your whereabouts. Please trust me." She nervously awaited her twin's response. She had never before employed such an authoritative tone with him before.

Lucy released a sigh as Matthew conceded, "You will have to ride back with me."

CHAPTER TWENTY

*B*lake awoke to cold water being splashed onto his face. It took him a moment to fully regain consciousness. When he opened his eyes, he found he was lying on the ground in a dimly lit cave with three burly men standing over him.

A voice from behind him spoke. "Well, well, well, the famous cartographer finally comes to." The speaker had a moderated, well-polished voice; this was no smuggler. There was something in his tone that Blake recognized but couldn't quite place. He tried to turn and look at the man, but his head whipped backward as his jaw was pounded by a large fist. Blood trickled from Blake's lip.

His captor said, "Don't turn around. Our instructions were not to harm you, so if you just follow our lead, all will go smoothly."

Focused on the three brutes in front of him, Blake slowly regained his wits. All three were similar in looks, possibly brothers or cousins. Their features forever burned into his memory. Blake assessed his odds of escaping. They were not in his favor. Perhaps silence would make his captors uncomfortable and he could gain critical information.

"Nothing to say, Devonton? You and Harrington made my job so much easier. I was anticipating having to subject myself to the idle entertainments of the London *ton*. I had not planned to return so soon; this means we have a few days to become acquainted before we sail. I'm sure you will find our company and accommodations satisfactory."

Blake rested his eyelids and kept his lips tight and closed. Who was this man? His accent was definitely British but with a slight Parisian influence, as if he had been in France for an extended period. It was risky to hold him captive on English soil for days rather than set sail straight away. Did they not have the required coin or connections? Was there another orchestrating Blake's abduction?

From behind, the gentleman commanded, "Give him some bread and water and then see he is moved without issue."

He was to be moved. But, where was he to be transferred? A blindfold was placed over his eyes and secured tightly. With no chance of Blake seeing his identity, his captor left the cave with quick, decisive steps.

Would the man's orders be followed? How loyal were the trio to the gentleman? Thirsty, Blake could only hope the bread and water would appear soon.

One of his captors hauled Blake up by the arm. With his hands bound behind his back, Blake made a motion to strike the man with his leg. As he made contact and the man's legs were swept from under him, Blake was freed and fell to his knees, pitching forward until his forehead hit the ground. A boot to the stomach was the reward for his attempt to escape.

Muttering to himself, "Bloody hell, Devonton. What

were you thinking, the odds were so slight?" *Damn.* His return to polite society had caused him to curb his tendency to talk to himself in the third person. A habit born out of only having himself for company. Now was not the time for its return.

While a rope was being synched around his ankles, he rubbed the back of his head against the ground to loosen the knot of his blindfold. Unfortunately, his captors were efficient, and he made little progress before he was lifted like a stuffed pig on a spit.

Having been in similar predicaments during the war, horrible memories came flooding back. His breathing became erratic at being restrained once more. Blake was no sloth but knew his success in escaping would be the result of him using his wits rather than brute strength.

The motion of flying through air abruptly ceased as he landed on his side. The wood beneath him creaked as he rolled onto his back. The smell of straw overpowered his senses as it covered him from head to toe. Blake hated the suffocating feeling. Why had they chosen a cart to transport him? Disguise was the most probable answer, or was it also to travel a great distance?

He tried to remain calm, slowing his breathing and mentally reminding himself he was back in England and not in some foreign country under attack by Napoleon. He needed to focus his thoughts so he could figure out how to escape. He worked relentlessly at the knot binding his wrists, but the motion was rubbing his skin raw.

After what seemed like hours in the back of the cart, he was able to breathe once more as the straw was removed. Roughly, one man grabbed him by the ankles while the other crudely carried him by his arm, which felt like it was about to come out of its socket. As he dropped to the floor, his blindfold slipped enough for him to see he lay upon a stair landing. Pushed, he was sent rolling down, each riser bruising his body. His descent stopped as he curled up in what felt like a corner, two walls supporting his aching form. He attempted to sit upright, scraping his back up against the cold stone wall.

His fall had loosened his bindings, and his wrists were now free. Slowly, he ran his hands over his thigh, squeezing to assess any damage. He bent his knee, pulling his legs closer to his chest, and he flinched as pain coursed through his rib cage. Taking a shallow breath, he continued to evaluate his condition and found no broken bones in his lower limbs. His arms and shoulders were badly bruised, but again he found no indication of any breaks.

Wood creaked as heavy footfalls echoed down the steps. Pulled upright by the back of his shirt, Blake slumped and faked unconsciousness.

The brute grunted as he hauled Blake's dead weight across a dirt floor. Metal clanged, and a key rattled as it opened a manacle which was wrapped and snapped shut around Blake's ankle. He was hauled to his feet, and another manacle was placed around his right wrist. The manacle was secured above his head, forcing him to stand. The slam of the door and fading footsteps up the stairs were the last things he recalled before blackness claimed his consciousness.

Blake awoke, dry mouthed, lips cracked, and blood oozing from his ear. How was he going to escape? Shifting his weight, metal scrapped against his skin. With persistence, he could work on a knot and gain his freedom, but to try to break the manacle with limited reach and no tools was an incredibly daunting task to his fatigued mind.

Soft blonde curls. Grey-blue eyes.

Instead of the girlish image his mind had drug up numerous times over the past decade when he found himself in similar predicaments, a mature woman in a lavender gown now flittered through his thoughts. His instincts told him she needed him. He had to escape. When were they to move him? A few days, he could survive a few more days… for her.

LUCY PEERED out of the coach window and sighed with relief as she spotted the London tower. With Matthew and Mr. Smyth present, she had been relegated to the coach for the entire journey. Her attention refocused on the dozing Mr. Smyth, who sat slumped in the rear-facing seat. He had been invaluable on the trip back to London, making sure the changes of horses and drivers were done with efficiency and care.

At the last posting house, Lucy had overheard Mr. Smyth state, "Lord Harrington, it would be best if you continued the journey in the coach."

Matthew's immediate response was, "We have been traveling at a bruising pace. You need rest, and I need to be outdoors. You are to travel and protect Lucy in the coach."

Lucy suspected Mr. Smyth's request was due to finding himself being used as a pillow the last time he was subjected to riding in the coach with her. She had inadvertently snuggled into Mr. Smyth's shoulder after falling asleep. At the time he had promptly assured her he did not mind at all and he welcomed her warmth—despite the fact that his hands were grasped tightly together in his lap. She was loath to admit it, but she found Mr. Smyth's presence reassuring and familiar, rather like a brother, which she had openly shared with him. Had her comment offended him? She really did like the man and resolved to apologize as soon as he woke up.

As the coach approached the front steps of their town house, Mr. Smyth still had not moved. Evidently he felt the coach's change in pace, for when the door opened, he bounded to the street.

She hadn't even managed to alight from the coach before Mr. Smyth hurriedly stated, "I'm off to see about the package for Lady Lucy," and disappeared down the street.

Matthew tugged on her elbow as he reached to assist her down from the coach. "Come on, Lucy. We have much to do. But first we must remove all this travel dust. Meet me in the library when you are ready." He limped up the steps, and she followed close behind. They were greeted by an enthusiastic Edward, only his excitement subsided at Matthew's slow movements.

"Matthew, what happened? Were you attacked by highwaymen?"

Matthew groaned, "No highwaymen…"

Edward peered around his brother to see Lucy. With brow creased, he asked, "Did Lord Devonton remain at the house party?"

At the mention of Blake's absence, Lucy's eyes watered. It was Matthew who came up with a plausible excuse for Blake not accompanying them. "No, Devonton had to return to his own town house to check up on the repairs."

"Will he return tomorrow?"

"Edward, I'm exhausted. I'm glad to see you too, but can you please let us enter? I need a bath." His reprimand came out rather harsh.

"Sorry, Matthew. I'll be off." Dejected, Edward turned and left his siblings milling in the foyer.

"He was just concerned for Blake," Lucy admonished.

Brushing past her, Matthew muttered a curse and

something about an apology. Tired and weary, she didn't have the energy to deal with her twin. She needed to see to Edward first and reassure him he had done nothing wrong.

She found her younger brother in the schoolroom alone. He was standing by the small window that let in a surprising amount of light due to its position.

"Edward?" The look on the poor boy's face made Lucy's eyes water yet again. How could Matthew have forgotten their brother was only eight?

"I was just asking. I didn't mean to upset Matthew."

"You did nothing wrong, Edward. Do you understand? Matthew is just upset because… well, because he and Lord Devonton are out of sorts at the moment."

"It's probably Matthew's fault. He is always saying things he doesn't mean. Well, that's what he tells me all the time."

"He says it to me too. And you are likely right it was Matthew's fault."

Lucy hugged Edward. Behind the door, boots scuffed the floor. Who was listening? A servant or was it Matthew? Had their brother overheard all the conversation or just her last few words? Footfalls faded down the hall. Did Matthew believe he was at fault for Blake's capture? If he had been the one eavesdropping, her comments must have had him reeling.

CHAPTER TWENTY-ONE

*F*aint footsteps became louder. A man in boots entered the darkened room.

Blake pled, "Water," his voice hoarse and his lip cracked and bleeding. The skin around his wrists was cut and bloody and had also become red and inflamed. His captors had alternated the manacles between wrists to prevent further damage. Even though his boots had provided a layer of protection for his ankles, they were not faring any better than his wrists.

Blake was stubborn and refused to become a docile prisoner. If there were another breath left in his body, he would continue to fight with his captors every chance he had. He tried to open his eyes to see who had entered, but his lids felt like sandpaper. Having been kept upright, he had not been able to rest. Lack of sleep and his festering skin made it difficult to devise a sound plan for escape. He couldn't remember the last time he was fed or had water. During the past few hours, Blake felt as if he was becoming feverish and his thoughts were muddled.

He began to mumble in a mix of English and French.

"Should have told her… *je l'aime*… I love her… shouldn't have waited to tell her… *je desire l'épouser*… I want to marry her… the most beautiful gray-blue…"

Hearing his ramblings, his captors threw cold water into his face. Blake continued to mumble incoherent thoughts. "…need to take her to see… *nez le plus mignon*… cutest nose…"

Blake was released from the manacles, and his knees buckled. Instead of falling to the ground arms wrapped about his waist. Although not entirely conscious, Blake still continued to fight, but with limited strength, he was easily blindfolded, and his wrists and ankles bound with rope.

The fever caused him to drift in and out of consciousness.

"Bloody hell! I told you lot we needed him healthy for the voyage. We will not be paid if he is in this condition. Get a doctor or a healer, *now!*"

The light click-clack of a heeled boots approaching filtered through his foggy brain just before a cool, gentle hand pressed against his forehead. How much time had passed? Attempting to open his eyes, an image of a woman of middling years materialized. She must be the village healer. She lifted his arms and bent to sniff his wrists. Methodically she removed his boots and then shook her head as she muttered, "Tsk, tsk."

"What is…" His throat burned, but he tried again. "Who are you?"

"Me name is Miss Willow. You're in rough shape, milord. I'll have to fetch some supplies. But I will be back."

Did he know Miss Willow? How did she know he was a lord? He didn't recall ever meeting a Miss Willow, nor were her features familiar. The darkness claimed him once more.

∾

A BURNING SENSATION at his wrist had his muscles jumping. He pulled back to swing at the villain who was torturing him. With one eye open, Miss Willow glared at the offensive hand, and Blake relaxed and let his hand fall to his side. Relief washed over him, glad that he had not hit the woman tending to his wounds. Palm facing upward, he reached for her, hoping she would come closer for him to speak. But Miss Willow pulled back and shook her head.

She held a foul-smelling tonic to his lips. "Drink, or there will be no tomorrow for ya."

He opened his mouth and gulped the thick liquid.

"Out of me way. Do ya want me to keep 'im alive or not?" Miss Willow pushed past one of the hefty men and went to work on his ankles, applying salve and bandaging them up tight.

What would intimidate the stout Miss Willow? Not the two brutes standing over her.

"He will need broth, and his bandages tended to."

His guards stood and stared at her. Without hesitation, Miss Willow poked one of the men in the chest and said, "Me services are not free for ya."

The scene was comical and nearly brought a smile to Blake's lips, but he was so bruised and swollen he couldn't feel the muscles in his face.

Tapping her foot, the woman didn't budge until the guard nodded his consent. Then with a broad smile she said, "Aye, y'll pay me handsomely to make sure he lives, or that other gent is gonna have ya..." The woman slid her finger across her neck. She had a flair for dramatics.

Bending down, she whispered in Blake's ear, "And you, milord, had better not die on me."

Another salve was applied to his lips, then the cool

touch of her fingers was replaced with a mug filled with warm beef broth. The taste was familiar, and it brought hope he would survive this ordeal.

∼

NEEDING to take a break from pouring over the papers scattered across her desk, Lucy raised her arms above her head. Her gaze locked with red bloodshot eyes. How long had Matthew been staring at her? He had refused to sleep or leave her side for days out of stubborn pride.

The afternoon of their arrival back in Town, Mr. Smyth had returned with the package of missives. Matthew had confronted the man. "What orders did you receive? Did you inform them of Lord Devonton's abduction?"

Calmly, Mr. Smyth responded, "Lord Harrington, I updated Home Office that Lord Devonton had been captured. I was given orders to remain here until Lady Lucy has completed her assignment—with your permission, of course."

Matthew didn't hesitate. "We will have a guest room made up for you. If you need anything, please do not hesitate to inform the staff."

Mr. Smyth clarified the extent of his orders. "My lord, I'm to watch over Lady Lucy and provide her with any and all resources necessary."

"What! Do they not think I can protect my own sister?" Matthew yelled.

Since that awkward conversation, the two men had constantly been hovering over her. How was she to work under these conditions?

Matthew interrupted her reverie. "Lucy, perhaps you should seek your bed and begin in the morn."

Lucy focused on the sheets before her, but her vision was blurred. "I cannot sleep. Blake is missing, and the sooner I can gather information, the better. I'm praying there will be clues in the missives that will lead us to his captors. I will not rest, and I need to…"

Her words faltered, and tears welled in Lucy's eyes. Before she realized it, Matthew had his arms around her, and she began to sob, resting her forehead on his chest.

After a while, she stopped crying and lifted her head, "Matthew, thank you for comforting me. You know I'm not normally a watering pot."

Lucy hiccupped, and after taking a deep breath she continued, "Blake is… he is so different from all your other friends." She continued to babble, "When I'm at an engagement, I find myself seeking him out. When I'm near him, the rest of the world disappears, and all that is left is the warmth of his gazes. At the Redburn house party, we would venture to the lake and just talk. Blake was always inquiring into my interests, into my thoughts and ideas. He takes note and remembers what I like and dislike. He often commented that he liked the fact we could discuss any matter, and he always encouraged me to voice my true opinions, even if he disagreed."

Lucy paused to see if Matthew was following her jumbled ramblings. She began to blush as she shared, "When Blake kisses me, he makes my skin tingle, and I…"

Matthew raised a hand to stop her from telling him more. With his other hand he rubbed her back in a circular motion, as their mama had when they were little. "I know exactly what you are saying. Despite Blake's aloof exterior, he is a most exceptional man. I am thrilled you see him as I do. But right now, he is counting on us. You need rest. Without it, you will not be able to think clearly and decipher the missives posthaste."

Matthew bent to kiss the top of Lucy's head, and then he raised her chin to face him. "I want you to know I've always been proud of you. I don't doubt your brilliance. I know you will succeed in decoding the missives."

His confidence in her resulted in a smile that crept across her features and revitalized her energy. Who had dared to capture Blake? Was he safe or being tortured?

Matthew addressed Lucy again. "If you do not want to retire to your bedroom, then I'll call for a light meal. We can share it here while we organize the documents. I want to help, Lucy. He is my very best friend, and I failed to protect him."

"It would be best if you sought out your bed. Once I have the information we seek, I assume you will need your energy and wits for the journey ahead."

CHAPTER TWENTY-TWO

*W*aves crashing against wood and the rolling motion of the channel brought Blake out of slumber. "Damn, I'm on a boat."

Tingling sensations crept up his arms as he began to move. He tested his restraints, only to realize he was bound by ropes across his thighs and chest, allowing no movement. His wrists and ankles were bandaged and he no longer felt feverish. How much time had passed? Hours? Days?

A hand on the back of his head prevented Blake from looking up. He could only see the tips of the man's boots, but they were hessian's and well polished.

"Yes, we are at long last on our way. I would have preferred to leave days ago, but the winds were not favorable. If the current conditions prevail, we should arrive in Calais soon." The voice belonged to the gentleman in charge. The man's stomach made an awful sound as he declared, "God, I hate sailing. Six hours on this ship is enough for me to last a lifetime."

Who was the traitor that dared to kidnap a lord? For what purpose was he being sailed to the Continent? Blake had not wanted to set foot on foreign soil again unless it was for pleasure. The idea of venturing to Evora with Lucy made his mouth curl into a grin.

The large hand at the back of his head forced him to stare into his lap, and his captor moved to stand behind him. The man shoved his head down farther before releasing it. "Do not attempt to turn around."

Blake rasped, "Calais is a bustling port."

"We shall arrive under the cover of night. Not to worry, Devonton, I'll ensure your accommodations will be comfortable enough once we reach land. It's a shame you were not willing to cooperate earlier. My man wouldn't have had an excuse to use you as a punching bag. I had hoped you would visibly be in better condition. Now I will have to wait until your body heals before I am able to turn you over." Why had his captor shared his plans? Would the blackguard confide for what purpose he had been taken?

Blake asked, "Turn me over to whom? Why do you need me?" He was extremely frustrated at not being able to deduce the reason for his abduction.

With a snicker, his kidnapper apprized, "Do not concern yourself, Devonton. All will be revealed in due time."

He tried to turn as footsteps retreated. The gentleman ordered, "Lights out."

A huge fist struck him, and stars appeared. Then blackness descended upon him.

Lucy wiped the back of her hand across weary eyes.

Someone was snoring. Loudly. It was Matthew. She observed her brother's form facing the fire, his head resting on a throw pillow from the settee and his jacket over him like a blanket. It was as if he was accustomed to sleeping on a hard surface and not in his luxurious bed that easily held his tall frame. When had he had cause to sleep on the floor? What type of assignments had Archbroke sent him on? Lucy frowned, not quite believing her eyes. *Why had I not trusted my twin? How had he not confided in me?*

Lucy released a deep sigh, banishing the depressing thoughts. As another snore rattled the walls, she thanked her lucky stars her rooms were in the opposite wing of the town house to Matthew's or she would never get any sleep.

Blake had been taken nearly a fortnight ago. They were exhausted; they had hoped to have the assignment completed before the original deadline of the nineteenth, but even working day and night, they were not able to decipher the missives.

Home Office had sent agents to the Lone Dove to monitor activity, but Archbroke's hunch that the plans had been altered was confirmed when there was no sign of Blake. They both knew the answers to their questions were contained in the missives. She was growing extremely frustrated and had been undulating between tears and pure determined focus. Matthew had been quiet but supportive, making sure she had everything she needed and providing helpful responses even when she seemed to be talking to herself.

Lucy stretched and saw Mr. Smyth snoozing in a chair by the door. He had remained present, although he did not involve himself in her work. He remained vigilant in his duties. He ensured the town house was not being watched. He acted as Lucy's messenger; she often sent him to the Home Office to obtain documents. Other times, when

Matthew was unavailable, Mr. Smyth, acting as a Harrington footman, would escort Grace to visit Lucy, ensuring her safety to and from her parent's town house. Grace was the only distraction Lucy allowed herself.

Despite having the two men by her side day and night, she longed for Blake. She didn't fully comprehend how the man whom she had spent relatively little time with could make her feel safe and comfortable.

Lucy called for her maid and a bath and quietly made her way up to her room. "Carrington, I've never had this much trouble decoding. I can't seem to see any correlation between the five documents, and while I've tried to decode them as if they were all independent, it just doesn't feel right. Argghhhh..."

"My lady, I think you are putting too much pressure on yourself. Perhaps you need to walk in the garden, get some fresh air. You haven't been out in days. It might help you relax and clear your mind."

Lucy lay back in the tub and tried to submerge more of her body in the hot, almost burning water. For days, she had felt a cold numbing sensation invade her body as if she were experiencing the feelings of another, and in her mind, she was convinced it was Blake. She feared he was unwell and his mental strength was being tested to its limits, just as her limits were being pushed. Lucy wondered how she had come to be in tune with the man in such a short time.

"My lady, it seems to me you have strong feelings for Lord Devonton. Might you pretend another was taken and not Lord Devonton?"

"Carrington, I have been trying! He needs me, and I'm failing. My thoughts are a jumble, and I keep remembering our conversations. They play over and over in my mind, and sometimes I think I can actually hear his laugh."

Carrington was frowning as she tried to follow the

conversation. "His laugh, my lady? What would he have to laugh about?"

"My jokes! The ones I shared with him by the lake at the Redburn house party."

"Your jokes. He actually laughed?" Carrington was grinning at her mistress.

Lucy frowned. She was fully aware that it was rare for anyone to understand her wit and humor. She often received blank stares or silence in response when attempting to share a joke.

"Blake may be the only person to really understand me, and… I miss him. I can't stop thinking about his all-knowing smiles, his intense looks, holding his hand, his kisses, and his… I miss everything about him terribly."

Lucy closed her eyes as Carrington poured water to wash out the soap in her hair. Carrington had always been the one Lucy talked to when she was working on missives in the past.

Abruptly, Lucy sat up in the tub, sloshing water on the floorboards. "Carrington, I need you in the library with me. Matthew has been there, but I need _you_. You are the one who has helped me all these years. Why have I not thought of this before…"

Carrington's eyes were misting—had she hurt her maid's feelings by not realizing this before? "I would be delighted to join you in the library, my lady."

Glad that Carrington would not hold the oversight against her, Lucy said, "We must hurry, Carrington. We need to get to it right away." Lucy stood and tried to exit the tub.

"My lady, there is still soap in your hair. Please sit so I can finish."

She sat back into the tub. "Yes, yes. Just hurry, Carrington. Blake needs us…"

~

DRY AND DRESSED in a simple lemon-colored day gown, Lucy sat in front of the fire as Carrington brushed her hair. The maid listened to her mistress recount the various details of the five missives. "My lady, do you think you could tell me the rest while we take a walk in the garden?"

Carrington's suggestion was perfect. Lucy always worked best when she was in motion. "Certainly, Carrington. We will just have to inform Mr. Smyth."

Lucy continued to share with Carrington everything she had determined and eliminated as they descended the stairs. Mr. Smyth was milling about in the foyer.

"Mr. Smyth, I've decided to take advantage of the weather and venture out to the garden. Carrington will accompany me." Lucy had not even bothered to stop to hear his reply as they made their way out to the garden. Even though the man walked without sound, she was confident Mr. Smyth would only be but a few paces behind them.

Carrington asked, "My lady, do you find it odd that five missives were intercepted all at one time? Before they would come to us at different times; it seems like a lot of work for five to be written together."

Lucy pondered Carrington's question. "Do you think they intentionally sent multiple, just to cause confusion or to delay?"

"Well, we have never had two missives that go together before, my lady." Carrington was quiet for a moment. She continued walking but was looking down at the ground and then slowed to a stop before saying, "My lady, I find it all unusual. The Lone Dove is a tavern used by our people, not the frogs. Why was Lord Devonton over on the Continent for the duration of the war, I wonder? Why would anyone have need of Lord Devonton, my lady?"

Lucy had asked herself those exact same questions many times over the past few days. The war had been declared over as soon as word came of Napoleon's exile to Elba. Were Napoleon's supporters behind Blake's abduction? Had he been taken to somehow assist the frogs in determining the terrain that would aid Napoleon, or was there another reason for Blake's abduction?

As they stood in the garden, Lucy took in a deep breath. Carrington had been right. She needed the fresh air to clear her mind. A light drizzle fell, and it was rather refreshing.

Unexpectedly, Mr. Smyth's hand was at her elbow. "My lady, I think it is time we return to the house." Mr. Smyth's hand was warm but firm. He kept looking behind them as they turned back.

"What is it, Mr. Smyth?" Lucy asked as she twisted to see what Mr. Smyth was concerned about.

"I'm not certain. I just have a feeling we are being watched. I want to return to the house immediately."

"Mr. Smyth, I think you are overcautious. Why on earth would anyone be watching our stroll in the garden?"

The look Mr. Smyth just gave her could only be described as incredulous. Did he think she was unaware of the dangers of working for the Home Office or being identified as being one of their agents? She was well aware of the risks and on more than one occasion had been reminded she was but one woman, but she was not one to ever give up. Lucy had worked diligently to establish her skills, not only to assist the Home Office. Others had benefited from her sharp mind and intuition.

Mr. Smyth was still muttering curses when Lucy

addressed him again. "Mr. Smyth, that is some colorful language. You must tell me what on earth you are saying."

"None of what I spoke is for the ears of a lady."

Carrington giggled, and Mr. Smyth made a hasty retreat.

CHAPTER TWENTY-THREE

Seated with his hands bound behind his back, Blake raised his head and stated, "The winds must have changed." From the sway of the ship, it was moving forward but at a plodding pace.

His statement garnered him no reaction from the guard, who sat with his head in his hands, elbows on his knees, and feet braced apart.

The gentleman in charge had remained out of sight since Blake regained consciousness. Attempting to gain information, he stared at his guard before saying in German, *"Der Verräter hat Sie stattlich zu vergüten, damit Sie ihm helfen."* *The traitor must be paying you handsomely to assist him.*

Garnering no response, Blake searched the man's form. Dark brown hair, forearms of an olive tint, hints of being from southern Europe. Blake continued this time in Spanish. *"Si me ayuda, le pagaré el doble. ¿Qué dice?"* *If you assist me, I'll pay you double. What do you say?*

Unexpectedly the man grunted, *"Nein,"* and then raised his eyes to meet Blake's and grounded out, "No."

His response had been spoken with no discriminating

accent. The brute had obviously spent time on the Continent and was versed in languages other than English.

Donning a mask of indifference, Blake asked in French, *"Comment vous appelez-vous?"* *What is your name?* Since Blake wasn't expecting a response, he continued in English. "I shall call you Brutus."

What would it take to garner a reaction out of Brutus? Insults?

Blake asked, "Tell me then, Brutus, are you to be my nanny for the entire journey?"

A fast fist approaching his face was the answer. With his eyes shut, Blake held still waiting for the impact. When he felt nothing, he opened his eyes only to see Brutus still seated but glaring at him. Spit landed in Blake's eye. He was not sure which was worse, a punch to the face or the foul-smelling saliva on his cheek.

Not one to give up, Blake continued to ask questions and mixed in a few insults. Brutus's only reaction was to place his hands on each side of his head and stick his forefinger in his ear. Only when Blake had inferred his mama might be a French courtesan did Brutus react with his fist. Frustrated that he was unable to convince the guard to engage in a conversation, Blake resorted to issuing more insults, only to receive a swift punch to the face or gut.

Unable to obtain information and sore from the abuse, he refocused his efforts on loosening the restraints. He had nearly managed to loosen the rope, but then his vision was full of stars.

When he awoke, he found himself knocked to the floor, on his side, and bonds tightened once again.

Blake stared at the blurred form in front of him. "Brutus, how long was I out for this time?"

Brutus pushed a plate of bread and cheese with his toe toward Blake. Was he to eat like an animal? Blake was starving, but he refused to behave like a dog. He had survived starvation before. The plate shifted slightly with the roll of a wave and then shifted back. The plate's movements hypnotized him into closing his eyes.

Instantly an image appeared like a ghost haunting him: it was Lucy, her sweet voice saying, "Don't give up." Memories of their discussions by the lake renewed his motivation to endure the beatings.

One question that Lucy had posed plagued his mind. *Why did you choose to tour the Continent during a time of strife?* At the time Blake had given her a vague response for he didn't want to ever lie to her. He promised himself if he ever saw her again, he would tell her the truth. It hadn't been out of selfish reasons to explore; he wanted to be needed. His skill was highly valued at the Foreign Office, which in turn fed his self-esteem. His fellow Foreign Office agents had relied upon his cartography skills. Some had even thanked him personally and had claimed that the accuracy and the detail contained in his maps were the only reason they had managed to escape detection or capture. It was their stories that had led Blake to continue to serve on the Continent. Milling about Town and engaging in the idle activities his peers seemed to enjoy held no appeal.

Head slumped forward, he again questioned his captors' motives. What information did they believe he held that they could not gain otherwise?

Lucy's voice drifted through his thoughts once more, "If you are able to recall every detail of every city without the assistance of a map, you would be the ultimate guide." A guide? Did they need him to lead them?

His thoughts veered back to Lucy. He desired her. The woman was the only person who was able to banish the constant feeling of loneliness that beleaguered him. Did he alleviate the emptiness in her heart due to James's death? It riled him to know he was competing with a dead man for her affections. Lucy would be a true life partner in all ways that mattered. If he was successful and she fell in love with him, he would be the luckiest man alive.

Blake's stomach growled, but he kept his blackened and swollen eyes closed. Was Matthew on his way to the Continent? Had either the Home or Foreign Office obtained any evidence to help identify his captors or who they were working for? There would be gossip if the Foreign Office didn't cover up his disappearance.

Had Lucy resumed the social route? How many days had he been gone? Over a fortnight. More than enough for her to forget about him. Visions of men flirting and dancing with her had his blood pumping harder. He began working at his bindings again. He had to escape as soon as they docked. He needed to return to London and claim Lucy.

Brutus righted Blake and the chair and then noticed the bindings had come undone. Without warning, Blake was struck, a hard blow to the temple. As he began to lose consciousness, he questioned just how many more beatings he could endure. But just as the thought pervaded his mind, the image of Lucy and the memory of her sweet kisses provided enough strength to continue.

MR. SMYTH ESCORTED Lucy and Carrington back to the house. The trio came upon Matthew, who was waiting for them. "Lucy, I have a few matters I'd like to discuss with you."

Carrington and Mr. Smyth glanced at each other before Carrington suggested, "A light luncheon, perhaps?"

The pair left Lucy and headed in the direction of the kitchen.

Matthew's gaze held her frozen as they waited until they were completely alone.

"Where would you prefer to retire to? Library? Drawing room? Or my study?"

Weighing her options Lucy decided, "The library."

She hadn't even settled into a chair before Matthew said, "Lucy, I have been waiting for you to share with me how you became involved with the Home Office. I cannot continue to wait for you to come forth. So how long have you been decoding missives for the Home Office?"

In the same no-nonsense tone, Lucy provided, "Years. I started the year James began discussing his desire to join the army. It all started one day when I was visiting Theo. Lord Hadfield was in the parlor where I was shown to wait for Theo. He was deep in thought, voicing his frustrations at the confusing missive he held. He did not notice my presence at first, and when I suggested he only focus on the first letter of each word, not only was he surprised at my presence but also at my solution.

"In the beginning, I just assisted Lord Hadfield, but then I began to receive missives directly from the Home Office. I enjoyed the work and the knowledge that I was helping our men at war."

She understood it was a lot for Matthew to absorb all at once. If Matthew was an agent, he would know Lord Hadfield had been a senior agent at the Home Office. Granted, it was not well done of Lord Hadfield to have carelessly disclosed his activities with the Home Office, but the old man had no qualms about discussing or involving Lucy in his assignments.

In an attempt to distract her brother from the details, she asked, "How is it you are involved with the Home

Office?" Matthew was excellent at keeping secrets and avoiding questions. He had mastered the ability to supply the least amount of information necessary.

"I too have been working with the Home Office for years. Coincidentally, Lord Hadfield, who happened to be my mentor, failed to mention to me his recruitment of you."

"He was not at liberty to discuss or disclose the identity of agents."

Matthew grumbled, "True." A frown marred his face as he continued, "Over the years, I must admit there were times when I had wished I could seek your advice. You are by far the smartest person I know. There was more than one instance where I would have benefited from one of your brilliant stratagems."

His compliments caused Lucy to blush. "I rely tremendously on logic, but in this instance, I think my logic is working against me, and I have this feeling I'm missing the obvious. This is the first time where I have had such a difficult time resolving the code."

"I've often found that going with my instincts is the best course of action."

Since he had avoided her first attempt to understand his role, she tried again. "What exactly is it you do for the Home Office, Matthew?" Would he answer her this time? She clasped her hands in her lap to prevent fidgeting and then let her eyes follow Matthew as he paced back and forth.

"It's hard to explain. I was first approached by the Foreign Office before Papa passed. I was to go to the Continent with Devonton. But once Papa died, I had responsibilities here, and I couldn't leave and put you, Mama, and Edward at risk. The powers that be at the Home Office realized I would not be venturing to the

Continent. Since I had been thoroughly vetted by the Foreign Office, the Home Office approached me to see if I would be willing to work on assignments for them. However, while I officially assist the Home Office, I have maintained my connections with the Foreign Office, and as a result, I have a unique role where I assist both."

Lucy was turning his answer over in her mind. Matthew had mentioned going to the Continent with Blake, but that alone did not confirm her suspicion that Blake worked for the Foreign Office. If Blake had been commissioned by the Foreign Office to provide cartography services, who else would have this knowledge? Could this be the reason he was kidnapped?

"Matthew, if I understand correctly, you take direction from both offices and have access to resources both in England and abroad. I would imagine it can be rather complicated."

"It is. There have been times when both offices have had agents working toward the same objective; however, they don't always communicate or agree upon how missions should be carried out."

Lucy considered the complexities of the two offices. "What if the missives we intercepted were not all from the enemy? What if some of them were from the Foreign Office in a code that differs from the Home Office?"

"What are you saying?"

"I don't know, precisely. I'm just throwing out ideas… it's still a little fuzzy in my mind, but somehow it makes sense." She rose and walked over to sit at her desk and began poring over the missives but now from a different perspective.

Carrington, laden with a tray, walked in and placed it on a side table. "My lady, would you like coffee or tea with your meal?"

Matthew was nowhere to be seen. When had he left? How long had she been alone? Crumpling the paper in her hand, Lucy yelled, "Carrington, you were right!"

"I was? How is it I was right, my lady?"

Smoothing out the crumpled parchment, Lucy explained, "The five missives were not all written by the same party. After reexamining them, I can tell two of the five were of French origin, and the other three are primarily in English. My theory is the Foreign Office was trying to pass along information to some of its agents at the same time as Blake's abductors were sending instructions."

Her heart was pounding against her chest. She furiously began writing and uttered, "Carrington, I need more paper. Go see if Matthew has any in his office."

CHAPTER TWENTY-FOUR

*B*linking, Blake was surrounded by darkness. The sway of the ocean was absent. His back hit a solid surface as he straightened. Male voices filtered through his fog-filled brain. Had they docked? Where were they holding him? Calais? His tongue rubbed again the gritty cloth stuffed in his mouth. Lifting a hand to remove the offensive gag, pain ripped through his arm and shoulder. *They left my hands unbound—why?*

Lifting his head and opening one eye while the other remained swollen shut, he could make out the outline of a door. He was being held in a room. Raising a hand to his face, he gingerly tested the tenderness around his eye. Puffy, but the structure seemed to be intact. He didn't consider himself vain; however, he did wish to preserve the looks he had been gifted with regardless if some considered him plain.

The voices were increasing in volume. What was being said?

He needed to get closer to the door. Aches and pains riddled his body as he rolled to his side. With his feet left unbound, he managed to position himself on his hands and knees and began to crawl. Who was beyond the door? Brutus? The gentleman traitor? *French*. He shook his head to clear it and closed his eyes in the hopes of sharpening his hearing. With his mind still foggy, he struggled to piece the conversation together, but there were a few words he recognized for certain. *Unharmed. Healthy. Journey. Ride. Fortnight.*

A fortnight! The risk of remaining in one location for extended periods was high. They must be holding him in an area they were confident his presence would not raise suspicion. *Healthy?* Physically, he was barely able to hold his head up, drained of all energy. Mentally, the lack of information as to why he had been kidnapped was taking a toll on his mind. *Journey? Ride?* His body riddled with cuts and bruises, Blake was in no condition to mount a horse. He would need food and rest over the next fortnight to rebuild his strength. What concerned him most was whether he had the mental strength to endure another fourteen days of captivity.

LIGHT FOOTSTEPS APPROACHED, definitely not Brutus. Uncertain if it was morning, noon or night, Blake let his eyes close as he slid to the floor. A tray scraped along the floor, and a whoosh of air brought with it a clean, sweet scent to his nose. A woman. The metal click confirmed he was again imprisoned in the small cramped bedroom. Where was Brutus? Why had a maid delivered his tray? Did she fear him? The idea that a woman was afraid of him tore at his soul.

He shuffled to the tray and picked up the metallic cup. As water flowed down his gullet, his stomach quickly revolted against the liquid. Too much, too soon. His nostrils flared as he inhaled deep breaths. After a minute or two, he eyed the meager fare of cheese and bread.

Lucy's voice filtered through his thoughts, "Croissant? Bread, light and airy? With paper-thin layers? I've never experienced such a thing." She had been incredulous of his description of the French creation.

Once again, the image of Lucy brought him renewed hope. Blake began to consume the food in painfully small quantities until all was gone. Shoving the tray away, he rolled his stiff shoulders. *Time to begin strengthening.*

Stretching his legs out and tensing the muscles that were weak from lack of use, Blake groaned as a stabbing pain shot down his right leg. Rubbing the aching limb, he found he was unable to reach past his knee before wincing as his back muscles seized up. Forced to lean against the wall, he let his head fall back. Deliberately, he began to relax each muscle, starting with those in his forehead and working down his body until he reached the soles of his feet. He wasn't going to escape in his current condition; he would have to bide his time and rebuild his strength.

HAVING SPENT the past week diligently working through each missive, Lucy jumped up from her seat. "Carrington, we did it! We figured it out! Not only have we figured out their destination, we now know who was behind Blake's kidnapping. We will need to contact…"

Lucy stopped short as Matthew and Mr. Smyth entered the library. "Matthew, where have you been? I've completed the assignment." Waving sheets of paper about, she said, "The Foreign Office was aware of the threat also and had placed agents…"

"Lucy, please slow down."

There was no time to argue with her brother. She needed his help to get to the Continent and swiftly. She briskly walked over to Matthew and shoved two sheets of parchment into his hands. "You can read the decoded missives yourself."

Matthew read:

<u>Foreign Office Missives</u>
Tracked Addington down. Plans to travel to Sandgate Cove.
Intercepted correspondence indicating Devonton is to be taken within the fortnight.
Agent should be advised—urgent.
Unable to identify Addington's contact. Lord H seeks permission to continue investigation on Continent, delay return.

<u>French Missives</u>
Transport arranged on Njord to Calais.
Asset to be delivered in good condition, healthy and able to travel distances.
Addington to receive payment upon delivery of asset.

Matthew frowned down at the decoded message. "Lucy, are you certain? Addington has not returned from France, and he is one of the Foreign Office's best operatives."

Lucy was assisting Carrington in packing her writing instruments but stopped at her brother's question. "I'm positive I'm correct. Matthew, if you know him and how he operates, it will be easier for us to track him down and locate Blake. We must pack posthaste…"

Matthew and Lucy's gazes collided. "Pack?" He took a bracing step toward her. "Lucy you are not going anywhere. You are to remain here with Mama and Edward."

"Why?" She began to plead, "Matthew, I can assist…"

Matthew's features were drawn tight. "No."

One glance at Matthew's stubborn stance and features and Lucy knew there was no way she would convince him to alter his decision. Deciding it would be far more efficient if she were to arrange her own departure with her own staff and team, Lucy gave Carrington a side glance, and her maid scuttled out of the room.

She didn't need the assistance of her brother or the Home Office. Giving her brother a placid smile, she replied, "All right, brother, as you wish."

Mr. Smyth's smirk caught Lucy's attention. Sending a silent plea not to speak his mind, Lucy continued to address her brother, "I shall retire to my room. Have a safe trip."

With questioning eyes, Mr. Smyth quietly opened the door and let Lucy pass. She dare not return his gaze, for if she did, he would detect she was scheming.

After placing her foot on the first step to ascend to her rooms, Lucy paused. Who should she send word to first? Reports of her brilliant stratagems had spread over the years. She was often sought out by various individuals to investigate complex or plain bothersome issues. Some cases were more challenging than others, but ultimately the majority were related to funds or a lack thereof. Figuring out the identity of an embezzler, blackmailer, or kidnapper had kept her occupied when she wasn't working on an assignment for Archbroke.

Captain Bane. She trusted the captain would get her across the Channel safely and undetected. In order to obtain all the necessary resources and information to locate and retrieve Blake, she would have to call in nearly every favor she possessed.

She and Carrington rushed about Lucy's bedchamber, packing for her departure. Neither noticed Mr. Smyth's arrival. "Lady Lucy, I need to speak to you."

Surprised and relieved at Mr. Smyth's entrance, Lucy asked, "Mr. Smyth, what is it?"

"My lady, as you are aware, I have orders to protect you. I fear you have no intention of remaining in England as your brother has asked of you. I am here to tell you I have never failed in my duties; thus I shall be accompanying you."

"If you suspect I'm planning..."

Mr. Smyth interjected, "I know you are, Lady Lucy, and I intend to be a part of those plans."

"Mr. Smyth, I'd be happy to have you along with us for the journey." Lucy turned her attention back to Carrington. "I need you to cover for me as long as possible."

Carrington pleaded, "Lady Lucy, please, let me accompany you. I want to be of assistance."

"Carrington, the best way you can assist me is by not letting Matthew know that I have left. I need you to remain behind and ensure I'm not missed."

Resignation set in and Carrington sighed, "Yes, my lady. I'll do my best."

CHAPTER TWENTY-FIVE

hey had said a fortnight. If I've counted correctly, today is day fourteen. Stripped to the waist, Blake stood, anxious to escape. While his skin remained spotted in varying shades of blue, green and yellow, he was able to lithely move about without pain. His strength had not yet fully returned, but he continued to push himself each day. He had adopted a routine of meditation, breathing, and exercises that used his own body weight to strengthen his weakened muscles.

The light footsteps from the hall indicated it was time for him to cease. Sliding on his ragged shirt, he leaned against the back wall as the door opened. "What do you have for me today?"

He had slowly gained the maid's trust. She now came into the room to deliver his meals; however, she never spoke regardless of what language Blake decided to converse in.

"Let me guess... cheese, bread, and water." He received the same three meals each day. When the maid moved to the bed and laid out a set of clean clothing for him, he stood. Blake straightened to his full height, and the maid skittered to the door. The lock clicked into place before he had even managed to reach the bed.

Shaking out the lawn shirt, he noted its design was uniquely French. They were getting him ready to leave. But where and when was he to be transported? He quickly shed the filthy, ragged clothes he had worn for weeks. Pouring water into an empty basin, he washed, eradicating most of the offensive odor he had acquired. *Am I ready?* Blake donned his new ensemble before sitting at the table to consume his meal. *Why did someone go to such lengths to abduct me?*

The question continued to plague his thoughts. He had spent hours upon hours working through multiple scenarios, none of which warranted the risk of being hung for treason, for that was the punishment for kidnapping a lord.

His mind whirled with other pressing questions. Where was Harrington? He had remained in one location long enough to be found. Why had the Foreign Office not dispatched more agents to assist? Now that the war was over, was he of no use to them? Would no one come to his aid?

Doubts and negativity would not help him escape. Blake rested upon the bed, placing his hands behind his head. He attempted to quieten his mind. The result was he fell into a deep slumber.

An image of lavender silk brushing up against his leg flashed before him only to be replaced by a vision of twinkling eyes that were slightly more gray than blue. Lucy's voice echoed through his mind, "Oh, Blake, to have been able to roam about a castle of that magnitude..." Gone were the tantalizing pictures of Lucy. In their place were his drawings of the Chateau de Coucy in Picardy, one of the holdings the Foreign Office had sent him to infiltrate and illustrate. Why would he recall that particular holding now? He opened his eyes, hopeful Lucy would be within arm's reach. It was only a dream.

Every night Lucy had surfaced in his sleep. His dreams often began with them sitting under a tree, chatting, laughing, and ultimately kissing. Some nights his visions were so vivid he could have sworn she lay next to him. Memories of the afternoon he spent in her room at Redburn House fueled his dreams. He envisioned her writhing under him as he tasted her, starting from her lush lips, moving down her neck, trailing her collarbone, and licking his way to her breasts. His dreams progressed beyond reality as he imagined sinking into Lucy, slowly at first and then with an intensity that only sought to bring her pleasure and ultimately release.

He was in the middle of a rather lucid dream when Brutus entered the room. Hauling Blake up to his feet, he barked, "Get up." Brutus spoke with the same peculiar accent as his employer, English with a tinge of French.

Blake rolled his shoulders forward and waited. Brutus had a short fuse and was not above cuffing him or knocking him out.

Brutus shoved him toward the door. Blake stumbled but rapidly recovered and asked, "Are we going for a stroll?"

As expected, Brutus's fist came flying at his jaw, and while Blake had enough time to avoid the blow, he stood and took the hit. Even if he had fully regained his strength, Blake knew he would not be successful in taking Brutus on alone. He needed to keep his wits about him but couldn't prevent himself from sharing, "It has been a while. My face was beginning to miss the feel of your…"

In no mood for witty banter, Brutus roughly grabbed him by the arm and pushed Blake out of the room. Squinting, Blake's eyes adjusted to the light streaming in from a window at the end of the hall. Were his days and nights mixed up? Had his captor intentionally reversed the order of his meals?

A row of doors on each side of the hallway indicated he had been held captive in what appeared to be a coaching inn. He had assumed he was being detained in a cottage, which was more common in coastal towns.

No sound came from any of the rooms they passed, and it was quiet belowstairs. Careful not to remind Brutus that he was free of his bonds, Blake leaned against the wall and descended the stairs slowly. Impatient with their progress, Brutus hauled Blake over his shoulder the remaining ten steps. Blake's feet hit the wood floor, and he was thrust once again toward the exterior door.

He repeatedly blinked, not having been exposed to direct light in weeks. A coach and four were waiting.

Brutus opened the coach door, picked Blake up, and deposited him in the vehicle unceremoniously. The door slammed shut, and the sound of wood falling into place followed. The door was barred, and the windows were boarded on the inside.

In the dark, he ran a hand over every surface, noting the upholstery was well worn. The coach began to move, and Blake had to steady himself, bracing his feet wide and placing a hand on the sidewalls. This was the opportunity he had waited for, a chance to escape. He set his mind to devising a plan.

HOLDING her mount steady with a slight tightening of her thighs, Lucy pulled her wool coat tighter as the wind was biting this evening. "Mr. Smyth, is everyone in place?"

"Yes, my lady. We had word from the innkeeper that he is to be moved tonight."

"Excellent. Any news of my brother?"

"No, my lady. I've not been able to confirm his arrival. I'm fairly certain he has not yet set sail as the winds and tides have not been favorable since we left."

Spying Mr. Smyth's odd expression, Lucy asked, "Did you have something more to add?" She often caught him with a conflicted countenance. He never expounded and had remained focused and respectful.

"Lady Lucy, I was…"

"Go on. Spit it out, Mr. Smyth. We do not have all night."

"Your appearance is difficult to reconcile. The image of you while at the Redburn house party is rather different from what I see before me now."

Clad in breeches and a white lawn shirt, there was no hiding her curvaceous figure. "I am the same person, regardless of my attire."

"My lady, I meant no offense. Rather I admire that you remain true to yourself no matter your surroundings." Mr. Smyth, who was normally quite direct, was bumbling through his explanation. He cleared his throat and then stated, "You are an excellent strategist and an exceptional leader. I am honored to be a part of your contingent."

Not sure of how to respond to the compliment, Lucy asked, "Shall we go over the plan once more?" She had taken extra care in planning this evening's mission.

"That is not necessary."

While Mr. Smyth need not go over the plan, she wanted to run through all the moving parts one more time to calm her racing thoughts. Information from one of the men she posted at coaching inns across the area had finally reached her earlier in the day. Blake was to be transported in an old and dilapidated coach with only a coachman and two outriders escorting him. Lucy had sent her outriders ahead to scout for potential dangers. With her contingent reduced to John, Evan, and Mr. Smyth, would they be able to overpower Blake's guards?

The beat of hooves eating up ground and the rattling of carriage wheels had her peering through the trees. Ready to take action and attack, Lucy surveyed the area once more. The coach moved faster than what she originally anticipated a ramshackle vehicle could.

They were in the wrong position. She motioned for her team to move farther down past a bend. Mounted, the quartet moved swiftly and silently, avoiding detection. The skin on the back of Lucy's neck began to prickle. Something was not quite right. She should have posted a man at the inn and ensured they were to overtake the correct coach.

Her men were awaiting her command. Should she give the order to overtake the coach or follow it to its destination? Second-guessing her plans now would harm her team.

With seconds to spare, she placed her fingers to her lips producing a sound similar to that of a birdcall. At her signal, John and Evan surged forward on horses trained to take direction with the slightest movements from her footmen. With their hands and arms free, the men tackled the outriders, dislodging them and their target to the ground.

After Evan had managed to disarm his target, he jumped the large, hulking man who was about to pound John to the ground. Arms and legs were flying about. Lucy held her breath until her men finally succeeded in apprehending the guard.

Her heart continued to pound as Mr. Smyth jumped from his mount to land beside the startled coachman.

Knocking the pistol from the coachman's hand, Mr. Smyth wrangled the reins and brought the coach to a halt. With quick reflexes, he caught hold of the coachman before he was able to jump and escape.

Sliding from her horse, Lucy began to weave through the trees, making her way closer to the men. The drumming in her ears became louder—she was about to see Blake. How would he react to seeing her again? Running her hand up her neck, Lucy made sure her braid was safely tucked under her cap. Would he recognize her? Palms sweating, she pressed her hands and herself closer against the tree.

Mr. Smyth approached the coach, opened the door and yelled, "Bloody hell! He is not in the carriage."

CHAPTER TWENTY-SIX

*M*iles upon miles of being jostled about. Blake estimated they would have to stop and change horses soon. Feet up against the door, he pushed hard, but there was no give; it was solidly held in place.

How was he to escape? He had been stripped of his possessions long ago. He calculated his probabilities of freedom—slight at best.

The coach was slowing. A male voice instructed their horses to be replaced with fresh mounts. The voice was unfamiliar. The sounds of the horses being led away and then more being rigged up had him hoping they would let him out to relieve himself.

Wood scraped against the coach door, then a bundle of food was hastily tossed inside and the door slammed shut. In his haste, Blake's captor had not replaced the wood barrier.

A man shouted, "*Bouge, pas de temps à perdre!*" *Move, no time to waste*. And the coach was back in motion. Blake devoured the day-old bread, cheese, and apple. With the door unbarred, he repositioned himself, ready to break free.

A bend in the road caused the carriage to sway. Blake's pulse began to race. This was his opportunity to escape. With strength powered by fear, Blake pushed the carriage door open. Freedom. He drew in a deep breath, preparing himself for the impact to come. He threw himself to the ground and began to roll away from the wheels. Through the haze of dust, he caught sight of the door closing as the coach righted itself. He scampered to the edge of the path and rolled into a shallow ditch. The exhilaration of the escape numbed Blake from feeling the pain that riddled his body.

He needed to get to the tree line. A crushing ache in his ribs had him fighting back shouts of agony as he positioned himself on his hands and knees. He scanned his surroundings once more. Relief flowed through him as there was no sign of the coach or his guards returning. Taking a shallower breath, he stood and hobbled into the woods. Slumped against a tree, he sat and waited for his heart to return to its normal pace.

Blake's gaze searched for any identifying land marks, but there were none. It was still too light to see the stars, and without any knowledge of the name of the town or coaching inn they had last visited, he was unable to determine his exact location. Giddy at having rid himself of his captors, he needn't worry, for he had traveled most of the Continent and every part of France. It would only be a matter of time before he could identify his location. Deciding it best to head back in the direction of their previous stop, he pushed himself to stand and was surprised at the lack of discomfort.

Making his way through the woods at a light jog, Blake was surprised and relieved to find his body in far better condition than he'd expected. Only an occasional twinge of pain in his right leg had him halting for breath. Midstride, he spotted movement among the trees. Was it an animal? No. A small boy. Slowly, Blake closed the gap between them.

Blake was within arm's length of the boy. He was just about to grab the urchin by the collar when a man shouted, "Bloody hell! He is not in the carriage."

The man's voice was familiar. Blake narrowed his eyes. Mr. Jones! What the devil was a Home Office messenger doing here?

The boy gasped, but it wasn't a boy. Reacting out of instinct, Blake wrapped one arm around a small waist and placed his other hand over a lush mouth. His forearm brushed against rounded curves—definitely a woman. What was this woman doing in the middle of the woods?

As the woman continued to wiggle, his intuition told him he had held her before. The woman struggled with a fierceness he had to admire. He leaned in and took a deep breath. Lavender.

His fears confirmed, he asked, "You came to rescue me?"

Lucy immediately froze. He wanted to turn her in his arms and kiss her senseless, but he couldn't risk her alerting anyone to his presence.

"I'm happy to have you in my arms, but you have just ruined my escape. I had hoped they would not realize I was gone until they had reached their destination."

Lucy's muscles tensed, and anger radiated from her. Her jaw moved slightly. Would she bite him to gain her release? The words *biting* and *release* had Blake picturing Lucy naked and nipping at his shoulder or arm. Indecent thoughts flooded his mind until he shook them away. Pain radiated up his leg as Lucy stomped on his foot.

Eyes squeezed shut, Blake whispered, "My sweet, I'll release you, but you must remain quiet."

Lucy gave a slight nod of acquiescence. Blake loosened his hold, and she spun around so fast her braid came loose. Wide blue-gray eyes blazed at him and raked over his features. Contrary to the fire in her gaze, Lucy spoke in a tone so cold it froze his heart. "You. Are. Welcome."

Lucy turned and stomped over to Mr. Smyth, who was gathering the captured men and tying them to a tree nearby. Blake must have looked like a fool, grinning after the woman who had ignored his command entirely.

This was not the reunion with Lucy he had envisioned. He had dreamed of her waiting at the docks of Dover for his return, her rushing into his arms and crushing her lips to his with a kiss. He definitely had not anticipated her to be dressed in a great cloak, hair tucked under a cap, hiding in the woods with men at the ready to set upon a bunch of hardened criminals.

Careful to remain unseen, he stood behind a tree that would afford him a full view of Lucy's activities. She directed her men, waving her hands about, but with purpose. Her gestures and mannerisms reminded him of Wellington, direct and concise, with no hesitation. Who wouldn't admire those qualities in a person, regardless if they were male or female?

Tapping his fingers against the trunk of the tree, he waited for Lucy to return to him. Would she disclose his position or keep his presence a secret?

~

WALKING STRAIGHT UP to Mr. Smyth, Lucy put a hand on his arm and said, "Mr. Smyth, I need to rethink our strategy."

Blake had startled her at first; she hadn't recognized him with a dirty, scruffy beard. Why had she not felt fear as his arm wound around her? Why had her heart fluttered when he spoke in her ear? Should she inform Mr. Smyth that Blake was hiding in the woods behind her?

Deciding it best to keep Blake's presence a secret for the moment, Lucy glanced up to see Mr. Smyth was awaiting instructions. She imparted, "Please see if you can gain any information, destination, names, et cetera from our guests over there. Let's reconvene in a half hour. I will be across the way, in sight of John and Evan, but I need space to think."

Mr. Smyth nodded and proceeded forward to interrogate the men. Lucy was not at all surprised to find he was fluent in French and was more than capable of accomplishing all her requests. Since they had left London, Lucy had also noticed the way Mr. Smyth stood a little closer to her. He gave her looks that lasted an extra second longer than necessary, and she ignored his very kind but direct compliments. She wasn't entirely sure how to handle Mr. Smyth's attention, but it only confirmed what Lucy already knew: she was only interested in receiving such attention from one man, and that man was Blake Gower.

Without a word, John and Evan trailed their mistress. They fully understood Lucy's wishes with just a look from her. They kept their distance but would be able to reach her within seconds if necessary. As Lucy made her way back to the edge of the woods, she found a fallen log upon which she plopped down and stretched out her legs, revealing her breeches. She sensed Blake coming closer; he didn't reveal himself, but he was close enough to converse.

In a harsh whisper, Blake asked, "What on earth are you wearing?"

Turning her head slightly to look behind her, Lucy did

not respond but just raised both eyebrows, followed by a smirk and a wink. Blake was rather handsome with a beard.

Lowering her gaze and tilting her chin to her chest so he would not detect her devilish thoughts, she rolled her head side to side, stretching her neck muscles. Now was not the time to fantasize or consider what Blake's beard might feel like against her skin.

She was not the only one distracted. Blake teased, "I do love the sight of your legs."

Hiding her grin, Lucy tried to sound serious and admonished, "Blake, I'm trying to concentrate. Either please be of assistance or move away."

"Are you asking for my help? Did you want to hear my thoughts on what we should do next?"

"If I didn't, I wouldn't have asked."

"I think it best my whereabouts remain unknown to your guests by the tree over there. I would have your associate obtain their destination. It would be risky, but then I'd replace the driver with one of my own and send your associate to accompany him in the coach, pretending to be me…"

All thoughts of kisses were banished as Lucy interrupted, "No, no, no… that won't do. That would put Mr. Smyth in a perilous position, and the risk is not worth the reward. Are you willing to hear out my plan? Or are you like my brother and assume I'm unable to formulate one?"

"I'm definitely not your brother and hope you don't see me in such a manner. You sound rather like your brother, asking multiple questions at once without waiting for a reply."

"Humph."

"I'm all ears, my sweet. Please share your plan."

Lucy questioned why he was not more serious. Was he

flirting with her now of all times? Putting her thoughts aside, she replied, "I was not expecting you to be wandering the woods. After briefly considering our current situation, I would have to agree with you that your presence should remain unknown."

Her last words gave her pause as a pang of guilt hit her in the chest. It was irrational, but she didn't like the implication that she wanted him to remain hidden from all. Shifting on the log, Lucy continued, "Once Mr. Smyth provides the information we seek, you will have to move south and meet me along the path. I will arrange a mount for you. Can you navigate through the woods to Saint-Malo? I have a ship waiting to return us to England. Blake, I'd not take any well-traveled paths if possible. Are you familiar enough with this area to do that?"

BLAKE KEPT HIS FACE BLANK; he was still trying to reconcile the fierce young woman sitting calmly with her back to him with the woman who had laughed and kissed him under the tree on Redburn's property. He was stunned by her brilliance and couldn't help but grin. "It would be my honor to escort you to Saint-Malo."

"Blake, I'm not asking you to accompany me to a ball or the theatre. I'm serious. Are you familiar with this area or not? We have the others' safety to consider in addition to our own. The traitor, Lord Addington, is a known agent with the Foreign Office, and as Matthew informed me, he is one of their best. He is based here in France. His reach and resources must be extensive."

He turned to stone inside. "Addington, the bastard. I met him briefly at a masquerade party, but he knows I never forget a face. No wonder he so cleverly avoided me.

While I have perfect memory by sight, I did not recognize his voice, but now that you mention his name, it all fits perfectly. Tell me what you want or need, and I will always honor your requests to the best of my abilities and protect you at all times."

It sounded to his ears he was pledging his life and fidelity. Good God, he was in love with the woman.

A declaration of his love tickled the tip of his tongue. Should he tell Lucy she was the reason he never gave up? He took in their surroundings; now was not the time nor the place to have that discussion.

The woman he loved was here on the Continent in search of him. But how was it she came to be here? Had someone sent her? Had she come on her own volition, and if so, why? He wanted—no, needed—the answers before he shared his intentions with her.

Mr. Jones approached, and she stood to meet him but did not venture too far. Smart girl. Blake pressed tighter against the tree, trying to hide his giant form.

"Lady Lucy, unfortunately, the bodyguard was not communicative. Despite my efforts, he refused to disclose for whom they were working. He did share he was the one responsible for hiring the driver. The driver disclosed their destination was Chateau d'Olhain. They were both unaware Lord Devonton was no longer in the coach. I wonder how he managed to escape; he looks more bookish than a man of action."

Blake flinched. Had Mr. Jones's specifically made a comment about his appearance to try to draw him out? Mr. Jones was standing rather close to Lucy and had reached out to escort her to the coach. While it was not a full moon, Blake had excellent night vision and no problem seeing the admiration in the man's eyes as he gazed at her.

Mr. Jones suggested, "I believe it would be wise to

move the coach farther into the woods and disable it by removing and splintering one of the wheels, but we should release the horses so they can make their way back to the stables. We can leave our new acquaintances by the tree; it is far enough from the road, unless you would prefer I take care of them now."

Lucy pulled her cap lower and adjusted her cloak higher around her neck. She moved with him toward the coach and out of range for Blake to hear the rest of their conversation.

Irritated that he could no longer hear them he pushed away from the tree. Had Lucy intentionally walked away so he would be out of earshot? What did she say to Jones? Was she flirting with him? Anger and an urgent need to possess her flowed through Blake's body. He nearly leaped out of the woods to lay claim to her. Not knowing how Lucy felt about him had him in knots, and every insecurity he had about himself rose to the forefront of his mind.

Blake had been alone for so long, but now he couldn't imagine his life without Lucy in it. She was essential to his being. She gave him hope and a future to look forward to. It was excruciating for him not to be able to declare his feelings and whisk her away and hide her at his country estate.

Blake shook his head, trying to clear it and calm his breathing, but his body was tight and full of pent-up energy needing to be released. Knowing his captor's destination, he surveyed his surroundings. He cleared an area on the ground and with a stick began drawing a map of possible routes from Calais where they docked to Chateau d'Olhain.

After completing the map, he slipped farther back into the woods and paced. Deciding upon the most likely route his captors had taken, Blake began to draw another map, this time routes from his estimated location to Saint-Malo. There were multiple routes they could take, but his dilemma was choosing. Should he lead them on a route that would allow him more time with Lucy, or the most direct route that would get them back to England, where he could propose, marry her, and then whisk her away to the countryside?

The prospect of being back in London and subjected to all the *ton's* amusements, balls, clubs, and evenings at the theatre made Blake's skin crawl. He had much to do at his estate, but first he must determine if Lucy returned his affections.

From the corner of his eye, Blake saw she had released the horses and discreetly led one of them in his direction. He waited for the horse to approach and then, using his scuffed boots, erased the maps he had drawn. With his decision made, he mounted and headed south to meet Lucy as she had instructed.

CHAPTER TWENTY-SEVEN

*L*ucy took a few more steps before she said, "Thank you, Mr. Smyth. I know my plan would not have been executed so successfully without your assistance. I really appreciate you being by my side. I feel safe with you."

Was Mr. Smyth blushing? Ignoring her observation, she continued, "I agree with your plan for the horses and the carriage, but disable two wheels, not just the one. As for the men, we need more time before they are able to shout for help."

The well-worn path indicated it was a route other travelers were likely to use.

Lucy glanced over at the men tied up. "Leave the larger one where he is. I do not want to move him and provide an opportunity for him to escape. Please ensure his restraints are tight and then move the others so they are bound to trees that are a good distance from each other where they cannot converse easily. If they are smart enough to save their voices when another party passes close by, they should be able to call for help. We are to head toward Saint-Malo."

Lucy made her way over to Evan, who gave her a boost. Mounted on her mare, she scanned the road and the woods. Her contingent at the ready, they headed south along the path.

It wasn't long before she spotted Blake waiting just to the side of the road a furlong away. She smiled broadly as she approached. She was a bundle of nerves on the inside. Even now, covered in dust, Blake made her pulse race. She still had not figured out how he had managed to escape but was extremely glad she had found him.

She turned in her saddle to address Mr. Smyth as they made their way closer to Blake. "Lord Devonton will be leading the way to Saint-Malo."

At the mention of Blake's name, Mr. Smyth frowned and then narrowed his gaze down the road. When they were alongside Blake, Mr. Smyth said, "Lord Devonton, I'm relieved to see you alive. I thought your captors had somehow misplaced you."

"Mr. Smyth? Or is it Mr. Jones?"

Before Mr. Smyth could reply, Lucy curtly stated, "For this mission, he is Mr. Smyth."

She was rather unsettled by a feeling of possessiveness. For all intents and purposes, Mr. Smyth was under her direction, yet he ultimately worked for the Home Office. As to how many identities he held, she didn't care to find out; all she knew was that while he was here, he was her Mr. Smyth. What a complicated life he must live. Would his real name shock her? How had he become involved with the Home Office? That was a puzzle for another time. At present, they needed to get to Saint-Malo expeditiously so they could return safely to London.

Lucy dismounted, and the gentlemen followed suit. "I

do not believe we have much time before it is noted you are missing, my lord, so if you will lead us to the most efficient route, we should be on our way."

"We are still under the cover of darkness. We will have to ride at a slower pace until dawn. I estimate it will take us three days before we reach Saint-Malo."

"Three days! If we take the road, it should only be two at the most. I would have expected through the woods to be more efficient. Are you sure you are knowledgeable enough to lead us?"

No man liked to be questioned. She probably shouldn't have voiced her concerns in front of the team. Would he be angry and yell at her in return?

Blake did not respond with harsh words. Instead, he stood a little taller and faced her directly. "Do you trust me? If not, then I will thank you for the mount and suggest we part here."

Part ways? Now? She had just found him.

Her mouth was agape, and no words were forthcoming. She had called upon nearly every favor she had, she had sailed across the Channel, her absence from Town would be noted, putting her virtue and reputation at risk, all because... because she loved him. She had finally come to the conclusion he was the only man she could envision having a future with.

She had muddled through the guilt of loving someone other than James. If she had been honest with herself earlier, she would have realized what she felt for James was deep admiration for a wonderful boy who had grown into an honorable man who would have married her out of duty and obligation, not love.

She wanted to stomp her feet and yell at the top of her lungs. Weeks of hard work, sleepless nights, and hours spent soul-searching, wasted. Blake didn't love her. He was willing to leave her here in the middle of France.

As the silence lingered between them, Blake gazed into her eyes. The glassiness was a telltale sign of the tears she refused to shed. It was like he had stripped her bare, revealing a vulnerability she rarely showed anyone. But there was something more. Love! He had seen that exact look in his mama's eyes.

His heart was torn at the sight before him. He wanted his fiery hellion back. He wanted to see her eyes filled with wonder and life, not unshed tears. He closed the gap between them and then gathered her in his arms.

His lips grazed her ear as he spoke. "Lucy, trust me."

She shivered in his arms. She still appeared dazed and filled with confusion and hurt, but she managed to nod.

She mounted her horse with his assistance. Both Blake and Mr. Smyth vaulted into their saddles. Blake took the lead, with Mr. Smyth by his side. Lucy followed behind, flanked by her footmen.

"Smyth, I assume you are here on Home Office orders?"

The man's response was to glare at him. Blake was in no rush, and so he waited patiently for Mr. Smyth to answer. "My orders were to protect and assist Lady Lucy. I do not believe Archbroke or her brother is aware of her present location. She is an extremely determined and resourceful woman."

Interesting. How had Mr. Smyth and Lucy become acquainted? Did the Home Office somehow employ her as they did her brother? How did they come to arrive on the Continent? Where was Harrington?

Blake's features must have reflected his thoughts, as Mr. Smyth continued, "I believe Lord Harrington was coordinating with the Home Office. He had planned to travel to the Continent and provide you with assistance. However, to date we have not seen nor heard from him. But I suspect he was delayed in Dover."

In an attempt to gain information from the man, Blake strategized that praising Lucy might loosen the man's tongue. She and her guard had fallen a ways behind, enough to provide privacy for the conversation he wanted to have with Mr. Smyth.

"Lucy is quite remarkable. I'm assuming it was not her beauty that has earned your devotion and loyalty, but her courage and bluestocking ways."

"I would have to be dead or blind not to have noticed Lady Lucy's beauty, but I can assure you she has already given her heart to another."

The comment captured Blake's full attention.

Mr. Smyth continued to confess, "I've never worked with a better strategist. I will admit that at first I was astonished by Lady Lucy's expansive network of individuals, all of whom were willing to accommodate her requests. I'm extremely grateful for the opportunity to have become acquainted with her and hope she knows she can always depend on me and trust me whenever needed."

Blake did not miss the not-so-subtle reference to trust.

Turning slightly in his saddle to catch and hold Blake's gaze, Mr. Smyth added a parting comment. "You said remarkable? I'd say extraordinary. You refer to her ways as bluestocking; I'd call them pure brilliance. Any fool would know the difference."

After his declaration, Mr. Smyth fell back to join Lucy, leaving Blake to ruminate on his comments. He rode alone, which he was content with. For the moment.

Streaks of daylight were just emerging when Blake led them to a creek where they could give their mounts water and a well-deserved rest. While the footmen took care of the horses and Mr. Smyth went hunting, Blake took the opportunity to approach Lucy. He had felt the daggers she had been throwing at his back with her piercing eyes the entire journey. "Lucy, I wanted to apologize…"

Lucy held up a hand, "Blake, I need your assistance in guiding us to Saint-Malo, but once we arrive, please do not feel obligated to continue on with us. You may do as you please."

Blake's belly ached as if she had just punched him in the gut. He shook his head; he could not believe she wanted to be rid of him. Had it been a gleam of love in her eyes he had seen or had he imagined it? He turned on his heel and walked away.

CHAPTER TWENTY-EIGHT

*B*lake and Mr. Smyth returned to their makeshift campsite. Blake emptied his pockets of herbs and edible plants. Mr. Smyth threaded the hares on a spit and left them to roast over the fire. John and Evan brought wood to add to the fire and a blanket for Lucy to sit on.

She didn't know what had possessed her to push Blake away with her words. Was it to retaliate? To cause him as much pain as his words had caused her? She wasn't usually so petty.

After their meal and with all evidence of their existence hidden, Blake announced, "We shall push forward at a much slower pace, but we will not be making any further stops until nightfall." He had addressed the group in its entirety, but Lucy felt there was a silent message among his words just for her. What fanciful ideas he caused her to have.

But as she ran his words over and over in her mind, his message became clear. With no coaching inns to change horse teams, they would need to travel at a much slower pace, thus increasing their time. She should not have questioned Blake about his capabilities. He was the most familiar with their surroundings. It was not well done of her to do so in front of the others.

She pushed her mount forward to speak to him. "Blake, I believe we should find shelter for the evening."

Without looking at her directly, he ground out, "As you wish, Lady Lucy."

Blake's use of formality was like a dagger to her heart.

THE WOMAN obviously didn't think he had any sense or knowledge of how to lead a team or ensure their safety. Why had he been crushed by her declaration that she wished to part ways in Saint-Malo? He had sworn long ago never to let anyone get close again. Instinctively, Blake had gone on the defensive, using the honorific to push her away, but that was not what his heart was telling him to do. Why was he unable to focus?

Turning his attention back to the matter at hand, Blake considered: southwest or directly west? He needed to make a decision. Should he consult Lucy? No, the woman caused havoc with his thoughts. He wanted her. He needed her. His gaze involuntarily followed her movements; a few tendrils of hair had escaped caressing her cheek and the back of her exposed neck. The scent of lavender teased his nose, and his gaze was drawn to her legs encased in breeches. Blake's body responded, making him move uncomfortably in his saddle.

The southwest route would afford more cover and privacy. Blake had been a fool. He needed to get Lucy alone, away from the others. Would he be able to convince her that, despite his words, he would never leave her?

He knew exactly what he wished for once they arrived

in Saint-Malo. He had two days to accomplish his personal mission. He had never failed one yet, and this was the most critical to date.

Surveying the ground just beyond the path they were traveling, Blake spied leaves and branches in an unnatural pattern. He slowed his mount and raised his hand to signal the party to stop. The area reminded him of the numerous bivouacs he had seen and stayed in during the war. He turned in his saddle to confirm their location—they were about halfway to Saint-Malo.

Blake dismounted and ordered, "Stay mounted."

Would she follow his command? When she remained seated, he walked farther away from the makeshift trail. Spotting ash and coal hastily dispersed, he stopped to assess the ground. Tracks, two males with mounts. Bending to pick up a piece of coal, he sniffed, a lingering burnt smell. The fire had not been banked long.

Blake approached Mr. Smyth. "Check the immediate surrounding area and set up camp. Have John and Evan gather wood for the fire."

He didn't wait for a response and went to help Lucy dismount. He raised his hands up, placed them around her waist, and pulled her off her mount. Her legs would feel like jelly after long hours in the saddle. He gently let her slide down his body until her feet hit the ground; instead of releasing her, he held her tight and bent his head as if to talk to her. Brushing his lips over hers, he held a breath waiting for her response. Elation flowed through him as she lifted onto her tiptoes and returned his kiss.

She broke the kiss but held on to the front of his coat, "Blake, I'm sorry. I shouldn't have questioned your abilities and definitely not in front of the others. I shouldn't have implied I wanted to part ways either. Will you forgive me?"

Blake cupped her cheek and solemnly replied, "Will *you* forgive *me*?"

Lucy nodded and put her hands around his neck as he bent down to kiss her. This was no apology kiss; this was an "I'll never let you go" kiss. He wanted to make her moan, and when she did, she also flattened herself to him. Blake couldn't stop his hand from skimming down her arm to settle in the small of her back and press her into him even more. His other hand rested at the base of her skull, tilting her head, allowing him to deepen the kiss.

Needing a breath, Blake pulled back. "I'm going to check on the men. Do you know how to tend to the horses?"

Instead of replying, the woman haughtily turned and led the mounts, swaying her hips just enough to keep his attention on her. The she-devil gave him a cheeky smile over her shoulder and winked. There was much to be discussed, but he was confident that in the end all would be well between them.

Had the men seen their interlude? Blake scanned the area, and his eyes landed on Mr. Smyth as the agent left the woods and headed in Lucy's direction. Changing directions, Blake reached her first.

"Lady Lucy, I've found a note that was hidden in a tree knot. I believe it is in code." Mr. Smyth handed her the parchment.

Lucy seemed to focus on the note as Blake tried to read its contents over her shoulder. She turned and gave him a look, telling him to give her space. She softly mumbled, "It does not appear to belong to the frogs. It's not an obvious or simple code."

Blake crowded her again. "May I see it?"

Why would she be hesitant to hand over the note? What did she know of French missives or codes? He pried the parchment from her hand. Looking over the numerals and symbols, he broke into a grin, and then he made a sound like a laugh and a growl combined.

"It's from your brother." Blake couldn't help but laugh at Harrington's note. "He knows you beat him to the Continent. He says he is sure that by now I've either escaped or have been rescued by you, and he has decided to remain on the Continent and track down Addington. In the last paragraph, he states he will see us back in London, and we had better be wed by the time he returns."

Lucy's eyes widened, and her jaw slackened.

Blake put a finger under her chin to close her pretty mouth. "He used a code we had devised back at Eton."

Apparently, she was not soothed. "Wed? Why would he say such a thing?"

"Lucy, you will be with me without a proper chaperone for many nights, both while we are here on the Continent and when we return to England. You must have known we would have to wed when you came for me."

"I was saving you."

"And you did save me, in more ways than you realize." Blake gently turned her by the shoulders to move toward the fire, where a pallet had been laid out. "Let's get some rest."

BLAKE GUIDED Lucy over to the pallet. She was so compliant; he guessed her mind was preoccupied with the content of Harrington's note, just as he was. If her brother knew where to leave them a note, Blake was not doing an outstanding job of obscuring their route. Then again, he and Harrington were often of like mind, and perhaps it wasn't such a surprise he would have determined Blake's destination. Given his assumptions about Blake's relationship with his sister, it was a rather obvious choice.

He let Lucy get comfortable while he went and spoke to the men.

"Is Lady Lucy well?" Mr. Smyth asked first.

"She will be."

John turned and addressed Evan. "She didn't look well. Shocked and dazed. Mayhap we should move her pallet closer to ours."

"I will see to her welbeing." He received three dubious looks. "We are approximately halfway to our destination. With others having recently traveled this path, we will take a more obscure route to Saint-Malo."

The three men nodded their assent, and Blake made his way back to Lucy. She was lying on her side, so he slid next to her, lying on his back, his shoulder a mere inch from her. They weren't touching, but he turned to look at her. Cream-colored flesh above her collar teased his eyes, her neck begging to be marked with his teeth. His breath moved the loose tendrils of hair. As if seeking out warmth, she moved so her back was up against his side.

He lay with his hands cupped behind his head. They itched to touch Lucy, but that would not be a wise decision given their surroundings. Mr. Smyth, John, and Evan surrounded them, with the plan that they each take turns remaining awake and on guard.

As Blake gazed up into the sky, counting the stars, he sought ways to distract his wayward thoughts. He would try anything to keep his mind off Lucy and her lush body lying next to him.

Lucy kept wiggling under the blanket, and every time her bottom came into contact with his hip, images of her kissing and straddling him popped into his mind's eye. As he gazed up, he searched for constellations, but instead, his mind wandered again; this time to images of Lucy slowly undoing his shirt buttons and placing light kisses down his chest and following the trail of hair that led below his smalls.

Blake felt his body was reacting, especially since she had turned over to face him, with one of her hands tucked under her cheek, the other rested on his abdomen. She appeared to be sleeping, but she remained restless. Blake was struggling to act honorably as Lucy continued to move against his side. He started to remember the taste of her on his lips and tongue, and instantly the need to touch her became too much. If he moved her, would she continue to slumber? What would her response be?

The campfire crackled, reminding him they were out in the open and her men lay just a few yards away. His body would not relent. He released his hands from behind his head and rolled onto his side. Gently he repositioned Lucy so her back was to his chest, and he snaked an arm under her head and neck to provide a pillow. She sighed and snuggled into his embrace. Blake wrapped his arm around her waist and gently pulled her closer, bringing her bottom up snug against his groin.

Lucy stiffened. Was she shocked by his body's response pressing into her? Praying she was awake, he expelled a sigh of relief as she wiggled farther back and languidly exhaled. The back of her thighs lined up with the front of his, and he whispered into her ear, "I want to touch you and feel your response to me. Would you like that?"

Without hesitation, she nodded her head ever so slightly. Ah, thank goodness the woman was awake. Clever girl. Was she conscious of the proximity of the other men? Did the thought of them being so close by send a thrill of excitement through her? She wiggled her bottom once more, and he had to swallow the groan he wanted to emit.

Every night he had spent apart from her he had thought of the evening they were alone in her room at Redburn house, and he ached to touch her intimately again. Even though they lay on the ground among the woods, to hold her again was like heaven.

Blake ran his tongue along her ear and whispered, "Evan is on watch and sound travels easily out in the open. If you need to, you can bite on my hand or arm. I won't mind. Promise you will be quiet."

As soon as Lucy nodded, Blake leaned back a little and unbuttoned her greatcoat. She slid her arms out, and he billowed it wide over the both of them, using it as a makeshift blanket, mostly covering her. Once he had the coat arranged to his liking, he pulled her lawn shirt up out of the band of her breeches and carefully placed his hand on her gently rounded stomach. Rubbing her cold skin, he tried to warm her with slow, lingering strokes from her navel up to just below her breasts. Her response was to stretch and align herself fully against his body.

Lucy begged in a whisper, "Blake, please!"

"You promised to be quiet," Blake growled, and flicked her pebbled nipple.

Her whole body tensed, but as he began to caress her breasts, she softened against him. Careful not to touch her nipples, he ran his hand over her lush breasts in a circular fashion and then in a figure-eight pattern. Lucy began to wiggle against him, and he put his hand on her hip to hold her still. He had fantasized this moment every night. He wanted to take his time exploring her body, to learn every inch of her and to discover what excited her.

His hands remained unmoving until she took a deep breath through her nose and ceased shifting. As she released the breath, he began to caress the undersides of her breasts again, but her response was to press her bottom into him once more. Unexpectedly, he pinched her nipple, and she let out a squeak.

"Remain quiet. Next time I will stop entirely." He wasn't sure he'd be able to carry out the threat if she did make a sound, but when she meekly turned her face into his arm, blood pooled in his groin.

He continued to squeeze, rub, and pinch her breasts. When she began to move, he placed his wide hand in the middle of her chest. With his thumb, he rubbed one nipple, and he used his little finger to attend to the other. His other hand dug into her hip to prevent her movement against his hard member. She was his. He didn't play a musical instrument, but her movements proved he knew explicitly what to do to produce a melody of sounds from her, all muffled by his arm.

She shifted, and he released his grip from her hips. Immediately she began to rock her bottom against him. She moved her head forward, and he started planting kisses down her neck and shoulders.

He was caught off guard when she grabbed his wrist and flattened his hand against her body. Placing hers on top of his, she guided their hands to her core. Blake was thrilled by her boldness and rewarded her by gently running a finger along her slit and then finding the sensitive bud that would drive her to the edge.

She was so wet, and the knowledge it was the result of his touch made his heart ache. A sudden feeling of possessiveness overcame him. He vowed no one other than him would ever have the pleasure of feeling her heat or have her this way. He would do anything for this woman in his arms, but first he needed to finish what he started and give her the most pleasure she had ever experienced.

~

Lucy woke to the sound of men laughing. From under the blanket, she peeked her head out just enough to see Blake talking with John, Evan, and Mr. Smyth. Blake gave the impression he was totally at ease. Was he regaling a tale about his adventures? The men appeared just as enthralled as Edward had been only a few weeks ago. She snuggled back into the blankets and feigned sleep as she listened to Blake's tale.

"I had slipped onto a cart into Paris and was enjoying the juiciest of peaches." Blake wiggled his brows at the same time, the men laughed. "No, seriously, they were the best peaches I've ever had. When we reached Les Halles, the farmer was not at all happy with me."

Mr. Smyth chimed in, "I've always considered Paris to have the best variety of peaches." He winked at Blake and then added, "It's said that even the queen and the Russian tsars have traveled to Paris to partake in these wonderful peaches."

Blake must have seen her move, for he began to stand. She shook her head at him. She didn't want to disturb the camaraderie, and she needed to tend to some rather pressing personal needs. She rolled from the pallet and slipped into the woods.

She was just emerging from the woods as Blake approached her. A deep blush rose to her cheeks as she met his gaze. The man did not listen to direction very well. "Good morning, my sweet."

"Do you recall the first time you referred to me as your sweet?"

"Yes, it was at the Duke of Fairmont's ball. And in fact, I recall you not objecting to me calling you my sweet."

"What? Of course I objected!"

"No, you only objected the *third* time I referred to you as my sweet. Do you have objections now?"

Lucy frowned inwardly. Surely she had objected the first time; she had just met him at the Duke of Fairmont's ball. "No, I have no objections now. However, it would be best if you addressed me in such a manner only in private until we are wed."

The wide grin Blake gave her told her how he honestly felt about their upcoming nuptials. He did not have the look of a man marrying her out of honor or duty. What they had shared last night under the stars had her eager to bed the man, wed or not. Playfully, she patted his chest right over his nipple and was pleasantly surprised as it budded just as hers had the night before.

"Be careful, my sweet. You wouldn't want to start something in broad daylight."

Feeling cheeky she asked, "Would you?"

Blake chuckled, and then he bent down to press a quick kiss to her forehead. There was still so much to learn about this enigmatic man who stood before her, but she would have a lifetime to do so. Right now, they needed to get back to England.

Lucy turned to find the men had already packed up and removed evidence of their campsite. Mounted, with their backs to Lucy and Blake, they waited patiently. "How long do you think they have been waiting?"

Blake lifted her by the waist and placed her on her mount. "Long enough."

Throughout the day Lucy stole glances at Blake. At times she would close her eyes and recall how his hands had caressed her in the most intimate ways. If he were to remove his shirt, there would be evidence of her efforts to remain quiet on his arm. Blake caught her looking at him a few times, and every time he leaned in to give her a quick, chaste kiss.

After a long day of riding, she was tired and covered in

dust. She ran a hand over her hair and felt bits of leaves and twigs poke her palm. What a disheveled mess she must look. But when she caught a glimpse of the devilish glitter in Blake's eye, it made her feel wanted. Blake, however, did not have the appearance of having been on horseback for days, and while there was evidence of him running his hand through his hair, it just resulted in a rakish effect.

Having been caught staring once more, Lucy asked, "Will we reach port by nightfall?"

Would he answer or respond with a kiss? Blake leaned in closer, and when his lips were a mere inch away from hers, he replied, "Not much farther. Mayhap an hour, two at most."

Releasing the breath she held, her gaze bore into his as he regained his seat. The man had the audacity to wink at her. Turning her nose in the air, she purposefully exposed the section of her neck that excited them both. At the flare of Blake's nostrils and the glimmer of recognition in his eyes, Lucy gave him a devilish smile and urged her mount forward so her footmen once again flanked her.

CHAPTER TWENTY-NINE

*E*ntering Saint-Malo, every muscle in Blake's body was tense and tingling. He glanced over at Mr. Smyth, whose eyes were a little too bright, as if sensing danger. If Matthew knew of his escape, then so must others.

Both men were vigilant as they maneuvered through the port. Lucy inquired if they could stop at an inn, take refreshments, and clean up, but Mr. Smyth was the first to object, and Blake just shook his head when she made the request. Despite her obvious desire to rest, she didn't make mention of it again and never uttered a complaint at being denied.

As Blake dismounted, he asked, "What is the name of the ship we are to board?"

She answered, "*Quarter Moon.*"

Blake wrapped his hands about her waist and assisted her to the ground. "English then?"

As if she wasn't standing on a foreign dock over-crowded with brawny sailors, Lucy raised her chin and said, "Why, of course." Turning away from Blake, she addressed John, "Is he here?"

"Yes, my lady. I see him posted right where he said he would be."

Blake followed her through the crowd. He admired the way she eased her way flanked by two footmen. They moved as one, and it was an impressive sight.

She walked across the gangway. "Captain Bane, let me introduce to you Blake Gower."

"Word on both shores was you were missing."

Blake raised one eyebrow and replied, "How interesting, Captain. How soon can we be off?"

Captain Bane's gaze moved pointedly to Lucy. She gave an infinitesimal nod. "You are in luck. We will be able to set off with the tide this evening. If the winds prevail as I predict, we should be in Dover by early morning."

Lucy beamed at the captain. "That is wonderful news. If your estimates are correct, which they normally are, we will be able to slip back into Town without notice."

It was apparent the two had worked together previously, and the captain took direction from Lucy and Lucy alone. Pride filled Blake's heart. It was a rare woman who could command such respect. He was looking forward to sharing a future with this complex and brave lady. Would she continue her association with the Home Office after they were wed? He could foresee times where their loyalties could be tested if he was to continue to work for the Foreign Office and she with the Home Office.

FINGERING THE PARCHMENT, Lucy sighed at the dirt under her fingernails. She was in desperate need of a bath.

"Why the deep sigh, my sweet?" Blake asked as he entered the captain's quarters.

Seated upon the bed, Lucy straightened and gathered the missives she had been pouring over for the past hour. "Blake! What are you doing in here?"

"What have you in your hands, Lucy?"

"Correspondence."

Blake's features transformed from amicable to harsh as he barked, "From whom?"

"Various individuals."

Lucy wasn't accustomed to being questioned or sharing information. But if she was to marry this man, she should trust him. When she lifted her gaze, hard cold emerald eyes bore into her.

"I had Captain Bane reach out to some informants. There is a note here from a Miss Willow that is of interest."

Eyes wide, Blake said, "The healer."

"Yes, but I can't quite understand her message. It's in a dialect I'm unfamiliar with."

With an outreached hand, Blake asked, "May I?"

Apart from Carrington, she had never had a partner to assist her before. The parchment shook as she held it out for Blake. Stepping closer, he wrapped his warm fingers around her wrist and with the other hand on her lower back pulled her to him.

"Lucy, I too am unfamiliar to working with another, but I promise to be your champion, to stand by you and protect you always."

The sincerity in his eyes shone through, and she turned her wrist, placing the paper directly in his hand. He didn't read the note immediately; instead, his gaze remained upon her. What was he waiting for? She wanted to share her fears and doubts. Would he allow her to continue to work for the Home Office? If he confirmed his association with the Foreign Office, what would it all mean?

But in truth, her thoughts were consumed by his lips, and she was desperate to have them upon her once more, and then they were. Blake was kissing her with an intensity that matched her desires. How had he read her thoughts? At that moment she didn't care, sliding her tongue in his mouth and touching his. The sweet taste of port consumed her. Rising to her tiptoes, she deepened the kiss.

With a groan, Blake pulled back and said, "I want you. You are to be my wife. I trust you know your own mind, but…"

Like a lightning bolt, the word came to Lucy, "Maps! Miss Willow was describing the search for a map." Blake released her, and she went to search for the travel sack she had left in Captain Bane's possession.

Blake translated the note out loud. "Deep slumber master repeated search plan."

"*Le plan* can be translated as scheme, plan, or *map*! I'm correct, am I not?" Lucy asked as she stood with another stack of missives. Shuffling them into order, she placed them across the bed. Together they read over each one.

Blake pointed to the page that Lucy had deciphered and labeled French missives, and announced, "These were not written by the French."

Lucy questioned, "How can you be so certain?"

"It was written using English grammar."

With her head tilted and brow creased, she scanned the letter once more. *How had she not realized that before?* Blake's kidnappers were not French. Lucy asked, "If not the French, who? For what purpose? If they were still searching for a map, why kidnap you now?"

"I haven't any idea, and those are all excellent questions that need to be puzzled out. Lucy, will you share with me all the missives and information you have received to date?"

With a smile, she nodded. Together they mulled over the stack of missives Lucy had in her possession. Rather than coming up with answers, more questions arose. She would have to seek out Archbroke upon their return with the hope that he would be able to piece it all together.

CHAPTER THIRTY

*E*nsconced in a hired hack, Lucy snuggled next to Blake as the cool early morning air seeped through the cracks of the aging vehicle. Mr. Smyth and the footmen were mounted and followed close behind.

As they approached Harrington's town house, Blake turned to Lucy. "My sweet, I have many errands to see to. I shall call on you soon."

"I understand." Lucy leaned in and pulled his head down so she could deliver a scorching kiss.

The hack came to an abrupt stop, forcing Blake to wrap his arms around Lucy to prevent them from falling. He murmured against her ear, "Lucy, you tempt me like no other."

Lucy giggled as his beard tickled her skin. It was in this compromising position that Mr. Smyth found them in as the door swung open. Lucy righted herself and took his outstretched hand. Blake didn't care to see Lucy's hand upon another man.

"Lucy, I shall return as soon as I can."

The smile he received from Lucy put his fears to rest.

Eager to be done with his errands, he mentally prioritized what he needed to accomplish: a bath, provide his report to his superiors, and propose properly to Lucy.

～

REFRESHED, Blake entered Brooks's and was immediately shown to one of the more private rooms in the back. Lord Hereford was standing by the fireplace. Blake and Hereford had on occasion worked assignments together on the Continent. Why was Hereford here and not his superior?

"Hereford, a pleasure to see you again."

"Likewise, Devonton. Glad to see you made it back to England. You were gone a day too long for the comfort of our superiors." Hereford's features hardened as he said, "I've been instructed to take your report."

"Where is…"

Hereford cut him off. "Currently unavailable."

Blake walked over to stand next to the window. Careful not to be in full sight, he peered out the window.

Hereford came to stand behind him. "Per our informants, you and Lady Lucy arrived aboard the *Quarter Moon* early this morn. Harrington is on the Continent, hunting Addington. You are to wed Lady Lucy. Do you have more to add?"

Hereford understood how unusual the situation was and provided Blake with the most convenient method of providing as little detail as possible. "No, I believe you have surmised all the pertinent points."

Hereford placed a hand on Blake's shoulder. "You are a lucky man. Lady Lucy is an exquisite woman. Congratulations."

"My thanks. I'm off to make it official. Before I do, tell me this, Hereford. The three of us were recruited out of

Oxford. You and I accepted, and I was under the belief Harrington had declined. How is it he is on the Continent hunting Addington and not you?"

"He left against direct orders."

"Whose orders? Orders from the Home Office?"

"You know we are not to discuss such matters, Devonton. I was to inform you of your orders. Remain in England. Wed Lady Lucy. Beget an heir."

Those were his orders? It was fortunate they aligned with his own immediate plans. Plans that not only included marrying Lucy but also identifying and exposing the individuals behind his kidnapping. He would not rest until he gained justice.

THE STORE SIGN above his head read RUTHERFORD JEWELERS. The lettering was elaborate, but what caught his eye was the intricate angel that sat in the hook of the J. Where had he seen a similar design? The tinkle of the bell alerted Mr. Rutherford of his entrance.

"Lord Devonton, may I introduce myself? I am the proprietor, Mr. Rutherford. How may I assist you today?"

Blake had perfect recall of features. He had never laid eyes on Mr. Rutherford prior—how was it he knew who Blake was?

The man answered as if Blake had voiced his thoughts. "Your papa and I played many a hand of whist together, and he was a frequent customer of mine. You share his features, but you have your mama's eyes." Mr. Rutherford chuckled as he continued, "As soon as a high-quality emerald was delivered, your papa would snap it up."

Blake retrieved the item from his breast pocket and

placed it in the jeweler's hand. "I'll need it to be cleaned, sized, and ready by this evening."

Mr. Rutherford held the ring as if it was one of the crown jewels. "An extremely rare diamond. Not large in size, but it is of exquisite quality. Your mama would have been delighted to know it was not lost and the future Countess Devonton will honor family tradition. Who, might I ask, is the lucky lady?"

"Lady Lucille Stanford."

"Ahh... Harrington's sister. She is a remarkable woman."

How was it that Lucy would be acquainted with Mr. Rutherford? There was much to learn about his Lucy. Were her activities limited to decoding for the Home Office?

The reflection of a string of moonstones caught Blake's eye. Mr. Rutherford retrieved it removed it from the display. "A wonderful bride's gift, Lord Devonton. Just like your papa. He always had a keen eye for beauty. Your items will be ready upon your return."

Blake left the jeweler with his senses on full alert. He peered up at the sign once more. The plaque in front of the Home Office, the haberdashery, and the snuff shop he had seen Archbroke enter on occasion—they all displayed a variation of an angel and a harp. What was the connection?

CHAPTER THIRTY-ONE

*L*ucy ran her finger along the book spines. The Home Office library was her favorite room.

She jumped as Archbroke said, "Lady Lucy. I'm glad to see you. I assume your mission was successful?"

The man had the uncanny ability to walk into a room without detection.

Her pulse was still accelerated as she answered, "Lord Archbroke, do not even pretend it was your idea to send me." The man might play the dandy when among society, but he was the heart and mind of the Home Office.

"It is evident not one member of your family follows my orders." His lordship was pacing and mumbling in contrast to his usual direct manner. "I am not at all happy about your brother defying my orders."

Matthew had disobeyed a direct order? "I thought you were the one who gave him the order to hunt Addington down."

"You thought wrong. Upon hearing of Devonton's disappearance, I gave the order for your brother to remain in England. Then I was informed he was in Dover and *you* had commandeered a ship to cross the Channel." Arch-broke stopped pacing and faced Lucy. "Did you just say *hunt Addington?*"

"Yes. In the package of messages you had me work on, I found missives from both Blake's kidnappers and the Foreign Office. It is the reason why it took me such an exorbitant amount of time to decipher, for they were a jumbled mess. I had assumed Matthew informed you…"

The Home Secretary exploded, "What Foreign Office missives?"

Not wanting to increase his distress, Lucy quickly answered, "The ones that indicated that Lord Addington was involved in Blake's abduction."

Brow furrowed, Archbroke began to pace again. "Addington? Explain why your brother would fail to inform me of this information." He stood right in front of her and took a deep breath, then asked, "When did you start referring to Devonton as Blake?"

"Since the day I agreed to marry the man."

Ignoring her tart reply, Archbroke's cool, clear blue eyes bore into her. "I'll ask you once more, why did Harrington not share this information with me?"

Lucy was not about to let the man intimidate her. Returning his steady gaze, she stated, "Archbroke, I have no idea. And as I said earlier, I assumed he had informed you."

Why had Matthew decided not to report her findings to Archbroke? The missives had been intercepted by Arch-broke's team. But the communication belonged to the Foreign Office and involved their agents. Who had Matthew provided the information to?

Archbroke continued to bluster, "I'm going to have Harrington's head. By God, if I speak to…"

To who? Who was the head of the Foreign Office? For

years Lucy had tried to figure out who it could be. Would Archbroke finally share the confidential information with her? If Blake was a Foreign Office agent, would he confide in her once they were married? Would their positions in their respective offices result in discord between them? She needed Blake to confirm his association, and soon.

Hands held tightly behind his back, Archbroke paced until he stopped and announced, "I have no choice. I'm going to send Mr. Smyth to fetch your brother home."

What? Archbroke was a stickler for rules. Sending a Home Office agent to foreign soil was a direct breach of protocol. "Are you sure?"

"I've yet to lose an agent, and I'm not about to now." Archbroke's hands were balled into fists as he walked out of the library.

Lose? Was Matthew's life in danger? What did Archbroke know that she didn't? He was like a steel trap, and it would be an utter waste of time and energy to try to pry information from the man unless he willingly provided it. She refused to run after him. Archbroke was not her only source of information. She would seek answers elsewhere.

CHAPTER THIRTY-TWO

Twisting the ring around and around on his little finger, Blake contemplated how best to propose to Lucy. *When do you want to marry?* An offer like that would not warrant an answer, especially not from Lucy. It was not romantic enough. *Will you do me the honor of becoming my wife?* Tried and true, but boring. He wanted to make his proposal memorable. He wiped his palm down his thigh. What he needed was a drink. No, he wanted Lucy. He bounded up the steps to Harrington's town house.

The door opened as he approached. Lucy was on her way out. Where was she headed to? Wasn't she exhausted from their trip? He was. His only source of energy spurring his feet to move was the anticipation of her formally agreeing to be his wife.

"Blake, what are you doing here?"

"I've come to pay you a visit. Are you heading out? May I accompany you?"

"Oh, I thought you were here to collect your belongings."

Blake took a half step back, frowning. "Why would you think that? Am I no longer welcome?"

Lucy walked up to him and pulled him back into the foyer. She gave Kirkland a look, and with that, the butler closed the front door and promptly removed himself from the area.

Blake's lapels were being crushed in her attempt to pull him closer. She gave him a quick peck before she pulled back and patted him on the chest. "No, silly. It would not be proper for my fiancé to be living under the same roof until we are married. You wouldn't want to cause a scandal or ruin my reputation now, would you?"

Blake loved this playful side of Lucy. She gave him a cheeky grin and linked her hands behind his neck. It was Edward who descended the stairs and caught them in the embrace.

"Eeeewww. Lucy, what is going on? Are you and Lord Devonton going to kiss? Shouldn't that be done in private?" Edward had apparently picked up Matthew's habit of rapidly issuing one question after another.

Lucy took a step back, but Blake did not fully release her. He kept his hands securely on her waist. It was a possessive gesture, but he couldn't keep his hands to himself.

She turned to face Edward. "Why are you not studying with Mr. Trenton?"

"It's his afternoon off." Edward leaned to the right a little to speak to Blake. "Lord Devonton, I'm glad to see you both have returned. Where is Matthew?"

"Lord Edward, it is indeed good to see you again. I believe your brother has left for the Continent to visit some friends."

"Matthew is always off visiting friends. I hope to make friends like him when I go to Eton."

Blake left Lucy and went to put an arm around Edward. "You will meet boys your age, and I'm sure you will make a friend or two that you can depend on like I depend on your brother."

Hope glittered in Edward's lonely eyes. "Do you really believe that could happen?"

"I haven't a doubt. You are the smartest, most honorable eight-year-old I know. Anyone who dislikes you is an utter fool." Blake gave him a hug and then said, "Excuse us, my lord. I need to speak to your sister in private for a moment."

"Not a problem. I certainly do not want to see you kissing her." Edward ran back up the stairs and out of sight.

Lucy suggested, "Shall we retire to the drawing room?"

She said drawing room, not a bedroom—he really needed to get some sleep. The thought of rest and beds had his imagination running wild. He took Lucy's hand and led her to the drawing room.

WHY DID Blake need to speak to Lucy in private? As they entered the drawing room, he gently pulled her inside and locked the door. Why had he locked the door? Had he gained information regarding Matthew's whereabouts?

Blake took a step closer and gently put his hands on her shoulders. He searched her eyes. What was he looking for? Did he know of her errand?

He leaned in and placed his lips on hers. Only the need for air caused the kiss to cease.

"Lucy, I cannot begin to describe the feelings you have instilled in my heart." He dropped to one knee, and took her left hand in both of his. "Lucy, I will love you with all my being, now and always. I promise to always assist you, in every way I can. Will you grant me the pleasure of having you as my wife?"

The depth of his sincerity and love was evident in his deep emerald eyes. His words were exactly those she needed to hear. A knot formed in her throat and her eyes began to water. She smiled and nodded.

Blake slowly slid the most beautiful ring on her finger. She bent down and whispered in Blake's ear, "Yes, yes, I'll marry you. I cannot wait to be yours."

She stumbled as he pulled her down. She found herself on her knees with him. Unhesitatingly, she placed her hands on his cheeks and brought his face down to hers. Lucy kissed him gently at first, just as he had taught her, but soon she was grazing her teeth along his jaw. Blake let out a deep growl; she had learned he loved her boldness.

He gently eased her to the rug. He lay next to her on his side, and she turned to face him. His hand caressed her hip down her leg and back around to squeeze her bottom. Lucy gave him a wicked smile and began to undo the buttons on his jacket and vest. As soon as it was possible, Blake was divested of both garments, and he went to work on Lucy's buttons and laces. Within minutes, she found Blake had managed to remove her dress and stays, leaving her only in a chemise.

Lucy wanted to touch Blake, and he let her hands explore. She ran her hands from his waist up to his chest under his shirt. She enjoyed feeling his muscles twitch as her palms caressed his chest. She even dared to circle and flick his nipple. Lucy loved the way his body responded to her touch, and the sense of power she had over this man was heady.

His muscles tensed and then he leaned back, putting a

little distance between them. "We should wait until we are wed and in a bed."

"When did you start rhyming? I don't want to wait. I want you now. Please, Blake. Please make me yours."

His stare was so intense. Lucy wanted him. They were alone and would not be interrupted. Why was he hesitating? She was on the verge of standing when Blake moved to pull up the hem of her chemise. She placed a hand on his to stop him from drawing her garment over her head.

"Lucy, I want to see you. I've imagined the sight of your lovely body, and my hands have felt your beautiful curves, but I want to see you, all of you."

His memory was faultless. Once he laid his eyes on her, the image would be burned into his memory. Would he mind her rounded stomach? She was not lithe. If he was to see her, she should be afforded the same.

"Blake, I…" Lucy wasn't sure how to formulate her desire. Instead, she sat up and pulled him into a sitting position. She reached out to remove his shirt. He did not balk, but he stiffened as if to brace himself from some sort of blow. With his shirt off, Lucy saw the multitude of scars that adorned his chest, arms, shoulders, and back. Her heart ached at the sight of the marks. She lightly traced the white lines and gently pushed him to lie on his back. She straddled him and began kissing the crisscross of white lines on his chest and abdomen.

Her movements had caused her chemise to shift higher. Blake's warm hands rubbed up and down her thighs. She would not be distracted from her own ministrations. It became harder and harder for her to focus as his hands roamed to her waist and then up under her chemise to cup her breasts. He began to fondle and squeeze her breasts; he flicked her nipples, and she immediately felt a pull in her core. She leaned a little farther so she could kiss him thoroughly on the mouth, and as she was raised slightly, he was able to pull her chemise over her head, which broke their kiss.

He sought out her gaze. "Lucy, are you sure you want to do this before the wedding?"

She didn't reply; she simply began to kiss him again. Blake moved under her, pushing up with his hips, which forced her to place her hands just above his shoulders to regain her balance. In this position, Blake's mouth was now in line with her breasts. He raised his head, and devilishly his tongue darted out. He licked one of her nipples and then brought her breast to his mouth and began to gently suck. With each pull of his lips, the dampness between her legs continued to build. He acted as if he enjoyed having her in his mouth, and then a moan escaped her lips. Blake continued to lavish her breasts. Her moans were becoming more frequent and louder. She didn't want him to stop. She bucked when his finger ran along her slit. When she began to rock against his hand, Blake moved with lightning speed, and their positions reversed.

She lay on the floor with him between her legs. What was to happen next? He hurriedly pushed his smalls and breeches down, and his shaft sprung free. Wide-eyed, she peeked up at him. Blake's physique was impressive. She had thought the Elgin Marbles extraordinary when she had viewed them, but the male form was far better in real life.

Blake reached between them and guided himself to her entrance. The pressure of his tip as it slid along her slit felt glorious. But when he pushed a little farther, her fears of his size arose again. He hesitated. Was he worried too?

Taking matters into her own hands, she quickly pushed her hips up, accommodating all of him. He was long and thick. A sharp pinch caused her to gasp. Her immediate reaction was to retreat, but he had moved to kiss her breasts again. She was so focused on that pleasure she forgot about the pain.

Blake continued to move in and out of her, driving a little deeper each time. He bent her legs at the knees and pushed them closer to her chest. She found the new position more pleasurable, and she relaxed, letting her knees fall more to the side that allowed him deeper access. Lucy could feel him increase even more as he proceeded to intensify the pace and depth of his thrusts.

Soon there was no pain, no burning, just pure ecstasy as tension coiled in her belly, and then all her nerves exploded with the most wonderful sensation. Her senses were slowly returning when Blake began to pump more vigorously, and when he released a low growl, she matched his movement, increasing the friction until a warmth flooded her.

Both of their breathing was labored, and Blake rested his forehead on hers for a moment. "Are you all right? Did I hurt you?"

Sated and lethargic, she stared back and smiled. "I'm well."

He rolled off her and used his handkerchief to gently clean between her legs. His hand smoothly glided over her apex, her nerves still alive and tingling.

She stilled his hand. "Blake. I want… I love you. I want you again."

His gaze searched hers. He rolled and leaned over to give Lucy a kiss. His tongue mimicked his earlier movements, and then he pulled back. "Not right away, my sweet, you will be sore."

She frowned and gave him a serious look. "Then when?"

"Soon," Blake answered.

With him half on top of her, she ran her hands down his back. "How soon?" Her hands continued to roam his body, which immediately responded to her touch. Lucy peeked down and with a wicked grin said, "Hmm. Now?"

"Love, I'll never be able to deny you." He placed his hand at her center and pinched the sensitive bud. She gasped. She pulled him down for a kiss, but before she released him, she lightly bit his lower lip as he had done to her once before.

Desire flared in his eyes. Lucy could not wait for him to teach her all the ways to evoke that response from him.

"You will be sore later."

"Will you?"

All she allowed him to say was "Minx" before reaching for him.

CHAPTER THIRTY-THREE

*B*lake took in Lucy's exhausted and relaxed form. He loved the feel of her in his arms. "You never told me where you were headed earlier."

She jumped up and began donning her clothes and fixing her coiffure. "Oh my, I totally forgot. I have to go to the Lone Dove right away." Gone was the lethargic woman, and before him stood a determined Lucy.

He leisurely sat up and searched for his shirt, waistcoat, and jacket. "The Lone Dove? Isn't that a tavern?" he asked and then added, "Lucy, you are not going there alone."

She gave him a look that should have him cowering. Apparently, she did not care for his tone or edict. "John and Evan are to accompany me. I never go to that part of Town without them. I'm not a ninny."

Blake captured Lucy's face between his large hands and kissed her nose. Releasing her, he said, "We are to marry, so let me be perfectly clear. First, I would never consider you a ninny. You are the smartest person I know, without a doubt." He gave her another quick kiss on the forehead this time and continued, "Second, it will be entirely up to you if you continue to have an association with the Home Office."

Yes, to have a life with this woman and the challenge of eliciting the look that graced Lucy's features at the mention of the Home Office was all he needed.

"Third, I love you, and I will always be by your side, so if you are off to the Lone Dove, I'm going with you."

"Did you just say you love me?" she asked, a little dazed.

"Yes, with all my heart." Blake was so happy he had at last admitted his feelings. While he had hoped she would return the sentiment, he was well aware she was still in shock. Taking in her appearance, he turned her around so he could do her buttons and tie her laces.

"Blake, you need to pull them tighter," Lucy said as he left her laces loose.

"Tighter? How are you able to breathe with ease and move about? Wouldn't it be better to have them a little loose?"

Lucy turned and purposefully rolled her shoulders, allowing the loose gown to gape. Wide-eyed, Blake turned her once more and promptly pulled her laces tight.

"Blake! Now I can't breathe. Oh, good heavens, where is Carrington?"

Blake released his stranglehold on her laces. "Please take a deep breath so I can determine the correct tension." With a frown, he finished his task and gently placed his hand on her elbow and guided her to the door. "Shall we be off?"

At her hesitation, he said, "I'm going with you, and that is how it shall be, always with me at your side."

He escorted her to the awaiting carriage, and he rapped on the roof of the carriage to indicate they were ready to leave. As the carriage lurched forward, Lucy was jolted into Blake's side. Putting his arm around her, he turned to look at her and smiled. He liked what he saw, a woman who had the look of having been thoroughly satisfied in bed, her lips swollen from his kisses and her eyes still a little glazed over. He couldn't help but be a tad proud of himself for being the one to make her feel that way.

He leaned closer to her and asked, "Are you feeling all right, my sweet?"

"Yes. I'm trying to process everything. Did you say that should I decide I wanted to continue to work with the Home Office, you would support and respect my choice? That once you are my husband, you will not dictate or forbid me from choosing? Did you say I was the smartest person you know?"

Blake grinned and quietly whispered, "Yes."

Lucy reached out and pinched him hard on the arm.

"Ouch! What did you do that for?" Blake rubbed his arm and then twisted so she faced him again.

"This must be a dream. A man willingly giving me all the freedoms I've ever wished for who still wants to marry me. You cannot exist. I've never heard of a man being so reasonable." She put her forehead to his and took a deep breath. "This is just too good to be real. Pinch me so I know I'm not dreaming."

A multitude of images of pinching her in various places raced through his mind, but Blake decided to just playfully pinch her waist.

Lucy sighed. "You *are* real, and I am going to do everything to make you happy, as happy as you make me."

Her declaration was music to Blake's ears, and the only thing that would have made it perfect was if she had admitted she loved him too.

❧

THE CARRIAGE ROLLED to a stop in front of the Lone Dove. Blake exited first and then turned to help Lucy down. They made their way into the inn and to a table in the back.

As they walked, Lucy glanced around the room, and then her eyes rested on the man in the corner holding a cup with a red handle to indicate he was the one she sought out. The man became visibly nervous when he noticed Blake with her.

Lucy swiftly said, "I need to meet with my associate privately before he leaves. Please wait here."

Blake nodded and remained seated. To Lucy's surprise, he made no complaint about her leaving his side. There had been a flash of recognition in Blake's eyes. Did he know her contact? Uncertain if the missive requesting this meeting had been issued by the Home or Foreign Office, she was highly suspect of the man.

She made her way along the back wall to the corner. At seeing her approach alone, her contact had remained in place. She nodded to several of the tavern's occupants as she passed them. They were all friends and would no doubt come to her assistance if need be.

As soon as Lucy was close enough, her contact spoke in a rushed voice. "Lady Lucy, I've been asked to establish contact with you regarding your brother."

Matthew. Was he hurt? Fear of what the contact might share had her sitting abruptly in the chair next to the man.

"Your brother has sent word that he believes Lord Devonton was captured to assist in completing a map of sorts. Lord Harrington anticipates he will be remaining on the Continent for an extended period as he hunts Addington down."

Matthew had confirmed what she and Blake had been able to decipher upon their voyage. By remaining on the

Continent, he was placing himself at risk. How had Arch-broke known?

Breaking her train of thought, the informant said, "My superior is fully aware of the burden this will place upon you. I have been assigned to act as your steward and assist you in whatever manner is deemed necessary during his absence." He was definitely from the Foreign Office. Arch-broke would have handled the matter in an entirely different manner.

Not knowing who exactly she was dealing with, she questioned the real intent of the offer. Lucy was not at all familiar with practices or internal operations of the Foreign Office. She had on occasion heard various Home Office agents speaking about the Foreign Office, but mostly they were grumblings as to the obscurity of its leader. She also recalled Matthew's comment that the two offices sometimes did not agree on a mission strategy.

With a smile plastered on her face, which was contrary to the steel edge in her voice, she informed her contact, "Please thank your superior for the offer. However, I will decline assistance at this time. My brother has many extremely competent stewards already in place to oversee the estate, and I have acted on his behalf in the past and will have no issue doing so again. Please advise your superior I do expect updates and direct correspondence from Matthew during his time abroad—not details, just reassurance of his health and well-being. I trust you will be able to convey my message accurately."

"Yes, Lady Lucy. Should you ever need my assistance, please do not hesitate to leave a message for me here addressed to Mr. Atkins. If there is nothing else I can do, I bid you a good evening."

"Good evening, Mr. Atkins."

Her eyes narrowed as she made her way back to Blake.

He had revealed his knowledge of her association with the Home Office, yet he had not confirmed his association with the Foreign Office. She should confront Blake. She had to trust he would tell her the truth. If she didn't trust him, she should not be marrying the man. If she wished to continue to work for the Home Office and he the Foreign Office, could a marriage between them thrive? She feared the answer. It had prevented her from asking him directly in the past. Would she have to choose between the work she loved and the man who fulfilled all her wishes?

As Lucy cautiously approached, a range of emotions flashed across her features. Was she agonizing over Mr. Atkins and his message?

What concerned Blake the most was the looks of uncertainty in his direction while she had spoken to Mr. Atkins. Since he was aware of her work for the Home Office, it was only fair he should inform her of his association with the Foreign Office; he was just not sure of how best to approach the topic.

Lucy stood next to the table. When Blake pushed out the chair opposite him with his foot, she stared at the seat and then her mouth fell open. He definitely liked it when he took her by surprise. He wasn't one to always follow convention, and Lucy had an independent streak he loved and would encourage. Anticipating her needs and desires would be challenging, especially if he wished to do so before she even expressed them.

"I t has been a long day, but I do believe I feel like celebrating our betrothal. Let's have a drink before we leave. Would you care to celebrate with me?"

She slid into the chair and braced her elbows on the

table, steepling her fingers together. "Is this what life will be like with you? Constantly surprising me to the point that I become speechless?"

"Perhaps. What will it be, scotch, brandy, or perhaps sherry?" Blake had raised his hand to get the attention of the serving maid.

"Brandy." The woman was bold, and he loved her for it. He could foresee their marriage would be a happy one. It would be imperative for him to remember to always treat her as an equal, a true life partner, not just a possession.

After Blake had ordered her a brandy and a scotch for himself, he leaned back in his chair and turned to face her. "So, Lucy, what did Mr. Atkins want?"

Eyes narrowed, Lucy asked, "How are you acquainted with Mr. Atkins?"

Would she ask him directly to confirm his association with the Foreign Office? No, she would be circumspect. Blake retorted, "Are you always going to answer my questions with a question?"

"Are you?"

Catching her gaze, Blake answered, "I believe we both belong to the same association."

Lucy nodded as if satisfied with his answer. What a smart girl to have figured out his connection to the Foreign Office.

She shared, "Mr. Atkins has been assigned to assist me with the estate should I need it while Matthew is on the Continent. He advised me that Matthew sent word while we were homeward bound that your trip was coordinated in an effort to establish a map."

"I'm glad our theory was confirmed. Addington?"

The maid delivered their drinks. Lucy sipped on her brandy like it was a cup of chocolate. Before she brought it to her lips once more, she said, "Matthew is still hunting."

Blake could count on Harrington to sort the matter out. The possibility that Lucy could be with child meant he had other immediate issues to tend to—getting her to the altar, quick.

His wife-to-be sat eyeing him over the rim of her glass, entirely in her element. She was more at ease here among a varied cast of tavern patrons than at any *ton* event where he had seen her. It may take more than one lifetime to determine what would bring Lucy the most joy.

But as Blake took mental pictures of his intended, he surveyed their surroundings. These people and her work were the keys to her happiness. Once they were married, they would just have to find a way to manage their individual associations and perhaps even bridge some of the animosity between the two critical government departments. For with one glance he was certain his lady would not be giving up her work with the Home Office anytime soon.

CHAPTER THIRTY-FOUR

*L*ucy had three weeks to prepare. Blake had sent off the notice to the papers, and now two piles of invitations were stacked before her. Grace entered the drawing room as if Lucy was expecting her. She had missed Grace and was extremely relieved that her best friend didn't seem out of sorts with her disappearance.

Standing in front of Lucy's desk, Grace directed, "Separate them into Nos and Maybes."

"Then they all go in the No pile."

"Lucy, you have to at least attend those engagements held by Lord Harrington's friends and supporters. Here, move over and I'll sort them for you."

Lucy gladly handed the piles over to Grace. How was it Grace kept all Matthew's friends and acquaintances straight? In short order, she had eliminated the pile to a few small dinner parties.

"Will you be attending those also?" Lucy nodded at the small stack.

"Of course. I wouldn't lead you astray, would I?"

"I wish Matthew were here." She had allowed herself

only a moment to sulk over the fact Matthew would not be present at her wedding and unable to walk her down the aisle. She had asked Edward to do it instead and had been rewarded with such a love-filled hug that she refused to be saddened by Matthew's absence.

"He should have been." The harshness in Grace's tone was startling. Was Grace aware of Matthew's activities? Why would she bristle at the mention of Matthew? Were the pair in discord? Matthew had made no mention of a disagreement.

With a forced smile, Grace said, "You shall have the most magnificent wedding without him."

Lucy asked, "Do you think he will succeed while on the Continent?"

For an instant, Grace appeared as if she was going to state something, but instead gave Lucy an innocent look and replied, "Succeed at what, my dear?"

"Oh, nothing of consequence." Lucy held up an invitation, "Supper with Waterford? Blake will not want to attend."

"You will just have to convince him."

When had Grace become so autocratic? Lucy was loath to share that she was learning that her husband to be could be extremely stubborn. Blake hadn't touched her intimately again despite her numerous attempts to seduce him.

She muttered, "Humph, easier said than done."

Picking up her gloves to leave, Grace said, "After your wedding, I assume you will be headed for Shalford Castle."

"Blake and I haven't discussed the matter."

"Hmm. Well, in any case, I will be traveling to the Continent with my aunt. She has decided that it would be good for me to… to see more of the world."

Grace bussed Lucy on the cheek and then promptly left

the room, leaving Lucy to ponder the real cause for Grace's departure.

~

THE DAY BEFORE THEIR WEDDING, Lucy was sitting in Matthew's study poring over estate reports from the stewards. Big hands rested on her shoulders. She jumped and turned to see Blake grinning like a fool. Ever since their return, she had been on edge. She worried about his safety.

Blake gently pushed her back and began to massage the knots he expertly located in her neck and shoulders. Lucy relaxed and let his fingers do wonders with the tension she had been feeling for days.

"My sweet, you need to take a break. Would you like to go for a ride in my phaeton or go for a walk in the park?"

Lucy let out a moan. "Neither, I just want to relax here with you." She turned to look at him. Did he see the desire in her eyes?

"Lucy, we discussed this, and we had agreed not until we wed."

"I know what we discussed; I just don't recall agreeing with you."

His fingers began to trace the back of her neck, his touch light, and then he slipped one hand around her front, following the line of her collarbone. Lucy let out a sigh and tilted her head to the side, silently begging for him to kiss her neck. He groaned and then trailed his lips and nibbled her skin from under her ear to the spot that inevitably made her tremble.

"Tomorrow is the wedding," he mumbled against her neck. "You will have to be a good girl until then." Blake's hand moved farther down to knead her breast as if it had a mind of its own. Lucy placed her hand over his, encouraging him to continue. Boldness always guaranteed Blake's acquiescence.

Was he reciting cities on the Continent? No, he was reciting the multiplication table. He must be tempted; why else employ such diversionary tactics? It was the first sure sign of weakness on his part in three weeks. If she tested his self-control, would she finally receive her wish?

But then he removed his hands and placed them behind his back.

At the loss of his touch, Lucy asked, "Blake, where are you going?"

He came around the desk to face her. "Nowhere, my sweet. The door is open, and I came here to speak to you about tomorrow. No more distractions."

Slowly lowering her gaze, she smiled at the bulge he could not hide. He was not immune to her attempts to seduce him. She needed him to stay. "What did you come to discuss?"

"I wanted to know if you desired to remain here in London or if you would be agreeable to leaving for Shalford Castle. I wasn't certain if you wanted to remain near your mama and brother, or if you would be able to handle matters remotely. I had hoped to have you alone for a short period." Blake's devilish grin indicated his thoughts were not all innocent.

Lucy had given this much thought over the past few weeks but had assumed Blake would decide and she would have to live by his decision. She really shouldn't be shocked by his consideration, but nonetheless, she was pleasantly surprised.

"I've spoken to Edward and my mama and informed them I might be leaving for your country estate if you so desired. Given the awkward situation with Matthew away, my preference is to go to Shalford Castle for a fortnight and then return to stay at your London town house until his return. This would allow me to keep abreast of any developments in his mission, help my family, and... assist the Home Office if need be." Lucy hesitated, as this was the first time she had mentioned her decision to continue to work for the Home Office.

Blake didn't even blink an eye. "That sounds like the perfect plan. I will advise the staff. I know I should be seeking Matthew's permission to steal the staff away from him, but I thought I should talk to John and Evan to see if they would like to come work for us. I had just assumed Carrington would be coming, but perhaps I should speak to her also."

Lucy jumped up from her seat, rounded the desk, and pulled him down so she could wrap her arms tightly around his neck and kiss him passionately.

"Blake, I don't know how you do it. You always antici-pate my wishes and make them come true. I would love to have John and Evan accompany us to Shalford Castle, and Carrington would never leave me, but she will be thrilled to know that Evan is coming too. I know Matthew won't mind; I pay their wages from my income and not from the estate funds."

Lucy had to pinch herself yet again; she had gotten into the habit over the past three weeks. Blake was continu-ally surprising her with his kind consideration of her needs and wants. She could not wait for tomorrow when she would become the Countess of Devonton.

LUCY ALIGHTED from the carriage outside Saint George's Church. She took a moment and stared at the tall columns and magnificent wood doors. The grandeur of what she was about to do hit her like a lightning bolt. Legally, she and all her possessions would become Blake's. She would vow to obey him; none of the other vows worried her except for that one. Despite all his gestures to show her what it would be like to be married to him, she became panicked and short of breath and turned back to sit in the carriage.

Edward took hold of her hand. "Lucy, are you ready? Everyone is waiting for us. We need to go inside." When she didn't reply, he scanned her features. "What is wrong? Are you ill? Should I go fetch a doctor?"

His rapid-fire questions made Lucy smile. He was so much like Matthew.

"I just need a moment. I'm sure I'll be well in a minute."

Edward began to hum a song, at first a little quietly, but when she smiled at him, he hummed louder. It was a melody Matthew often hummed as he went about his day. She recalled the day she had asked him what the name of it was.

Matthew had chuckled and replied, "I believe it's called 'Billy Taylor,' but it is not a ditty you would hear at any of the *ton* affairs."

How many other off-handed comments or clues had Matthew shared that she had not thought to question? Focused on keeping her own involvement a secret, she never suspected her twin's activities were similar to her own.

Edward was humming the chorus, and Lucy joined in. By the end of the song, her smile and equilibrium had returned.

Walking up the steps to the church, thoughts of Blake waiting for her had her increasing her pace. Sunlight streamed through the stained glass. The rainbow of colors cascading in landed on the guests, who consisted of half the *ton*.

Edward escorted her down the aisle, passing the eight gentlemen Matthew had identified as potential suitors at the beginning of the Season. Each of them gave her a knowing smile and nodded their approval of her selection in a husband. Lucy nearly stopped short when her gaze fell upon Lady Mary. Why was Lady Mary standing so close to Waterford?

The only two people of import missing were Matthew and her childhood friend Theo, who remained in mourning for her papa. Her eyes glued to Grace's as Edward tugged on her hand and led her down the aisle.

Edward placed her hand in Blake's. A feeling of warmth and security radiated throughout her and filled her heart. The ceremony was a blur for Lucy. She was certain the priest had conducted the ceremony with the usual aplomb one would expect at a *ton* wedding.

Lucy remembered looking up at Blake as he said his vows and her whispering, "I love you" before stating hers. He rewarded her confession with a wicked smile and then he bent down and kissed her in front of one and all.

As soon as their lips touched, Lucy felt at ease and a sense of calm wash over her. Her hand engulfed by his, they proceeded to leave the church side by side, just as he had promised.

EPILOGUE

*L*ady Devonton turned the knob to her new bedchamber and pushed the door open. Cautiously stepping into the room that would traditionally only house Blake, she was surprised to see it sparsely furnished.

Carrington was on her heels and pushed her mistress farther into the room. "My lady, it appears you will need to wield your magic upon the town house as you did Shalford Castle."

"Yes, it appears we will have to refurbish each room." Lucy pulled the dark blue velvet draperies. She placed a hand along the edge of the window and measured it against the length of her arm. *Not wide enough.* How was she to read by moonlight?

"I will assume Blake's preference for me to sleep alongside him will continue to apply while we are in Town."

When Carrington failed to comment, Lucy turned to

find the room empty. Where had Carrington disappeared to? A piece of white parchment lying in the center of the enormous bed caught Lucy's attention. Had it been there when she entered? She had scanned the room for threats but didn't recall the paper having been there before.

At the edge of the bed, Lucy had to bend at the waist to reach the letter.

It was in this position that Blake found her as he strode into the room. "What a lovely view, wife."

Lucy jumped back and ignored her husband, walking directly to the window as her fingers ran along the crease in the parchment. Her eyes widened at the sight of Matthew's bold, masculine script.

Countess Devonton

The chill which invaded her body at the sight of Matthew's handwriting was dispelled as strong, reassuring hands rested on her shoulders. Blake's breath seeped through her skin, warming her as he asked, "Love, would it be easier if I read it to you?"

Lucy glanced up at her husband, and her heart fluttered. She was still adjusting to referring to Blake as such, but there was no uncertainty at the depth of his love and concern for her. Just as he had for the past fortnight, he was again showing her how in tune he was to her concerns and needs. She needed to read the note herself. With a slight shake of her head, she drew in a deep breath, and released it slowly as she carefully smoothed out the parchment. She raised Matthew's note slightly higher to allow for them both to read.

Dear Lucy,
I hope this message finds you well.
I must thank you for your consideration in leaving me three

*neatly tied presents. I am happy to report I was able to
retrieve them and have since placed them in safe keeping.
Please inform your husband his dear friend Brutus suggested
I go south and visit Spain.
Blake's knowledge of the area would have been of great
value. However, do not worry, for I'm not alone. Our dear
friends Lord Hereford and Mr. Smyth will be accompanying
me on the journey.
Pray for my speedy return.
M. Harrington*

Blake's thumb grazed her cheek, brushing away the tear that had escaped.

Turning and burrowing her forehead into Blake's chest, Lucy said, "He's alive."

Muscles that had been sore from weeks of tension began to relax. Lucy's anxiety over Matthew's safety had mounted as the weeks had passed with no word from him or either the Home or Foreign Offices. Carrington? Where was she? Tense again, she tried to step back, out of Blake's embrace.

Blake's hands held her arms tight as he asked, "Love, what it wrong?"

"Carrington! She was here and then not. Matthew's note mysteriously appeared." Lucy twisted at the waist to face the door.

"Shhh… Carrington is well. I saw her and Evan heading to the kitchen on my way up."

Lucy whipped about to face the bed, causing Blake to release his hold on her.

"How did someone manage to deliver Matthew's missive undetected? Who dared enter our room?"

"We will interview the staff."

Excellent idea. Why had she not thought of it? With

little rest over the three-day trip from Shalford Castle, her wits were a tad slower than normal. She was about to make her way to the door when Blake's hand snaked out and grasped her elbow.

"Tomorrow. We both need rest."

She let Blake guide her to the bed. Lucy turned her back to her husband, allowing him access to her laces.

With a cheeky grin, she replied, "Rest?"

Blake's eyebrow arched. His nimble fingers began to work on removing her dress and stays as he had done on numerous occasions during their stay at Shalford Castle. While in the country, Lucy had alternated her time between overseeing renovations and lying in bed with Blake. Blake's appetite for bed sport was insatiable, but they had also spent many hours talking and learning each other's habits, fears and dreams. Life with a Foreign Office agent meant there would always be the possibility of another mission or mystery to solve. Her heart thudded as she continued to ponder upon her future.

Lucy remained stock-still until Blake had removed every stitch of clothing.

A light kiss upon her bare shoulder brought her thoughts back to the present. She turned, placing her palms on Blake's chest, pleased to find a staccato beat that echoed her own. When she raised her gaze to meet his, Blake raised both eyebrows in question. Lucy lowered her gaze and focused on slowly removing his clothing. She drew out each movement, for she loved hearing the hitch in his breathing every time her fingers grazed against his naked skin.

As soon as Blake was devoid of clothing, he reached for her, only to grasp air.

Having anticipated Blake's moves, Lucy released a

giggle as she quickly hopped up onto the bed and burrowed under the linens.

Blake settled himself beneath the covers on his side and snaked an arm about his wife. "Come here, Minx."

Willingly she snuggled into her husband's arms and put all worries aside. Certain whatever they were to encounter, they would do it together, side by side.

READ ON FOR AN EXCERPT FROM
MYSTERIES OF LADY THEODORA

AGENTS OF THE HOME OFFICE SERIES

AGENTS OF THE HOME OFFICE

MYSTERIES OF LADY THEODORA - EXCERPT

*F*acing the drafty drawing room window, her back to her aunt, Lady Theodora discreetly pinched the bridge of her nose and closed her eyes. The heartbreaking image of the late Earl of Hadfield on his deathbed refused to dissipate.

The numbness that had seeped into her mind and body that day, leaving her devoid of emotion, was still with her. All her energy was devoted to fulfilling her promise to her papa.

Theo recalled running her hand over the well-worn volume. While there were no visual markings on the cover, the pads of her fingers had rolled over faint ridges and lines of a carefully molded impression. She squeezed her eyelids tighter as she reflected on the image still seared into her memory, the outline of a horse with a falcon perched on its back, circled by laurel leaves, a replica of the mark she bore. The electric jolt of recognition shot through her once more, making her heart beat erratically and her eyes open.

Words contained in the book came to mind:

Only trust those with the Mark.

Train daily.

The sharp sound of a book snapping shut made Theo whip around in the direction of her aunt.

Lady Henrietta Arcot Neale's usually cheerful voice now contained a touch of desperation. "Theo, I do wish you would accompany me to town."

"Beg pardon, Aunt Henri. What was it you said?"

"I was trying to inform you that Landon will insist we return to town with him."

"I'm perfectly happy to remain here. I prefer the fresh country air."

"Well, that might be the case, but we can't hide here any longer." Reaching for her cup of tea, Aunt Henrietta continued, "I haven't been subject to the *ton* in years. To be honest, I was rather relieved when my papa disowned me."

Theo smiled at the memory of her uncle, George Neale. His marriage to Aunt Henri had upended her ties to her ducal family. A second son who embarked on working as a barrister was not an appropriate husband for the daughter of a duke. But theirs had been a love match, and the Neale family had embraced Henrietta from the moment they met her. Her kindness and intelligence were valued by the Neales rather than considered a nuisance.

The teacup rattled against the small saucer in her aunt's hand. Theo was apparently not the only one unnerved by the *ton*.

But Theo's cousin Landon, the newly minted Earl of Hadfield, strode into the room, saving her from having to respond.

"Mama." Landon bent to give his mama a kiss on the cheek, then made his way to Theo's side.

Looming next to her, Landon twisted to peer out the window and quietly asked, "Fantasizing about being

271

outdoors? Wishing you were anywhere but here, trapped in a stifling drawing room, listening to my mama?"

"Landon, I was mentioning to Theo that we must venture to town and find you a wife."

Landon stiffened at the word *wife*. "Yes, we *all* should take up residence in town for the Season. Christopher has reassured me all is in order for our stay."

Theo was amazed at the ease with which he bore the brunt of his new responsibilities. Landon had not only inherited the title but also the neglected estate and the burden of caring for Theo. The only item he had not received was the family volume.

At the mention of Landon's younger brother, Theo couldn't prevent her lips curling into a grin. Christopher was of a similar age to herself and had been a boon companion during their childhood. Was he still a carefree fellow? She hadn't seen him but for a brief moment during her papa's funeral a year ago.

Theo straightened her spine, took a deep breath, and prepared to reiterate her arguments for the hundredth time as to why she should remain in the country. "Cousin, I'm perfectly fine remaining here at Hadfield Hall. Papa often ventured to…" Having read the family volume, it was clear her papa had not only left her behind to travel to London but often ventured much further in his investigations. On an outward breath, she finished. "…to town without me."

Landon's hazel eyes were no longer on Aunt Henrietta. Instead, they bore into Theo. "Don't be ridiculous. I will not leave you here alone with the servants."

Theo donned a mask of cool indifference. The unfeeling woman she had portrayed this past year was in stark contrast to the bubbly little girl he had played with in their childhood. Remaining aloof was the only way she had conceived to keep Landon from finding out the truth about her inheritance. It was imperative he did not find out about the family volume and their familial duties to the Crown.

In the driest tone she could manage, Theo asked, "Why must I accompany you?"

His grin revealed the dimple that rarely graced Landon's features. "You will assist me in becoming better acquainted with my peers."

"Me? I've only been thrown to the wolves once, my debut Season. You were fortunate not to have been there. It was a complete disaster."

Landon's dimple deepened at her response. Damn the man; he had managed to crack her cool exterior. Why was he so determined that she participate in the Season? Was he intent on marrying her off? Landon had mentioned he had set aside a modest dowry for her. It was impressive how he had managed to fatten the estate coffers within such a short period. Her cousin was not averse to hard work and had used his personal funds to invest in some lucrative ventures. They proved successful, resulting in his amassing a small fortune worthy of the Hadfield title.

"Theo, you will accompany us to town come Monday. I'll hear no more excuses as to why you should remain here in the country. Am I clear?"

As if she was swallowing toads, she answered, "Yes, cousin."

Theo fought the urge to fidget as Landon's gaze raked over her. He eyed her haphazard coiffure. Would he notice her raven-colored hair was now streaked with lighter strands due to the hours spent outdoors practicing?

Her mourning clothes sagged in places where her body had reduced as a result of her training regimen. She ran her hand over the well-worn material. The nervous reaction drew Landon's attention closer to her garments.

Landon sighed. "I will ensure you are both outfitted with new wardrobes."

Aunt Henrietta chimed in, "Landon, you will escort us to the theater—balls and such—will you not? As the patriarch, it is now your duty."

"Mama, I will be busy in town. I still have a law practice to run with Christopher in conjunction with all the estate matters."

Her aunt's nostrils flared. "Christopher is quite capable of running the practice without you. You now have other responsibilities. One of them is to find a wife and produce an heir."

Theo lowered her gaze to the floor in an attempt to avoid her aunt's attention. However, Aunt Henrietta had not forgotten her. "And you, my girl, will accompany me into town. We shall set out after we break our fast on Monday."

Not having grown up with a mama, Theo hungrily sought out Aunt Henrietta's opinion and favor. Her aunt had willingly taken on the parental role and treated Theo as one of her own children. Theo was extremely grateful, for it allowed her to relinquish the management of the household and gained her the freedom to train.

Raising her eyes to meet her aunt's, Theo said, "If that is what you wish, Aunt Henri."

Upon hearing Theo's agreement, her aunt smiled and clapped her hands together. "Now that is settled, who would like a cup of tea?"

Now was her opportunity to escape. "If you will excuse me, I think I will go outdoors and take advantage of the clean country air while I can."

As Theo made her way to the door, Landon ordered, "Don't stay out too long. You will need to start preparing for your departure. Monday will be here before you know."

Midstride, Theo turned, and nodded. *I have three days to plan and prepare.*

Would you like to read more?

Mysteries of Lady Theodora
Available November 2019

ABOUT THE AUTHOR

RACHEL ANN SMITH writes steamy historical romances with a twist. Her debut series, Agents of the Home Office, features female protagonists that defy convention.

When Rachel isn't writing she loves to read and spend time with the family. You will often find her with her Kindle, by the pool during the summer, or on the side-lines of the soccer field in the spring and fall or curled up on the couch during the winter months.

She currently lives in Colorado with her extremely understanding husband and their two very supportive children.

Agents of the Home Office series
Desires of Lady Elise (Novella) - July 2019
Secrets of Lady Lucy - September 2019
Mysteries of Lady Theodora - November 2019
Confessions of Lady Grace - Spring 2020

facebook.com/rachelannsmit11

twitter.com/rachelannsmit11

instagram.com/rachelannsmithauthor